How Would They Escape Detection?...

For a moment Damaris despaired, and then an audacious idea came to her. It was so simple and so daring that she spoke before she had a chance to think.

"You are right about the way being full of danger. Since our roads seem to lie together, couldn't we prevail upon you to act as our escort?"

Captain Hartwell stopped in the act of mounting his horse to stare at her with raised brows. Behind her, she heard her father's muffled exclamation of surprise. Did he forget that he had taught her this? When in wolf country, join the wolves. And what better protection was there against roundheads than a roundhead officer? She smiled at him, her dark eyes soft with pleading. "Please, Captain," she murmured . . .

There was silence. Damaris held her breath. Then, the captain drew a breath that sounded very much like a sigh . . .

Dear Reader,

We, the editors of Tapestry Romances, are committed to bringing you two outstanding original romantic historical novels each and every month.

From Kentucky in the 1850s to the court of Louis XIII, from the deck of a pirate ship within sight of Gibraltar to a mining camp high in the Sierra Nevadas, our heroines experience life and love, romance and adventure.

Our aim is to give you the kind of historical romances that you want to read. We would enjoy hearing your thoughts about this book and all future Tapestry Romances. Please write to us at the address below.

The Editors
Tapestry Romances
POCKET BOOKS
1230 Avenue of the Americas
Box TAP
New York, N.Y. 10020

Beloved Enemy

Cynthia Sinclair

A TAPESTRY BOOK
PUBLISHED BY POCKET BOOKS NEW YORK

Books by Cynthia Sinclair

Beloved Enemy
Promise of Paradise
Winter Blossom

Published by TAPESTRY BOOKS

An Original publication of TAPESTRY BOOKS

A Tapestry Book published by
POCKET BOOKS, a divison of Simon & Schuster, Inc.
1230 Avenue of the Americas, New York, N.Y. 10020

ISBN: 0-671-53017-8

First Tapestry Books printing June, 1985

10 9 8 7 6 5 4 3 2 1

POCKET and colophon are registered trademarks
of Simon & Schuster, Inc.

TAPESTRY is a registered trademark of Simon & Schuster, Inc.

Printed in the U.S.A.

Beloved Enemy

Chapter One

THE SLENDER YOUNG WOMAN WITH THE RED-gold hair watched by the open window and wondered whether she would be alive by the end of the day. From the window everything seemed peaceful in the hazy September sunshine, and no one traveled the dusty road that led from the village of Bridgenorth to Worcester in the northwest and Burrey in the south. She knew this could not remain so for long. Soon Oliver Cromwell's roundheads would come marching down the road, and when they came it would be the end of all her hopes.

"Damaris." She turned quickly at the feeble whisper and bent over a white-haired man lying on a cot behind her. "Water, daughter," the old man murmured.

There was a water pitcher by the cot in the

otherwise bare corner which had been curtained off as a makeshift sickroom. She slipped an arm around him and supported his head so he could drink. His weak trembling terrified her. Colonel Guy St. Cyr had always been as tough and as unyielding as an old English oak, and now his strength oozed from the wounds in his side. It had been all she could do to get him this far from the battle of Worcester. Owen Marsh, a villager who was a royalist sympathizer, had given them shelter for a week. But they could not hide forever.

"You must get away now, Damaris." Urgently, Guy St. Cyr clutched at his daughter's hand. "The Commonwealth troops will be here before long." His gasping voice sank even lower. "You mustn't be here when they come."

Gently she laid his head back on the hard pillow and smoothed the worried lines from his forehead. "Save your breath, Colonel, sir. I'm not about to leave you."

"Stubborn chit." He attempted a glare. "Dammit, I'm your father and you owe me obedience."

When she smiled, her tense face relaxed into softness, and a deep dimple appeared in her chin. Almost-black eyes crinkled at the corners. "So you always say."

The old man shook his head. "My fault. You're a woman, not a soldier's son. Why did I bring you to Worcester?"

"I insisted on coming, don't you remember? A good thing, too. Who else could have found you after that battle?"

She couldn't help the tremble in her voice as she remembered that search, and she knelt down and put her cheek against her father's. Never had there been such a terrible day as that one. When the news that the Stuart king's forces were being routed had begun to trickle into Bridgenorth, she had persuaded Owen Marsh to borrow a horse and cart. They had driven to Worcester when almost everyone else was trying to escape out of the town's narrow gates, and there she had looked for him amongst the dead and dying. When at last she had found him, he was lying bleeding at Barbon Bridge where Charles II had made his courageous stand.

The sick man patted her cheek. "We could have done it, Damaris. If it hadn't been for the cursed traitors masquerading as our own, we would have marched through Gloucester and to London to reclaim King Charles's crown." He drew a painful breath. "But, thank the Lord, the king was persuaded to escape. He'll get away to France and he will fight again."

"And you'll be there beside him."

"I have always been the king's man," he muttered. "First I served King Charles I, and I was his faithful servant until Cromwell villainously had him executed. Now, I follow his son, Charles II." His voice became agitated. "It is because of him that you must leave me and get away, Damaris. I have information that is important to him. . . ."

"Hush-h," she soothed and saw his eyelids flutter feebly shut. She sat with him until she felt sure that he slept, and then she bunched her skirts in both hands as she hurried from behind the curtain and into the communal room where the Marsh family ate and cooked and slept. As she did so, Owen Marsh's wife compressed her lips and drew her young children closer to her. Damaris understood. The St. Cyrs' staying here meant danger to this small household.

"My father is much better today and will be able to travel soon," she began. "I'd like to hire the cart that brought us out of Worcester . . ."

"There's not a cart nor a horse left in Bridgenorth. The royalists took them when they were trying to escape." The woman lowered her voice. "It's said that Cromwell's men are searching the banks of the Severn and all the river towns and villages. They'll come here for sure, and if you're found, my man and these babes and I will suffer."

"I understand." She started toward the door, but the woman clutched her arm and demanded to know where she was going. "I'm going to ask whether someone in the village knows of a horse and cart for hire or sale."

"You can't do that. Some people here are in league with the roundheads. If they get suspicious, those Judases will go straight to the authorities."

Damaris fought off the fear that had settled about her. "I'll be careful, I swear, but for all our sakes I must find a way of getting my father away."

How? The question chewed a hole in her

4

weary mind as she stepped into the narrow village street. Then, inspiration came. In the center of the village stood the Silver Dragon Inn. Innkeepers usually knew everybody's business even in these unsettled times. And if she told the man she was prepared to pay . . .

That was another problem. By her calculations, she had less than seventy pounds plus a necklace of gold and small pearls which had once been her mother's and which she did not wish to sell except as a last resort. She must bargain, that was all, and bargain shrewdly. Holding tightly to this thought, she walked into the Silver Dragon.

The ordinariness of the inn reassured her. A few locals were sitting at a rough table while a short, thick-set man behind the counter nodded in her direction. "Now, then, mistress," he said.

There was no friendliness in his voice, but she gave him her prettiest smile. "I need to hire a cart, Master Innkeeper. I thought that you would know if any were available."

But he was already shaking his head. "Can't be done," he said gruffly.

"I'll pay well . . ."

Rudely, he interrupted her. "I don't care if you pay me with diamonds and rubies. There are no carts. There are no horses anywhere. Can you understand that?"

She understood, but she couldn't give up so easily. She leaned both her hands on the counter and raised her voice. "But there must be something. Think again. I must have transportation, no matter what it costs. I must leave Bridge-north."

"Why the hurry to get away from Bridge-north?"

The deep voice caught her by surprise, and she turned quickly to face the new speaker. A man had risen from a shadowed corner of the inn where he had been sitting, and as he came toward her the first impression she had was one of height. Height and brawn of muscle, of broad shoulders that looked enormous in the inn's narrow common room. Then, he stepped into the light and she noted that his gray eyes were both interested and questioning, and that he wore the uniform of a Commonwealth officer. God save me, she thought, a roundhead officer!

"I hadn't expected to meet a lady in a village inn." Dark eyebrows rose quizzically. "I am Jonathan Hartwell, captain in the Lord Protector's forces, and what the innkeeper says is true. It has taken me some time to find a replacement for my own tired horse."

Her mind felt numb and useless, and her heart skittered wildly. This man had already picked her out for a lady even though she wore a simple linen dress and stood here hatless, gloveless, unescorted. He must not guess anything else. She made herself smile as she asked, "But you were successful in finding a horse?"

"That is because I'm on special business for the Lord Protector." In spite of the drabness of the Commonwealth uniform, he wore it with a kind of dash, and his dark hair had an un-

Puritan curl to it, framing his hard-planed, fine-featured face with an elegance she hadn't associated with roundheads. The questioning look in the gray eyes deepened. "And you?"

She took a gulp of air and tried to appear at ease. "My name is Damaris—Langley," she lied.

He gave her a very military bow that was still somehow graceful. "You seem to be in a hurry, Mistress Langley."

"My—my father and I have been traveling, and now he is sick. He is an—a cloth merchant, and our home is in Portsmouth." She paused, saw him nod and continued, "He had the ill luck to fall ill near Worcester, and our servants were afraid because of the fighting and ran away with our carriage and all our goods. A kind villager took pity on us and housed us here in Bridgenorth. Now, my father yearns for home. He feels that his sickness can be better attended there."

Did he believe her? She couldn't be sure, but he inclined his fine dark head courteously enough. "I can understand how you feel traveling at this time. England has been torn apart by the invasion attempt launched by this pernicious Charles Stuart who calls himself king. But now that he's been soundly defeated, we can all breathe more easily."

She caught her lower lip in her teeth to steady it. "Thank the Lord," she managed.

Did he suspect her? She wasn't sure, but he had not asked to see her father or ordered her arrest—yet! Then he said, "I wish I could help you, but I am on special business for the Lord

Protector. Tomorrow or the next day, though, troops under General Lambert's command will be coming here. They will be able to help you."

She felt sick. They were coming, the round-heads, and they would capture her father and drag him off to London to some vile prison or the headsman's ax. She turned away from him, and clenched her hands at her sides to regain control of herself. She must not weep in front of this man or do anything to make him suspicious.

"You're very distressed." There was a new note in the many-shaded voice, and she sensed that he stood very close to her. She was suddenly and inexplicably aware that if she took a step backward she would be in his arms. For a heart-beat's time her mind registered the thought of being held against the unyielding hardness of that broad chest, the strength of his rugged yet graceful body. Then she shook herself back to reality and concentrated on what he was saying. "Is your father very ill?" he was asking.

"Yes, sir." Her voice trembled at the truth of this. "He's ill and I'm afraid that—I don't wish him to die away from home. It is true that the Commonwealth troops may help us, but they may also be too busy with their—with their duties."

He was silent for a moment. "Perhaps you are right," he admitted. She turned to stare up into the silver-gray eyes and saw that he was frowning. "Where are you staying?" he then demanded. She didn't know how to answer. To tell him where they were hiding would be foolish, and yet not to reply would arouse his suspicions. Before she could decide what to do, the innkeeper bowed and smirked.

"She and her father lodge with Marsh, the farmer, sir." Damaris felt a coldness clutching at her heart. If their stay in Bridgenorth was common knowledge, anyone might betray her. She tensed, waiting for the roundhead captain to ask more questions, but he merely acknowledged the innkeeper's words with a brusque nod.

His eyes were on Damaris as he said, "I don't know what I can do, but will you trust me to try and help you, Damaris Langley?"

He was asking her to trust an enemy. She felt suddenly giddy and tried to force herself to steadiness. Tried—and could not. As she found herself swaying, his arm went around her waist in support. "You will make yourself ill." In that dazed moment she thought that he sounded— kind. But it was not this unlooked-for kindness that caused the sudden leap of her pulse, the confused tumult of her senses. That came from nearness to the man himself, from the way he held her so close that she felt herself surrounded by his strength and his power and the scent of him—leather and a clean, vibrant fragrance of the outdoors.

"Go back to this Owen Marsh's house and wait," he was telling her. "I will do what I can."

With effort, she drew herself free of the circle of his arms. "Thank you, Captain Hartwell." She managed to walk more or less steadily to the inn door, then paused to look back at the tall man and saw that he was watching her, and that the interest was plain in his silver-gray gaze. Foolish to look to an enemy for aid, but what other options did she have? If the captain would help them, there might still be a chance.

"He must help," she whispered aloud as she turned her steps back to the Marshes' cramped house. The roundheads were coming. If she didn't get her father away now, they were lost.

Chapter Two

"HE WON'T COME," GUY ST. CYR SAID.

Damaris did not answer. She was sitting beside him on the hard wooden floor, fanning away the flies that clustered into the little space behind the curtain. "Why should he?" the colonel continued. "He's a roundhead and from what you say he's on business for Cromwell, chasing royalists. If it had been a royalist cavalier, I could understand his wanting to be chivalrous and help a fair lady in distress—but these damned Puritans have no eye for a pretty girl. That's only one of the things that's wrong with them."

She couldn't even smile at his small joke. Her heart was beating a wild, irregular rhythm that almost stopped whenever she heard hoofbeats or even footsteps outside the little house. She thought of orderly roundhead regiments marching toward Bridgenorth and clenched the fan so tightly that her knuckles shone white. "He said he would come," she finally whispered.

Guy St. Cyr snorted. "You trust the word of a damned roundhead? Damaris, I thought you had more sense."

"Hush!" At the sound of hoofbeats, her heart leaped right into her mouth. She got to her feet and walked swiftly to the window, then caught her breath. The miracle she had prayed for had come to be. She looked down on a sturdy plow horse attached to a farmer's market wagon.

Beside them on a large dark horse was Jonathan Hartwell. As she stared in disbelief, he looked up at the window and swept off his hat. Catching up her skirts, she ran from behind the curtain and out of the door to meet him. "Captain Hartwell—" she began, then stopped. There were no words to frame her thanks.

"I'm sorry it took a long time. You see before you what probably is the only horse and cart in the entire county." His deep voice was both rueful and amused, but it was not amusement that he felt but surprise. The joy that blazed from this woman's eyes lent her an almost incandescent beauty, and it was almost an effort to add, "That rogue at the inn was right in saying that neither diamonds nor rubies can buy a nag these days."

"Then how did you acquire this one?" She stroked the ploughhorse's nose and felt the rough but sturdy construction of the cart.

"By shamelessly using the Lord Protector's name. I hope he never hears of it."

"He will not from me." She felt lightheaded with relief and thanksgiving. "Whatever it costs, Captain, I will gladly . . ."

He shook his head. "Keep your money. No doubt you'll need it between here and Portsmouth. Now, will this Owen Marsh drive you there?"

Suddenly the relief died away. They were not out of danger yet. Before them lay miles and miles of driving across rutted roads and hiding from roundheads—or lying to them. She forced the fearsome thought away and straightened her back. "No, sir. My father and I will go on together."

Dark brows drew together. Her brave words notwithstanding, he knew that she was afraid. "Do you have any idea how far it is to Portsmouth? A sick man and a young woman—it's folly," he argued.

She could hear Guy St. Cyr's feeble voice calling to her and she said, "It will be all right. Thank you again, Captain Hartwell, and goodbye."

She could feel those silver-gray eyes watching her as she turned her back to him and hurried into the narrow space behind the curtain where she bent over her father. "He did come, and we have transportation," she whispered urgently. "We must leave at once." He nodded wordlessly and she added, "I will call Owen Marsh to help me carry you to the cart."

"No need." She had not heard his footsteps, and the deep voice both surprised and frightened her. She saw her father's gaze swing to the curtained doorway and she was thankful that though Guy St. Cyr had fought at Worcester, he had been so long in retirement that he was not apt to be recognized. Besides, suffering from his wounds had changed his appearance dramatically. Even so she held her breath and only let it go when Jonathan Hartwell continued, "I'll help you."

"Are you a physician, sir?" Damaris was thankful that her father was playing along, using his most feeble voice.

"No, but I've nursed many a man's wounds on the battlefield." The tall man stepped closer, looking hard into the gaunt and wasted face of the wounded man. "I'm Jonathan Hartwell, a captain in the Lord Protector's armies."

She saw the tightening of her father's lips, but he spoke up gamely. "Then we follow the same truth."

"Amen." The gray eyes left the sick man's face and turned to Damaris. Caught in the silver intensity of that look, her pulse leaped alarmingly. "He's not in a condition to travel," the roundhead captain was saying. "Perhaps you'd do better to wait after all. General Lambert will have a regimental doctor with him."

"And why should the army waste its time on me?" Guy St. Cyr made his voice sound querulous. "I'm a peaceful merchant, always have been, and I don't hold with any kind of fighting. I only want to go home. I'm ready to leave this moment."

Through the half-open curtain, Damaris could see the frightened faces of Owen Marsh and his wife and children. The woman made a pleading, praying gesture that said plainly, please leave.

Forcing a confidence she did not feel, Damaris turned to the roundhead captain. "My father is right," she said. "We have little to take with us. As I told you, our—our runaway servants took all our goods with them."

"Very well." He turned to the cowering Marshes. "Goodwife, help Mistress Langley take the blankets from his bed and spread them on the cart." Carefully, he slid his arms under the old man. "Tell me if I hurt you, Master Langley."

The colonel made no sound and Damaris, aided by Owen Marsh's wife, hastened to pad the rough boards of the cart with the blankets. When she had finished, Jonathan Hartwell laid the old man down on his makeshift bed. He was frowning, Damaris noted, as he asked, "How is it with you now, friend?"

"I am as God wills," Guy St. Cyr whispered.

Damaris began her thanks again, but the captain interrupted her. "If you travel like this, the sun will blaze down into his eyes, and he'll have sunstroke within two hours."

"I was going to cover his face with my hat . . ." She held out her small but serviceable bonnet, but he shook his head.

"You'll be out in the same sun." He hesitated a moment, amazed at himself and wondering

15

whence came this urge to protect Damaris
Langley. Then he strode to his horse and withdrew a cloak from his saddlebags. "This will
serve your purpose better," he told her.

Guy St. Cyr was shaking his head feebly. "We
cannot be beholden to you like this." The captain
did not pay any attention, but arranged the cloak
over the supposed sick man like a rude canopy.
"Truly," the old man went on more strongly, "I
cannot take your cloak, sir."

The big man's voice was suddenly grim. "I'd
do the same even for some wretched royalist I
found by the roadside. Why not for a believer in
the true faith?"

Damaris spoke up before her father could
protest again. "We thank you for all you've done,
Captain. I hope we have not kept you from your
duties."

She sensed that he was close behind her as she
turned to mount the rough driver's seat, but she
didn't know how near he was until she felt his
hands under her elbows. His clasp was strong,
sure, more disconcerting than anything else that
had happened in this perilous leavetaking.
Though she was used to casual assistance, no
man's touch had ever conveyed this inexplicable
sense of strength, excitement and, strangely
enough, safety. She felt giddy and off-balanced
and tried to draw in a bracing breath, but her
treacherous senses were assailed by the clean,
virile scent of the man himself. For a moment he
held her close to him and then, with a powerful

movement, he was lifting her onto the rude wooden seat.

Silver-gray eyes met hers, and she saw the strong, fine mouth curve into a smile of rueful admiration. As she struggled to compose herself, he gave her his distinctive bow. "Godspeed, Damaris Langley," he said.

"Move, horse, please—please, move!"

With all her strength, Damaris tugged at the horse's reins. The animal strained forward, and Damaris tugged again, but the cart would not budge. The back left wheel was stuck fast.

It was so hot. Too hot for September, Damaris thought bitterly as she tried throwing her weight against the cart from behind. Dust clung to her and to them all, and flies buzzed about them unmercifully. She didn't even have the heart to swat them away as she gazed unhappily at the huge rut into which the wheel had fallen. "How am I going to get free of this?" she asked aloud.

"Damaris?" With despair, she noted how weak Guy St. Cyr's voice had become. "How far from Burrey, child?"

She straightened her aching back and forced a smile as she went to his side. "Not far," she said gently. "Are you thirsty? Mistress Marsh gave me a flask of water, and it's cool and sweet."

"I trouble you too much." The grieved note in his voice tugged at her heart. "I lie here as helpless as a babe while you struggle. It's not fair, my daughter. You are only one and twenty

—you should be living a life of ease and pleasure. By rights you should be married to some
kind, good man. But I give you no dowry, no
ease, nothing but poverty. War. Hardship . . ."

She felt near tears of worry and frustration.
The colonel's color was worse, and he was
sweating in spite of the makeshift canopy above
him. What to do, she wondered, as she supported
his head so that he could drink.

Burrey could not be far, and yet she could
not leave him by the roadside and go for help.
She cast a despairing look down the road and
then felt a jolt of renewed hope as she saw
that a group of five men were walking toward
them.

But when she started to hail them, the colonel
caught her hand in his. "Daughter, these are
evil times. They could be roundheads. Hide . . ."

As he spoke one of the approaching men gave
a halloo to his companions. "They don't look like
soldiers," Damaris replied uncertainly.

The weak hold on her hand tightened. "If I am
recognized or taken or if I die, you must get to
France to His Majesty. You must tell him . . ."

A rough shout interrupted the feeble words.
Damaris's heart sank. The newcomers were
dirty, ragged, unkempt, and their leader wore
two daggers at his belt. The butt of a pistol
protruded from his greasy, half-open doublet,
and even at this distance she could see the
greedy way they eyed the horse-drawn cart and
its driver.

"Had trouble along the road, missy?" The

leader of the group had a wide grin, made wolfish by sharp, dirty teeth.

She wished she weren't alone and helpless. She wished she had a weapon—anything with which to face them as she got between them and her father. "Yes, unfortunately. Our servant has just gone to Burrey for help."

"La—a servant—a likely story." The leader mimicked her speech and his friends howled with laughter. "And the wheel is stuck. Good fortune for us, bad fortune for you, missy. We've been looking for some transport to ease our weary feet. Hand over that water, for a start . . ."

He stepped forward, one dusty hand outstretched. It was a ruthless hand, large, with dirt circles under the nails. "You're not going to touch this cart, or this water," she snapped.

"How's that now?" The roughneck leader was not laughing anymore, and she was sickened by the odor of liquor and dirt that came from him. "I'm not one to be denied what's my due, am I, boys? If I'm crossed, I could turn ugly."

"Enough talk," one of his friends growled. "Let's take the cart and horse and get on, Jed."

"Not so quickly. It's a while since I had me a pretty piece like this one." The leader's tongue snaked across thick lips. "This cart should make a fine bed once we pitch out the old man. I'll have her first and then you boys can take a turn."

Guy St. Cyr tried to rise. "Run, child," he gasped, but Damaris did not move. Could not.

She felt petrified, rooted to the spot. "Go! If you stay, they'll—Damaris, run!"

"Now, ain't that touching?" The man called Jed came nearer still, his grimy hand upraised as if to strike the wounded man, but she wedged herself between him and the cart. "Pretty gal, aren't you? Got some spirit, too. Always preferred a lively wench in bed."

"Don't touch him. Don't hurt him—please." The man just grinned and reached for her. As his dirty hand clamped down on her arm, one of his cohorts called out a warning.

"Rider coming down the road, Jed."

"Just one? We can handle him if we have to, but maybe we won't. You hide behind the cart, boys. And you," he said, giving Damaris's arm a cruel twist, "be quiet, or the old man is finished. And you'll wish you were, too. I can make things so bad for you you'll want to die."

Numbly she watched the rogues draw daggers and pistols and hide themselves behind the cart. The rider came closer and the man called Jed gave Damaris another shake. "Smile, damn you. Smile at him so that he'll pass us by. Do as I tell you or I slice up that old man like sausage."

Despairing, she saw horse and rider grow more distinct. There was something familiar in the way he sat his horse and even in this terrible moment she wondered at it. Then, she choked out a cry, for the rider was Jonathan Hartwell. The man called Jed twisted her arm back cruelly. "You do that again and I'll break it," he threatened.

"I couldn't help it—you hurt me." Surely he would see them and stop to help them? She strained forward as he galloped closer.

Jed twisted her arm again. "Damn your eyes, smile. Now, as he passes . . ."

He was nearly upon them. Stop, please, she begged him silently. She nearly called out to him as he glanced incuriously toward them, and she held her breath. But next moment he had passed them, and hot air and dust washed back over her in his wake.

Beside her, Jed laughed in appreciation of his own cleverness, and she knew true despair. How could he not have recognized her? But perhaps he had. He could not have seen the hidden rogues, and he must have felt that Jed was helping her right the cart. "Oh, dear God," she whispered.

"He won't help you, lovely." The ruffian leader jerked his head at the cart as his grinning confederates emerged from their hiding places. "Heave out the old man."

"Shall we cut his throat or let him watch?" One of them laughed as he grabbed the old man's shoulders. "Maybe we should just . . ."

There was a sharp crack behind them, and Damaris saw the ruffian who had just spoken let go of the colonel and clutch his chest. As he slowly sank forward, there was the thunder of hoofbeats, a flash of steel. The other villain who stood beside the cart went down, howling, as Jonathan Hartwell swept past them in a blur of speed.

"Hell-damned bastard . . ." She saw Jed heft his pistol and had scant time to cry out a warning.

"Captain, behind you . . ."

She screamed at the cruel wrench on her arm as Jed dragged her in front of him to make a living shield. "Now I got you where I want you," he purred. "Too bad you came where you wasn't wanted, you damned, interfering bastard . . ."

The tall man on the horse hesitated, and she could hear Jed laughing. "No," she shouted and twisted back as hard as she could, throwing the man off balance for a moment. It was only for a split second, but in that scant space of time the man on horseback moved so swiftly that she could scarcely believe her eyes. And just as the snarling Jed fired, Jonathan's sword came arcing down.

As Jed fell, she whirled clear and ran toward the cart. "Father . . ." but he only clasped her hands tightly, anxiously. She shook her head in answer to his urgent questions. "No, I'm all right. He came back . . ."

Grateful, still afraid to believe, she looked over her shoulder at the powerful figure on the dark horse. He had cantered some distance away in pursuit of the last of the ruffians who had attempted escape, firing his pistol as he ran. Now the man lay by the side of the road, and Jonathan Hartwell was returning, sheathing his sword and returning a pistol to his belt as he came. He dismounted and looked at Damaris searchingly. "Are you hurt? Did that swine harm you?"

Reaction made her legs feel rubbery and she was grateful for the strong hands which supported her. "No. You came before—we're unhurt. And you? I saw those men fire directly at you . . ."

There was something savage in his smile. "To their sorrow, they were poor shots. They won't trouble you again."

"Desperate times breed desperate men." The colonel strove to prop himself up on his elbow, fell back. "We are truly fortunate that you returned to aid us. Sir, my thanks. My daughter means more to me than my own poor life."

The Puritan captain bowed acknowledgement, and again, Damaris was struck by the power and grace of that bow. "I am sorry if I gave you a few bad moments, but if I had turned aside when I first recognized you, that filth would have hurt you before I could move to help. I had to catch them by surprise." He looked deep into Damaris's eyes. "Are you all right, truly? You are as pale as a ghost."

She was unprepared both for the concern in his voice and for her own reaction to it. The weakness in her legs had gone, but now another weakness seemed to flow through her like slow fire, and again she felt the confused imbalance of all her senses. With effort she said, "I'm perfectly fine, but the wheel of the cart is not. It became stuck in this rut in the road, and we couldn't move."

"That's an easy matter to remedy." He studied the wheel for a moment and then said, "Take the reins, and when I lift the wheel, lead the horse forward."

She obeyed him at once, and as she turned back for further instructions, she saw that Jonathan had thrown off his coat and rolled up his shirtsleeves so that his powerful biceps flexed against tanned skin. He got a good grip on the wheel and then called, "Pull now, girl!"

Damaris urged the horse forward. A step, another—and then a loosening, a grinding, rushing release. The wheel was free. "Oh, well done, Captain," she exclaimed joyfully.

For a moment their eyes met, and he smiled. It was a warm and friendly smile full of shared cameraderie. Then he frowned. "You must be careful," he warned her. "The road is full of both ruts and vagabond rogues. I won't be there to pull you out of trouble when next it befalls you."

The genuine concern in his tone warmed her. "I'll remember," she said.

"Fortunately, there's a checkpoint further on ahead, and from there to Burrey is but a few miles," he then told her, and all her feeling of relief ebbed away. Her eyes met her father's in sudden fear, and she could almost read his thought. If the roundheads at the checkpoint suspected them, questioned them, they were lost.

How would they escape detection? They had no identification, nothing to prove that they were peaceful merchants. For a moment she despaired, and then an audacious idea came to her. It was so simple and so daring that she spoke before she had a chance to think.

"You are right about the way being full of danger. Since our roads seem to lie together, couldn't we prevail upon you to act as our escort?"

He stopped in the act of mounting his horse to stare at her with raised brows. Behind her, she heard her father's muffled exclamation of surprise. Did he forget that he had taught her this? When in wolf country, join the wolves. And what better protection was there against round-heads than a roundhead officer? She smiled at him, her dark eyes soft with pleading. "Please, Captain," she murmured.

"It's not possible." Was that regret or irritation in his voice? She couldn't be sure. But then she wasn't sure herself of her own temerity in suggesting this mad scheme. "Look, I must be about the Lord Protector's business."

Now Guy St. Cyr added his own plea. "We have troubled you much, I know, sir, but for just a little longer—for my daughter's safety until we reach Burrey," he begged.

There was silence. Damaris held her breath. Then, the captain drew a breath that sounded very much like a sigh. "Very well. Since I, too, go to Burrey, I will accompany you there." He pointed toward the trees ahead. "The checkpoint isn't far, just through those woods and over the downs. I will ride ahead to see that the road is safe for the cart to follow."

Before they could thank him he had spurred his dark stallion and had trotted on ahead. Damaris clambered up onto the cart and shook the reins, and the horse plodded forward. From behind her came the colonel's chuckle. "That was boldly done, daughter. A gamble—but you won."

"I had a good teacher." She kept her tone light for his sake, but she had never felt less like laughing. She knew as she watched the tall, powerful man astride his dark horse that she must guard her tongue and her actions. She did not underestimate Jonathan Hartwell as an adversary.

She held that thought as the rough, pitted road narrowed and then began to veer toward the woods. Calling softly to the horse, she eased its pace and blessed the coolness of the trees. Her father would feel more comfort, now, as they passed under the shadow of immense oaks that had been old when the Tudor kings and queens ruled England, when Charles I had lost his crown and his head to Oliver Cromwell, now Lord Protector of the land. She found herself breathing a wish that someday Charles II would ride as monarch under this same green canopy, and as if he had read her thought she heard her father sigh deeply.

"The king must have escaped to France by now. Daughter, you must get word to him—I know why the battle of Worcester was lost. The information is vital to him and the coming restoration."

"Hush—he's coming back," she warned, and

the old man fell silent. As the distance between them lessened, she sensed a tension in the way the powerful figure sat his horse.

She was certain that this was the result of his promise to accompany them to Burrey, but when he spoke, his voice was merely thoughtful. "Woods like these are said to be crawling with runaway royalists," he told her. "After Worcester, those that were not killed or severely wounded fled for their lives into any cover they could find."

"And is that your mission for the Lord Protector—hunting escaped royalists?" It was hard to school her voice to simple interest, but she managed it.

"I certainly seek them, but my mission is such that it's known only to me and my chief. I only pointed out something I've told you before—that England is unsafe for travel just now, Damaris."

There was something in the way he spoke her name that was unsettling, and her own response to it was even more so. As the deep voice seemed to caress the words, she felt the slow fire again in her blood. "Are we far from Burrey?" she asked quickly.

"We are coming to the edge of the woods, and then there are some downs to be crossed. After that, there'll be the checkpoint—and then the town."

Though he was watching the road, she sensed that his attention was all on her. "You know this way well," she said for want of something better to say.

27

The silver-gray of his eyes turned to her. "I've traveled the road many times." A pause and then he added, "And you? Do you always accompany your father when he travels?"

Carefully, she nodded. "Sometimes. His trade takes him to all parts of the country. He is old and—and not strong. It is a comfort to me to be there to take care of him."

"A worthy but unusual thought. Doesn't your mother worry about the two of you?"

She spoke without thinking. "My mother died many years ago when I was a child . . ." Then she stopped, frightened at what she had almost added. Almost she had said, "She died when my father was an officer in the army of King Charles I."

"He'll be all right," he said, and she realized, gratefully, that he'd misinterpreted her hesitation. "He needs a doctor, that's all—ah, here we come to the edge of the woods."

She shaded her eyes for a moment against the dazzle of late afternoon sun. Under the dome of blue skies rolled vast downs and rambling valleys. Green with late summer grass, they stretched far into the horizon, ending in low wooded hills to the north and in what looked to be ruins in the west. "Those are the ruins of Whiteladies Monastery," Jonathan Hartwell explained. He began to lead away from the ruins, and Damaris looked about her in delight. The fragrance of crushed grass, the sweet scent of late wild roses and early autumn flowers rose about her, and a large golden butterfly danced up to sit for a moment on the cart beside her. In a place like this it was hard to believe that war and death and suffering had ever taken place, that Worcester had ever been.

"It is a beautiful country." There was quiet conviction in the deep voice. "No other land can touch it, no matter what the season. Autumn will bring color and woodsmoke and the scent of apples—and then the quiet blessing of winter before the spring."

She stared, forgetting her own caution. "You sound more like a poet than a soldier."

Strong white teeth flashed when he smiled. "Do I? Perhaps a life of war makes me regret the beauty that is wasting while we hack at each other with swords. You may laugh at me if you like, but it's true."

"No. I—I feel as you do," she murmured.

"You sound surprised. But surely you realize that all manner of men and women who love England have united under the Lord Protector? Not only known Calvinists and common men, but many of the nobility, too, share his vision for this country and join in damning Charles Stuart."

His words brought her back to reality. She had almost forgotten to whom she talked. "It won't be long till we get your father to a comfortable bed in Burrey," he was saying. "We should soon reach the checkpoint."

Was that supposed to reassure her? Then, as the carthorse toiled over a green, rolling down she saw it before her. Standing some distance away, their drab uniforms as unmistakable as their arrogance, stood Commonwealth soldiers at attention. Near them was a man on a bay horse who now spurred toward them.

Jonathan Hartwell reined in his own mount and waited. Damaris drew the carthorse and tried to reassure herself that all would be well. As long as they were in this captain's company, they would be allowed to pass.

As the thought filled her mind, she heard the hoarse shout. "Who desires to pass this checkpoint?"

"Who wants to know?" Jonathan Hartwell responded instantly. "Your name and rank, sir?"

The rider of the bay mare drew up some distance from them, his hand was on the pommel of his sword. He was a tall man, red-haired and cadaverously thin. Between strong cheekbones, cold green eyes took in the cart and its occupant, Damaris, then shunted back to Jonathan.

"I am Captain Clandennon serving under General Lambert. I am in command of this checkpoint, as you can see," he said in a rasping voice. "None may pass without my order."

"In that case, you'd better watch the roads more carefully," Jonathan said. "This woman and her sick father were beset some miles back by robbers. While you are looking for royalists to hang or send off to Barbados as slaves, you might also attend to the filth that dirties the Lord Protector's highways."

Damaris caught her lip in her teeth at his

tone, and she saw Clandennon redden along his high cheekbones. "And who do you think you are?" he snapped.

Jonathan drew some papers from his pocket. "My orders. As you see, I'm Captain Hartwell, under the orders of the Lord Protector himself." As the other officer examined the orders he added, "You have quite a number of men at this checkpoint, Captain. Are you expecting a hundred royalists?"

"Sir." Returning the orders, Clandennon saluted with some reluctance. "You're free to go, of course. But who are these with you?"

Green, catlike eyes surveyed Damaris. She felt unaccountably cold, as if she had touched a snake. "They are Master Langley, a cloth merchant, and his daughter," Jonathan Hartwell was saying. "They travel under my protection."

"I must question them even so." Clandennon dropped his voice as if there was danger of being overheard. "We cannot be too careful, Captain. It's said that the royalists are desperate. One rumor has it that the son of the Stuart is fleeing dressed as a woman."

"Surely you cannot expect a big boned, six-foot man to masquerade as THIS woman." There was wry amusement in Jonathan's tone. "I've heard a lot against the son of Charles Stuart the first, but sorcery isn't one of them."

"Witchcraft is nothing to laugh at." Clandennon's mouth tightened in rebuke. "And I suspect everyone." Again, Damaris felt that chill. "You have heard that Milord, the earl of Derby, he that was great Lancashire, is taken and will go to the block for his treason. But Buckingham is still loose—and with him that devil, the earl of Larraby, and Colonel Reisling, one of the Stuart's finest officers." He paused and added almost as an afterthought, "And then there's an old, little known warhorse called Guy St. Cyr . . ."

Damaris's heart stopped beating under the man's cold stare. All thought evaporated from her mind leaving her numb and faint as Captain Clandennon continued, "It is my earnest hope that I myself will catch these enemies of the New Israel and bring them to the headsman's ax."

Chapter Three

IT TOOK ALL HER CONTROL TO MEET CLANDEN-
non's eyes without flinching and to speak with
some semblance of calm. "I'd be glad to answer
any questions you might have, Captain," she
said.

Clandennon glanced at Jonathan, who
shrugged. "As long as it will not take too long. I
have work to do, Captain, and I have promised
to escort this lady and her father as far as
Burrey." He tapped long fingers against his saddle bow to add, "So you seek Buckingham and
Larraby and Reisling and—what was the other
name? St. Cyr. I have not heard that name, but
I'll take your word that he belongs in this rogues
gallery also."

"St. Cyr was a follower of the first Charles
Stuart," Clandennon explained, "a faithful dog

who received his colonel's rank for service done to his so-called king. He is no peer and he doubtless had little wealth, for I hear he lived in relative poverty somewhere in the north till his master's son tried his luck at Worcester."

In the cart, Guy St. Cyr moved restlessly. Jonathan shrugged. "If you caught those men, Captain, you'd be doing all of us a favor. But they may well be in France by now."

"This I doubt. Rumor has it that they have all flocked around their so-called king and are still at large somewhere between here and the sea. They won't get away. Every bridge, every possible roadway, and especially every port is bristling with our men. Also, there's a price on the bastards' heads. A thousand pounds will go to anyone who aids in the Stuart's capture, and five hundred apiece for those villains Larraby and Buckingham." His voice grew even more rasping as he added, "The wicked shall perish, and the enemies of the Lord shall be consumed by fire."

The cruel words followed Damaris as she slid down from the cart and walked around to stand beside her father. She fought to keep fear out of her voice as she said, "Father, here's a Captain Clandennon who wants to ask us some questions."

Guy St. Cyr nodded. He was waxy pale, but he was also calm, and Damaris was filled with bitter pride in him as she turned to the captain who had dismounted and was coming toward

34

them, "He's very sick, sir. Please don't tire him."

Clandennon did not deign to answer her until he had asked her father many detailed questions about the cloth trade. Then he turned to her.

"What's the matter with your father?" he demanded.

She had her answer ready. "He has a fever, sir, which took him when we were close to Bridgenorth . . ."

"That is near Worcester," he interrupted. The feline eyes narrowed. "Were you near the fighting, then?" She told him the story of her supposed servant's flight and he listened intently, his eyes roving from her face to her father's.

Jonathan shifted impatiently in the saddle. "Good lord, my friend, how long is your discourse going to take? Can't you see these two are no more royalist than I?"

Clandennon looked annoyed. "Merchants often know more than they show," he muttered, but he stepped aside. Damaris felt the green eyes boring into her back as she hastily remounted the cart.

Jonathan saluted the silent officer. "Well, Clandennon. We may meet again."

"As the Lord wills." The gaunt captain saluted. Then, as Damaris flicked the reins and the carthorse started forward, he added, "It is for His glory that I will find those royalist knaves and bring them to the dust."

She wanted to speed the horse, to hurry away

from that hoarse voice and those cold-burning eyes, but she restrained herself. Any suspicious movement would mean detection not only from Clandennon but from Jonathan as well.

"How far to Burrey, child?" the old man asked from the jouncing cart, but it was Jonathan who answered.

"Not far at all." He pointed down the road and far in the distance she saw what looked to be a cluster of houses. The end of the journey, but still so far away, Damaris thought, and as she looked up read concern and reassurance in his gray gaze. "It will be all right," he told her gently.

She remembered all he had said about the king's most trusted supporters, how he had approved of what Clandennon was doing. Yet something within her, too deep and too elemental for reason, spoke of trust. To trust an enemy was great folly—but before she could complete the thought, a home-flying bird swooped low, almost in front of the carthorse's nose. Startled, it threw up its head and whinnied loudly with fear. She hauled in on the reins hard and the animal subsided, but her hands and shoulders ached with the strain. She wished she could stretch her back and rest her wrists, but there was no time for that. She set her teeth and shook the reins again, urging the horse forward.

There was a muffled exclamation from the man on horseback beside her. "Stop the cart," he said, and when she obeyed he dismounted and tied his horse to the side of the cart.

"What are you doing?" she demanded, but he only gestured for her to move over.

"We'll go faster if I take the reins." he said. "You are exhausted. Meanwhile, take this—September evenings become rapidly cool."

She protested as he shrugged out of his doublet and placed it across her shoulders. For a moment she registered his hands, sure and strong on her, and then he was flicking the reins and calling to the horse. As it moved smartly down the road, the wounded man in the cart muttered in pain.

Damaris turned in her seat to arrange the captain's doublet over the old man. As she did so, the cart gave a lurch, and she was flung backward. She tried to regain her balance, could not—and then a strong arm was about her, supporting her. "Easy, girl," Jonathan said.

Swaying and lurching with the uneven movement of the cart, she could only cling to him for support, and he registered her firm softness, her strength and her vulnerability. He felt wonder that this dark-eyed girl could move him so, and yet in some elemental way she fascinated him. He could feel her heart beating rapidly against his, and he tightened his arm around her assuringly. "It's all right," he told her.

Through the barrier of too thin cloth she registered warm male hardness and powerful muscle pressed tightly against her breasts, and when she tried to draw breath she could smell, feel, even taste his nearness. She could not speak. She could not even think.

"Damaris, is everything all right? I heard you cry out," Guy St. Cyr questioned anxiously.

The pressure of the hard arm eased. "No problems, friend," Jonathan replied. "Your daughter lost her balance for a moment, that's all."

She drew away from him at once. Small shivers were racking her, little implosions of heat that did not give her warmth or comfort. She found that she had wrapped her arms around herself as if for protection against the male presence beside her on the rough wooden seat. But there was no protection. As the cart swayed and jolted along, she was thrown up against him, into his whipcord tough side and his powerful thigh. Balance, she told herself grimly, as she drew away. Somehow she had to maintain her balance.

"Perhaps I should ride in the cart with my father," she murmured. "There is little room here on the driver's seat."

"Less room back there in the cart." She thought she read amusement in his voice. "You'd only hurt him if you tried that. No, mistress. You're a prisoner here with me."

The word cut through the confusion of senses and the tangle of her emotions. Prisoner—that was what she would be, and her father, too, if she made one wrong move with this man. Now she regretted asking for his protection. Even though he had helped them clear the checkpoint, Captain Jonathan Hartwell was dangerous.

"There's Burrey," he said, and pointed. "There's a passable inn there that I know of—the Tall Oak, where we'll find food and a bed."

"Many people seem to have the same idea," she observed, for as they approached the town there seemed to be a flurry of activity in the streets. Men were shouting at each other and there were horses, too. Enough horses for an army.

As the thought filled her weary mind she felt Jonathan stiffen. "I had not known they would be quartered in Burrey," she heard him mutter.

She turned to him. His eyes were narrowed against the dark, his lips tight. "What are you talking about?" she asked, and without his answering knew. No wonder there were men—and horses, too. "Commonwealth troops are quartered here," she whispered.

"So they seem to be." He sounded displeased. "Bad luck for us, unfortunately. Now the inn and every house in this town will be full."

There was nothing she could think of to say, and they drove through the town in silence until they came to an establishment with a sign on which a tree had been painted. "Wait here," he told her. "I'll see what I can do."

From inside the inn came a burst of laughter. Roundhead laughter. She flinched involuntarily, and he said, "Hold the reins tightly. You don't want the horse to bolt."

As the powerful figure shouldered his way into the inn, she turned to the suffering man in the cart. "As soon as we find shelter, I'll try to find a physician for you."

"No, child." The weak voice was also firm. "The roundheads may question any physician who examines a stranger to the town. Even now, they watch us."

He was right. By merely sitting in the cart she had attracted unwelcome attention. At least two dozen male eyes were focused on her, and one of the roundhead soldiers now strolled toward them. Damaris felt cold at the base of her spine as he looked up into her face, and she forced herself to return that stare and remain silent. Finally, he grinned.

"Look what we've found," he chortled. "Now, I wonder what you're doing here?"

There was liquor on his breath, and instinctively she shrank from him, for the bold glitter in his black eyes reminded her of Jed. Not wanting to anger him, she said, "I'm looking for lodgings, sir . . ."

"Why, lovely, you can have my bed," he purred.

". . . for myself and for my father."

The soldier roared with laughter. "Likely story, a pretty wench like you. Father, is it? What you need in your bed is a lusty man who can show you how much fun 'tis being a wench."

"And do you call yourself a soldier of the Commonwealth?"

She had not heard him come up to the cart, and neither had the drunken roundhead soldier.

He spun around and attempted bluster. "Who the hell are you?"

"Stand at attention when you speak to me!" Automatically responding to the ring of authority in the deep voice, the soldier tried to snap to. "So. You swear, you bother women, and you're disgustingly drunk. Who's your commanding officer?"

More roundheads had drawn close, and one of them said, "Forgive him, sir. We've been on the jump all the way since Worcester, and that's more'n two weeks ago. We've been combing the woods around here and the riverbank for royalists."

"Caught one, too—Reisling, his name is," another one chimed in. "I hear he's going to be taken straight to London." He made a slitting motion across the throat and laughed.

"For that piece of good news, I'll overlook this—just once." Thoughtfully, Jonathan watched as the soldier reeled gratefully away and then turned to Damaris. "As I feared, there's no room in this inn," he informed her. "I've found a place for you in a woodcutter's hut nearby." He took the carthorse's reins and led it down the street. "I'll take you there now."

"And you—where will you stay?" she asked.

He sounded somewhat preoccupied. "You needn't worry, I'll find quarters elsewhere." He drew to a stop before a small house and turned to help her down, and she was grateful to note that his help was completely impersonal. "The

41

landlord of the Tall Oak sent someone to warn these people that you were coming," he went on. "They're expecting you."

The narrow door of the house opened as he spoke, and a small, middle-aged man peered fearfully out. Behind him peered a woman and three small children. "Is your worship Captain Hartwell?" he quavered.

Damaris took it upon herself to answer. "I am Damaris Langley, and this is my sick father. We are very grateful for your kindness in giving us shelter." Guy St. Cyr groaned as Jonathan lifted him from the cart, and she caught her lower lip in her teeth. "He is very sick," she said urgently. "Please, if you have a bed on which we can place him . . ."

Silently, the figures in the doorway melted away, and Jonathan followed. The lintel was so low that he had to bend to enter, and Damaris noted that the woodcutter's house was smaller even than that of Owen Marsh. Yet it was pleasantly cool and held the sweet clean scent of new wood. A blanket had been hastily strung up across a corner of the one-room house, and behind it was a wide bed and a smaller cot. The rough, homespun bedsheets were clean, and by the light of a smoky lamp she saw that a jar of wildflowers had been set nearby on the floor. Somehow the sight of that homely nosegay reassured and steadied her.

"I hope this serves, your worship," the woodcutter was saying anxiously. "These are not very good beds, your worship, but they're all we have . . . and here is a blanket for your sick father, my lady."

"Can I help you make him comfortable?" Jonathan Hartwell asked, but Damaris shook her head. She was afraid that the strain of travel had reopened the wound in her father's side and that it had begun to bleed again. If so, every moment that the captain stayed close by increased the risk of discovery.

"Now that we are sheltered, I can take care of him. You yourself need a place to stay," she pointed out.

He didn't press her. "The horses need to be attended to," he agreed. He started to leave the small enclosure and then half turned to face her. The smoky lamplight shadowed the hard planes in his face, turned his face to deepest bronze. "Damaris . . ."

In spite of herself she caught her breath. She was acutely aware of him as he stood there, one hand pushing the curtain aside, his powerful masculinity making the tiny space even smaller. She swallowed and tried to speak calmly. "What is it, Captain Hartwell?"

"I only want to urge you to sleep well—you are safe here." His lips quirked in a brief smile and then the curtain swung down behind him and she could hear his footsteps walking away.

She found that she had been holding her breath. She let it out in a deep sigh as her father whispered tensely. "For sweet Christ's sake, daughter, the bandages have slipped. Quick, before anyone comes."

43

She set to work feverishly, removing the colonel's coat and shirt and undoing the bandage. The wound was again bleeding as she had feared, and as she rebound the wound and then wrapped him warm in the blanket, he murmured, "That roundhead captain is a good man. Too bad he is not on our side."

"If he was, he wouldn't be able to help us with the magic of Cromwell's name," She did not want to talk of Jonathan, and she was grateful that her father fell silent as the woodcutter's wife came in with bowls of steaming soup.

She thanked the woman and spooned her father's soup before drinking her own. She could hear the woodcutter and his children eating. On the big bed, the colonel slept, and she knew that she, too, should try to do so. The warmth of the soup was welcome, the room secure. But though she lay down on the narrow cot, she could not will her body to relax into sleep.

Her body screamed for rest, but her eyes would not stay closed. She could remember too well Jed's predatory hands, Clandennon—and Jonathan Hartwell. Above all that had happened this day, the dark-haired captain strode through her tired memory like a strong-limbed panther. She heard the concern in his voice as he rescued her from Jed and his ruffians, felt his arm go about her in support. And she remembered the feel of being pressed against his hard body.

A moan from the colonel brought her upright on the cot, but when she bent over him, she realized he slept. Why couldn't she sleep also? If the town was full of roundheads, they must leave soon, perhaps in a day or two, and she needed to conserve her strength and plan for their future. If the colonel grew stronger, perhaps they could go as far as Stourbridge and seek out help along the way. Family friends, the Kirkes, lived near that town. But could she put Aline and Robin Kirke in danger by appearing at their door?

It was a question she would have to answer soon, but not now. Her mind felt heavy and she knew that she must somehow relax herself for sleep. Perhaps, she thought, if she went outside, breathed fresh air, it would help.

The embers of the cooking fire still flickered on the hearth, and by its glow she saw the woodcutter and his wife asleep in one corner, their children on a thin pallet beside them. Careful not to awaken them, she slipped to the door and pushed it open. There was no moon tonight, but stars shone white against the darkness. By their light she could see houses, and beyond them the road, a dusky ribbon in the faint starlight. Near the road stood what looked to be a stables. I will walk that far and then go back and try to sleep, she promised herself.

Burrey seemed deserted as she began her walk, and gratefully she drew deep breaths of night air, cooled and scented with new wood and loam and crushed grass. Almost, she could believe herself in some peaceful countryside, somewhere far away from danger and violence. "It's almost like home," she whispered out loud.

"Where is home, Damaris?" She spun around at this intrusion, at the deep voice that echoed her thought. He was standing nearby, against the narrow building that she had thought was a stable, and now he came toward her, a shadow against the greater dark. "I'm sorry if I frightened you," he went on, "but I was surprised to see you. I'd thought that you would be resting."

"I'm too tense for sleep." He nodded, as if he could well understand this. "And you?"

"I was seeing the horses bedded for the night." She could not see his face but she could hear the smile in his voice as he added, "It's so dark I would not have recognized you if you had not spoken. There is both sunlight and shadow in your voice, and like you it is hard to forget."

She ignored this and the ungovernable leap of her pulse. "Our hosts have been very kind to us," she said instead and saw him nod.

"The people of England are kind. And decent, most of them." He spoke quietly but with the same depths of feeling she had heard earlier that day on the downs. "They are the backbone of the land. Even in these troubled times, they keep faith that the day will come when the nation is one, at peace."

Sickened, she thought suddenly of the bloodbath that had been Worcester. She thought of herself hunting amongst the wounded and the dead, remembered the smells of smoke and gunpowder and blood, the screams of hurt men and dying horses. "Will that day ever come?" she muttered.

"The Lord Protector is doing his best to bring it closer." She realized with sudden fear how close she had been to speaking her mind. Near this man, she was not safe! She forced herself to rigid attention as he went on, "You spoke of home just now. I, too, remembered a place where I used to go as a boy. It was a small place, out of the way, and the stars were as bright, the evenings as fragrant and fresh. Is that how you remember your home, Damaris?"

In spite of herself, she found herself nodding. "Yes."

"And this is your home in Portsmouth?"

"No," she began automatically, and then bit her lip. Now she had no choice but to describe the small holding in the north which had been home until Guy St. Clair sold it to help raise money for Charles II. Carefully, she said, "When I was a child, my father and mother and I lived near York. My mother said that the finest roses grew in the area."

"Tell me more about this home."

What else could she do but tell him? "It was a small place and perhaps poor in the eyes of others, but the perfume of the roses stole into my chamber at night, and there were songbirds that nested in the garden. I had a small white dove of my own, as tame as could be. She would take fruit from between my lips." She couldn't help smiling at the memory.

"Fortunate bird," she heard him murmur, and his voice echoed her smile.

Now that she had begun to remember, she

could not seem to stop. "One moonlit night, my mother and I walked in the garden together and she held me in her arms. I remember the scent of her hair, and the way she kissed me. I was so happy and so safe in her arms that night, but then just a week later she died of a fever. My father was not home and the servants feared to tell me. I wept for her for days before they let me know the truth."

His voice was gentler than she had ever heard it. "It must have been hard for you—and lonely."

"For my father, too. That is why we are so close. We only had each other, and now . . ." She checked herself but not before the full thought formed: now he is terribly hurt, perhaps even near death.

It was too much. The shell of her courage cracked open, and fear poured in. And, worse than fear, the terrible, sad loneliness that she had felt long ago as a child searching the empty halls for her mother. It caught at her heart, and she felt the tears blur in her eyes.

She could not let him see her cry. But as she turned away, she felt his arms drawing her back. "Damaris, it's all right. All humans are lonely sometimes—it's God's curse and His gift." He drew her against him and she did not resist, did not want to. "A curse because it hurts, a gift because it makes us strong."

He had known loneliness, too. Yes, surely, he had. Otherwise he would not hold her like this, stroke her hair as if he understood. And there was something more that kept her where she was, the feeling that here was safety and comfort. The distinctive, vital, clean fragrance of him filled her senses like stardust, gentled the tense, weary corners of her mind and spirit. She felt herself unfolding, easing, loosening in a way she had not for weeks—perhaps even for years.

"You should go and rest, my heart . . ."

Her eyes leaped to meet his at the endearment, were held by the light of his eyes. She felt her head tipping back of its own weight, and her lashes swooped down to veil her eyes as his lips found hers. A gentle kiss, almost chaste—she registered the sweetness of his mouth, and she shivered again as deep within her something seemed to shift, to open.

"Jonathan—" She didn't know that she had spoken his name aloud, but he heard and his arms tightened around her as their kiss changed. She felt it change. Her mouth opened against his sweet insistence and against the exploration of the tongue which boldly quested the perimeter of her lips, then roved deeper, invading the rich warm honey of her mouth. Fire flowed through her veins and burst through her senses, leaving her shaken.

One hand reached up to smooth the fiery waterfall of her hair, then traveled down her spine, stroking lightly over the rounding of her hips and up again, over the slender waist and the sweet, high curve of her breast. Sensitive fingers caressed the firm mounds, and she pressed closer, yearning for what she did not know until his light touch answered her unspoken quest by brushing against her nipples.

His mouth left hers to kiss her temples, her chin, her throat and he found her incredibly sweet. In his twenty-eight years he had held many women like this, yet now they seemed faceless and without substance beside the reality of this slender girl who trembled in his arms and whispered his name with such longing.

He bent to cover her still-clothed nipples with his open mouth, and she all but cried out in her greediness for the caress that seemed to burn through the cloth. She caught his dark head to her and held him prisoner, twining her slender fingers in his crisp curls, and deep in his throat she heard the deep purr of pure male enjoyment.

His mouth deserted her breast, came back to seek her lips. Melded together, they breathed one breath as tongue and teeth and lips tasted, sipped, worshipped. "My dear one," he called her.

As she drew breath to answer, she heard a soft whinny and the sound of restless hooves moving nearby. She started at the sound and drew back, but he only held her closer.

"It's nothing, Damaris. No one will disturb us . . ."

But by then she saw what it was. Beyond his shoulder his great dark horse stood near to the stables. Her eyes might still be dazed with passion, but they could clearly make out the fact

50

that Jonathan's horse had been saddled and bridled.

She turned to him, eyes wide. "You said you were seeing to the horse," she exclaimed, "but you were lying, weren't you? You were going to ride away tonight."

Chapter Four

"IT WAS A FINE NIGHT FOR A RIDE," HE SAID. Even if his voice had not altered, she would have sensed the falsehood in the way his arms loosened about her. Why the lie, she wondered, and then cold understanding swept through her. He must have seen that the colonel bled and been on his way to Clandennon with the damning information so as to claim the reward on her father's head. Perhaps he had kissed her to keep her from guessing his midnight errand—or perhaps so that she would trust him and confess to what he already suspected. She pulled back from him and looked up at him, and there was nothing in his suddenly shuttered face to reassure her.

"I don't want to stand in the way of your ride,

Captain." She was furious with herself for having gone into her enemy's arms freely, even joyously. What in God's name ailed her? A small breeze touched her cheek and brought with it again the fragrance of the September night, stirred within her senses the memory of shameful passion. She found that she had wrapped her arms about herself in a futile, protective gesture. "You had better be going," she went on.

"I've changed my mind." He was frowning. So, she thought, I did stumble onto something he wants to keep hidden.

"Damaris," he said and there was steel in his voice. "I must ask you not to mention to anyone that you saw me ready to ride. I have enemies in Burrey who'd gladly try to hinder me in my duty. I'd hoped to ride away unseen, but if you are out walking, others might be, too. I can't risk leaving now."

Not trusting herself to answer, she gave a brief nod. He wasn't content with that. "I want your word," he said sternly.

She was grateful for the anger she felt against herself and him, anger that kept her spine rigid and her chin high. But she seemed to taste ashes as she said, "You have my word. I will not tell anyone I saw you ready to slip away like a thief."

"Bravely said, Mistress Langley." She couldn't tell whether he was amused or angry. "I suggest you return to your father and try to rest. I ride at dawn, so I will say good-bye now."

"Aren't you afraid that you will be seen at

dawn—by your enemies here?" she snapped. It wasn't wise, but the words erupted out of the bitterness she felt at her own helplessness. He closed the distance between them with two strides and caught her by the hands.

She nearly cried out at the strength of that pressure. In the darkness he was a formidable figure full of menace as he loomed over her, but it was not this that made her shiver. His strong clasp evoked a different response, and she was shamed and sickened at her weakness. Fearing him, hating the cause he fought for and the master he served, she still wanted him to pull her into his arms.

She tried to wrench her hands away, but he held them too tightly. "Let me go," she wanted to cry out at him, but the words came out a whisper.

It was suddenly so silent. In the distance some restless bird made a plaintive sound, and she could hear the beating of her own heart and his even breathing. She thought she heard him murmur her name and knew that she was lost. If he drew her to him, she would go back into his arms no matter what. Her head slowly tipped back, and without her conscious will her soft mouth trembled. Waited.

Then the pressure of his hands on hers altered. "You must be careful on the road tomorrow," he told her, and his voice was carefully bland. "If you are going to Portsmouth, the safest thing to do would be to cross the Severn River at

Elmshead Bridge and then follow the river road until it forks to the left. Hold to that course until you reach Stourbridge." A pause, and then he asked abruptly, "Can you use a pistol?"

She was so surprised that she blurted, "Yes," before she remembered that merchants' daughters would not even know what a firearm looked like. Hastily she tried to explain. "I became familiar with firearms when I started journeying with my father."

Loosening one of her hands, he drew a long-barreled pistol from his doublet. In the starlight she could see the glint of silver on its handle. "Keep this with you and use it if necessary," he said, and laid it in her hand. She registered its cool butt against her palm, his strong fingers pressing her fingers around it. "Good-bye, Damaris, and go carefully."

Perhaps it was a trick of the darkness that made his eyes soften, his hard mouth curve in a smile that was somehow rueful and tender. She spoke in response to that perhaps imagined tenderness. "Godspeed, Jonathan," she whispered and caught her breath to see the light blaze in his eyes.

He bent forward as if to kiss her again, and in spite of everything she felt her head tilt back to meet his lips. But he only bent his dark head over her hand, turning it so that his lips brushed the palm. For a heartbeat's time she felt the warmth of his mouth, the tender-rough brush of his cheek against that sensitive softness.

Then, he released her hand and stepped back into the shadows and was gone.

Next morning brought bad news. "The town's going to be crowded, a lot more crowded, before nightfall, my lady," the woodcutter's wife sighed when she brought gruel and coarse bread for the colonel's breakfast. "Those Commonwealth soldiers are on the march again, and they'll be in Burrey today. We'll have to put up with their demands and their noise—and their prisoners, too, I'm told."

Damaris's head ached. She had not slept well during the night, and once toward the dawn she had started awake to the sound of hooves galloping away past the woodcutter's house. She had prayed that they could rest here a day or two, but now this seemed impossible. Not only were the roundheads coming, but there was also the fear that some prisoner would recognize Guy St. Cyr and inadvertently give him away.

The colonel himself was anxious to leave. "I feel much better now that I have rested," he told his daughter when the goodwife had left them. "Besides, I have an idea. We have friends on the road. Do you not remember that Aline and Robin Kirke live near Stourbridge? I do not like to impose on old friends, but in these circumstances they will take us in, I know."

"I, too, have thought of them." Her mind dwelt longingly on the pleasant country couple who had known her parents for many years and who had been so kind after her mother died. "But," she added reluctantly, "our going there would expose them to danger. It is a crime to help escaping royalists. Rather than endanger our friends, I'd thought to follow the road toward Bristol and Bridport and then to the sea."

"You heard that green-eyed devil Clandennon yesterday—they'll be watching all such roads. No, daughter, our only chance is the Kirkes." The old man drew painful breath. "It is not for myself nor even for you, child, but for the king. Robin and Aline honor His Majesty and will gladly run any risk for him. In Kirke Hall we can wait out this storm, and you can rest." He patted her pale cheek. "There are lines under your pretty eyes, and I know you have not slept for worrying."

Not only for worrying—the thought touched her mind, and for a moment the image of a tall, dark-haired man hovered perilously close. Then she put both thought and memory away. "But can you travel?" she asked, anxiously.

"Better to be dragged about in a cart than to the headman's block," was the grim reply.

Before telling her hosts that her father felt rested this morning and anxious to be on his way home, Damaris took out the pistol Jonathan had given her the night before and made sure it was loaded and ready to fire. In the daylight she saw that it was a fine weapon, well balanced and deadly, and with the design of a tree over a sword worked in silver on the handle. Perhaps it was Jonathan Hartwell's family coat of arms, or—the thought was disquieting—perhaps he had taken it from some captured royalist.

Hastily, she hid the weapon in the sash of her dress and went to seek the woodcutter who readied the cart for them and then assisted in carrying the colonel to his bed of blankets there. He also gave her directions. "You'll see Elmshead Bridge on t'other side of Burrey Woods," he explained. "After the bridge, there be the road as plain as day. And steer clear of the Commonwealth army if you can. There are decent men in the ranks, but there's some rough customers, too. You don't want to tangle with them, my lady."

No, she was sure she didn't want to do that, Damaris thought, but she didn't have much to say about the matter. As they jolted out of Burrey toward the river road, she sighted the first dusty columns of Cromwell's men marching toward Burrey. The soldiers seemed well disciplined, and the officers kept stern order, but the sheer numbers were terrifying. And then, there were the prisoners. Damaris heard her father grind his teeth in helpless rage as wretched men with hands bound and necks yoked by ropes stumbled past.

"Damn Cromwell to hell," Guy St. Cyr swore bitterly. "Half of those men are too sick and too hurt to walk. He cares nothing whether they live or die."

Jonathan's words from yesterday filled her mind. These men would be taken to London and imprisoned or sold as slaves to labor under the hot Barbados sun. That was what awaited captured royalists. That was what waited for Guy St. Cyr if he were recognized. She gripped the reins so tightly that her knuckles shone white, and she forced herself to drive slowly. She couldn't risk some officer noticing her haste and ordering her to halt for questioning.

Once a nearby officer shouted an order to stop, and all the blood in her body seemed to drain away until she realized that the command wasn't for her. Another time an exhausted prisoner stumbled against the side of the cart and begged feebly for water, and she had to pretend indifference and drive on even though she was torn with pity and horror. She willed herself to concentrate not on the marching troops but on the river; if she got to the river, she would be all right. She just had to get to the fork in the road and turn left . . .

It was over an hour before she reached the fork in the road, and she breathed a prayer of thanksgiving as she guided the carthorse onto the side of the split that would lead to the river. The narrow roadway led through a peaceful green meadow. The fear inspired by the roundhead soldiers eased as she drove through the sweet-scented grass and then down a slope toward a copse of trees. Now she could see the glimmer of water below her. "We've come to the river, Father," she exclaimed joyfully.

"At last. So far, so fair." Then he added quickly, "What is it? What's wrong?"

"Roundheads." It wasn't easy, but she managed to keep raw panic out of her voice. "Scores of them are watching the bridge."

From her vantage point Damaris could see that though most were being allowed to go on, a few were being told to stand aside for more detailed questioning. And these people were being searched. She watched as a thin man was stripped of his doublet and shirt. Merciful God, she thought, we're lost if they search Father and uncover the wound.

"We can't cross by the bridge," he was saying. "Backtrack and see if we can find another bridge or a shallow part of the river."

She got down from the driver's seat and led the horse back the way they had come. The trees screened her retreat, and she held the carthorse's nose so that it wouldn't neigh and betray their presence. When she was sure that they were out of earshot, she began to descend toward the river again and soon stood on the bank.

There were no roundheads at this particular part of the Severn and it wasn't very wide, but the current was swift. She urged the horse upstream for a mile or so along the bank until voices up ahead made her stop, and peering through the trees she saw that they had come upon yet another roundhead checkpoint. These roundheads were guarding a shallow part of the river and were deployed all over the riverbank and back into the woods. Her heart sank as she realized that there was no way she could pass them without being seen.

St. Cyr frowned a question when he saw her face. She tried to smile. "We're going to have to backtrack again. I'm sorry."

Please, she prayed within herself, let there be some place where we can cross. But there was nothing, only eddying, whirling river and enemies on either side. She hesitated, wondering what to do. Should they stay where they were and hope that the roundheads would move on? But she knew that was foolish. The colonel had taught her that the longer one stayed in enemy territory, the greater the chance of capture. And even though she had a weapon, she knew she could not bluff or threaten their way through enemy lines. There was only one hope, and that was to attempt a crossing halfway between the bridge and the other checkpoint.

She explained this to the wounded man and he agreed but said, "I wish that I could help you in this. Are you sure you can manage the horse?"

"I'm your daughter, colonel sir, and have been around horses all my life." She tugged the horse by its bridle, coaxing and urging it into the water. The animal balked and neighed at the swift-flowing current, and even while she talked to it soothingly she winced at the way the cart jolted on the riverbed stones. the water rose from Damaris's knees to her thighs and then to her waist. "Come, horse. Be a good horse," she urged. "Now, come . . ."

Then she cried out as her foot turned on a slippery stone. She stumbled and fell forward, realized she couldn't touch bottom. Grasping the reins she tried to swim alongside the cart, but the horse panicked. Neighing and rolling the whites of its eyes, it tore its reins free and began to swim away from Damaris.

"Father!" She tried to reach for the reins again, but now a strong current seized her and bore her downstream, away from the floundering horse and the cart which bobbed helplessly behind it. "Father," she screamed again.

He was shouting to her to save herself. She tried to think of some plan and could not form a coherent thought, but as she struggled to break the vise-grip of the rapid current, a name rose unbidden in her mind. Jonathan. Jonathan.

"Hold on, girl!"

Her head jerked up at the sound of that well remembered voice. How could he be here? she wondered dazedly. But there was no mistaking that voice or the broad-shouldered rider who was urging his horse into the river. She didn't know where he'd come from, but renewed hope made her frantic. "Hurry," she cried. "Please hurry . . ."

"Hang onto my saddle." He was almost next to her as he spoke, and now a long, brawny arm reached out and pulled her free of the river current. "Now we go for the cart."

The cart had lost its buoyancy, was almost going under as he turned his horse and made for it, but next moment he had grasped the reins and was turning the carthorse toward shore. Damaris let go of the saddle to swim beside the cart and to hold the wounded man's head above water, but this was hardly necessary. Under Jonathan's firm hand, the carthorse dragged both itself and the cart into the shallows and then onto dry land.

"We're safe." She still could not believe it, and she repeated the words a second time. Her father shook his head in feeble wonder.

"Where did he come from, your captain?"

"He's not MY captain."

And as if to underscore this Jonathan spoke roughly from his position up front.

"What made you attempt such a foolish thing? You could have drowned—would have if I hadn't come along. Didn't you see the bridge a half mile downstream?"

Death had been so close that she involuntarily spoke the truth. "The soldiers were on the bridge . . ."

He frowned. "What's this about the soldiers?"

The colonel intervened. "My daughter was concerned about the way the soldiers were conducting interrogations. Some of those stopped for questioning were being stripped and searched. We are rather helpless; a woman and an old, sick man . . ." He paused and added, "We owe our lives to you again."

Damaris watched the captain's dark brows form a frown, but she couldn't read the expression in his steady gray eyes. "There was no need to risk drowning. The Commonwealth army is not made up of brigands."

Silently she began to wring the water from the colonel's blankets. She did not look in his direction, but she was sure that Jonathan Hartwell was getting ready to ride away again as abruptly as he had reappeared in their lives. She could not explain why this troubled her, and she kept her face averted and went on trying to make her father more comfortable until she heard the big captain swear under his breath.

She looked up then, and he said impatiently, "My horse has thrown a shoe—it must have happened in the river. Now I'll have to find a blacksmith before I ride on."

"I'm sorry—" she began to say, but he turned abruptly from her, and tied the reins of his horse to the cart.

"By your leave, sir, I'll be a passenger on your cart once more," he told the colonel.

He did not ask her leave nor did he glance at her as she mounted the driver's seat beside him. He seemed to be deep in thought, and she was grateful for his silence at first, but as they plodded through a green meadow and onto a wide, apparently well traveled pathway, this lack of words served only to accentuate her awareness of the rugged male presence beside her. She glanced at him and saw that the river water had plastered his clothing to his body so that his powerful torso was almost intimately revealed. The musculature of his back, the wall of his chest, his flat belly and the strong column of his thighs—it was almost as if he rode naked beside her.

Quickly, she averted her eyes, and as she did

so he said, "Why did you not stay on in Burrey? You were so anxious to get your father safe. Now you hazard him again—and your own life."

"The troops were coming into town and were being quartered everywhere. There was sure to be no room for us," she faltered. "Besides, I thought that Stourbridge would be closer home." Silver-gray eyes turned to her, and she forced herself to meet them. "And you? I thought when you rode away at dawn you went on the Lord Protector's business."

"Life has many surprises, Mistress Langley." At long last, he smiled, but it was a wry twist of his fine lips. "I say good-bye to you one night— and here I meet you in the river again. I suspect that in that dowsing you also wet the pistol I gave you?"

It was her turn to smile. "You're right, I did."

"Well, nothing is lost—and we seem to be together again. Until I find a smithy, anyway, and we can dry ourselves before the forge fire. It's a warm day, but your father needs dry clothing—and you, too. There's not a dry stitch on you."

His eyes were appreciative suddenly, and his smile was no longer wry but warmly, fully male. Made acutely conscious of the fact that her body too was being revealed by her wet clothing, she resisted an urge to cross her arms protectively over her breasts. He seemed to read her thought, for his smile became a grin, and his gaze roved over her. Boldly the silver eyes caressed her white throat, her high breasts, then dropped to the rounded curve of her hip and the line of her long, slender legs.

She knew that she should be indignant, even angry, but there was no place for annoyance amongst the other sensations working their magic within her. In spite of the chill of her wet clothes she felt a warmth, a langour that seemed to fill her veins with honey. Her breasts felt heavy, pressed taut against the thin stuff of her dress, and as he reached out toward her, she found herself leaning forward to meet the caress.

But he only smoothed back a strand of her hair. His touch was light, almost tender, and so was his voice. "There's something to be said for a swim if the company is right."

She frowned. What kind of remark was that for a Puritan to make? She pulled herself back from his disturbing proximity. "You are right about my father, Captain," she told him, coolly. "I pray we reach the blacksmith and his fire soon."

He pointed. "We're in luck, it seems."

They had turned a bend in the road, and the road broadened into what looked to be a village. It was no more than a handful of small, thatched houses bordering fields of ripe corn and golden wheat, and some distance from these dwellings was a smithy set up under a large, many-branched oak tree. About him stood or sat or lounged at least three dozen roundhead soldiers.

Her heart was going like the blacksmith's

bellows, and she felt as if she were shrinking into herself as Jonathan urged the carthorse closer. "Wh-what are they doing here in this poor place?" she finally ventured.

"Repairs." Jonathan nodded to the line of men and horses who waited their turn by the smithy's forge. The smith himself, a huge farrier with an enormous apron of tanned hide over his naked torso, was hammering away at his anvil while his apprentice applied the bellows to his forge. The hammer rose and fell in steady rhythm, raising sparks as it rang on steel. "The Lord Protector's men have horses that need shoeing. But what's this?"

There was the sound of shouting and men and women came running out of their houses and into the clearing near the smithy. All of them carried sticks and logs, and they threw the wood into a pile. "It looks like a bonfire." Then Damaris caught her breath. "Oh, dear Lord— they are dragging some poor soul out of his house . . ." Her voice rose in horror.

"Look again," Jonathan said, calmly. "It's just old clothes stuffed with straw and wigged to resemble Charles Stuart."

Feebly, the colonel tried to rise from his place in the cart. "What is this you say?" he gasped.

Damaris turned to try and calm him and Jonathan guided the horse closer to the round-head soldiers. "Perhaps these fellows can tell us what is happening here."

He hailed the man at the end of the line of horses, a short, close-shaven, round-faced fellow with cropped hair. Learning Jonathan's rank, he was eager to explain. "Sir, it's good news that makes the villagers light their bonfire. First, we have captured important prisoners . . ."

Damaris followed his pointing finger and gulped back a cry of pity. Five men, their hands bound tight before them, linked together by rough rope halters, stood to one side in the full and pitiless sun. It was plain that they had been badly treated. One man's forehead had been gashed open, another slumped half fainting in his bonds. She saw Jonathan's eyebrows rise, his nostrils flare, but he spoke quietly.

"Is it necessary for them to stand, and in the sun? Better sense to let them rest so that they have the strength to walk."

"Captain's orders, sir. We're not to let them take a rest or have any water until evening." The little round man looked a little abashed. "One of them's that bastard, Colonel Reisling."

With difficulty, Damaris supressed a shudder. Colonel Reisling had been one of Charles II's commanders at Worcester, and though he did not know her father personally, he might recognize the older man. She must get him away quickly—but how? She glanced at Jonathan and saw that he was nodding approvingly.

"I see. A prize to make this celebration worthwhile," he said.

"But not THE prize." The hoarse voice was familiar, and it gloated. With sick surprise Damaris saw the unmistakable and cadaverous form of Clandennon step out from among the waiting soldiery and approach them. The man's green eyes glowed with inner fire as he added, "We said we would meet again, Hartwell, but we did not say on what joyous occasion. The man of blood has been captured!"

"The king taken!" Guy St. Cyr's voice was low, but Damaris darted a look at Jonathan to see if he had heard. He had not. His gray eyes were blank with astonishment.

"Well, what say you, Captain Hartwell?" Clandennon was enjoying himself. The pointed tip of his tongue came out to touch his thin lips. "Is that not cause for celebration?"

The villagers had collected enough wood, and now one of them threw a lit match into the heart of the timber. Smoke rose, and then a gush of flame. Suspended over the flame, the effigy of Charles II wavered and turned black. Damaris could not tear her eyes from the quickly charring figure of straw, and she heard a low moan rise from the captured royalists. Oh, God, she thought, it can't be true. The king can't really have been taken prisoner.

"If this be no rumor, it is news to make a man weep for joy," Jonathan's deep voice was saying. "Did you yourself have a hand in this, Clandennon? You are to be congratulated. Honored."

"No, it was not I, though I apprehended Reisling and his rogues myself. The son of Stuart was taken further on, near the coast. He was attempting to bribe his way out of the country and escape to France. Of course, he will be taken to London to face the Lord Protector's justice."

"And may he meet his father's fate," one of the soldiers added fervently. "May *his* head, too, be cut off by the executioner's ax."

The villagers now began to dance about the bonfire, leaping and kicking their heels as they circled the flames. They shouted out a Puritan hymn, and Damaris saw Clandennon's thin lips writhe into a satisfied smile. "These are honest, God-fearing folk," he began, but he was interrupted by a low, uncertain voice from among the prisoners.

Surely, the man couldn't be singing? But he was. Damaris recognized both tune and words, and her heart squeezed tight with pity and pride as the proud cavalier song was hurled forth like a challenge: "Come pass about the bowl to me, a health to our distressed king. Though we're in hold, let cups go free, birds in a cage may freely sing!"

"Silence that man!" Clandennon snarled, and a soldier slashed down with his whip. "Colonel Reisling, you will sing another song when you meet the ax, just as Derby did. It's said that the market crowd cheered as the traitor's head fell into the dust."

"No doubt they would have cheered to see any other poor soul lose his head. People are fickle, Clandennon." There was an odd note in Jonathan's eyes, and Damaris saw a muscle twitch in his cheek. He can't stand cruelty either, she thought, and wondered why this should matter so much.

"Well, my friend, I give you congratulations for your prisoners and ask your cooperation. My horse threw a shoe and I need the good smithy's services immediately."

Green eyes moved coldly over Jonathan and his companions. "You are very wet on a sunny day," Clandennon murmured. "It almost seems as if you forded the river without the use of a bridge."

"Does it, so?" Jonathan got down from the cart and drawled the words into the thin officer's suspicious face. "Perhaps I had my reasons— which I do not believe I need explain to you."

"Most honest folk use the bridge." The narrow tongue darted again, and this time the catlike eyes came to Damaris. They moved from her face to her thoroughly wet bodice, lingered on her breasts. She felt sickened, as if she had come into contact with filth, and she crossed her arms across her bosom and drew back against the hard back of the cart as Jonathan spoke again.

"As I said, friend, I would have my horse shoed immediately. You know the orders I carry." There was steel just under his quiet voice, and Clandennon did not answer. Instead, he came toward the cart and stared up into Damaris's face. She fought off an instinct to shrink away as he said, "And you, mistress? Are you, too, loyal to the Lord Protector?"

"You know we are, sir." She managed to sound calm, a little annoyed. "We told you yesterday, when we met . . ."

"Yet you, too, found it necessary to swim the river. Interesting. Tell me, would you also join these villagers in their dance of triumph?"

She could not help herself. "No," she cried, and then hurriedly added, "I don't know how."

Glittering green eyes drew nearer. "I'm sure that at least you will join us in damning the man of blood? In praying for his execution?"

He stopped and waited for her reply. And not only he—she realized that all of the assembled men including Jonathan were watching her. The laughter and singing from the rejoicing villagers seemed an unreal backdrop for this terrible drama. She had to say the words, or they were doomed—doomed like those poor brave prisoners. Yet how could she curse her true and sovereign lord?

Clandennon leaned forward avidly. "Well, mistress?" he purred. "Can you possibly be a friend to Charles Stuart?"

Chapter Five

"MAY GOD DAMN THE SON OF CHARLES STUART!"

Damaris turned sharply as she heard her father's hoarse voice. His face was ashen gray, his lips moved with effort, and she knew she must follow his lead. Lord forgive me, she thought, as she lifted her chin and tried to speak lightly. "Of course I damn the man. La, sir, why all this fuss?"

"A good question." Jonathan untied his horse from the cart and tossed the reins to one of the nearby roundheads. "However, the bonfire is well thought of. We are wet, as you justly observed, Clandennon, and a chill can be dangerous for a sick man. I'd take the loan of a cloak or two as a kind act."

Several soldiers offered Jonathan their cloaks.

One he settled about Damaris's shoulders, and the others he placed in her arms before turning to watch the bonfire. Damaris wrapped the cloaks about the wounded man in the cart and, as she did so, sensed that Clandennon was watching her. He was far from satisfied, she knew. He'd hoped to add the supposed Langleys to his prisoners, and he was still suspicious of her. She was desperately anxious to be away, but she knew that haste would be incriminating, and so she took the colonel's wet blankets and carried them closer to the fire, spreading them on the ground to dry in what she hoped was a casual manner. She would have retreated to the cart then, but Jonathan stopped her.

"Stay awhile and watch the dancing and dry yourself." There was distaste in his tone, and his face was like stone as he watched the laughing villagers prance around the flames. "I'll wager that these folk were among those who cried, 'God bless King Charles the Second!' not long ago."

She looked at him uncertainly, not knowing what to say. "Captain Clandennon is enjoying it," she began.

"No doubt he is." The disgust deepened in his voice. "But not everyone shares his tastes."

Before she could respond to this, there was a stir from the small knot of prisoners. One of them, the man with the slash across the forehead, slowly sank to his knees on the turf. "Water . . ." he muttered.

"Shut up, you!" The roundhead soldier with

the whip moved menacingly closer. "You heard Captain Clandennon. No water till we make camp tonight."

The blood seemed to flow away from Damaris' heart. As the prisoner moaned hoarsely, she moved without her conscious will, hurrying back to the cart and searching blindly for the flask of water she had brought out of Northbridge.

"What are you doing?" Jonathan asked, sharply. "Don't interfere, Damaris. This is no concern of yours."

The hand that was holding the waterflask shook, and so did her voice. "That poor wretch is dying for water."

"He's Clandennon's prisoner." She moved forward toward the fallen man and he repeated. "Leave it, I tell you."

She paused a moment to look into stern gray eyes and saw in their depths a small, raw flame. She was not sure if that anger was for her, and she did not care. Indignantly she said, "You said yourself that you would give aid to any wretched royalist by the roadside—do you now go back on your words?"

"Stop." Clandennon's familiar hoarse voice cut short her words. "Put back the water and get back on the cart, Mistress Langley. Col. Reisling must suffer. And so must the brutish Scots who have dared to try and invade England by following their so called 'king.'" He came closer, and she could almost feel the heat of his fanatical eyes. "Woe to the man of blood. The forces of the

New Israel were clothed in God's might and prevailed at Worcester over His enemies."

Damaris swayed forward. "No," Jonathan said, so quiet that it stopped her. She suddenly came wide awake to the dangers she faced, and she knew she must not take another step. Unable to bear the sight of suffering she could not aid, she turned away. Forgive me, she cried silently. If I help you, I'll betray my father.

"In the name of God, water. Of your sweet charity . . ." the voice was fainter, now.

In the cart, the wounded man moved restlessly. "For the Lord's sake, daughter," Guy St. Cyr groaned, and Damaris knew what was in her father's mind. Better to be imprisoned, better to die, even, than to turn away from such misery. Her fingers clenched the waterflask tightly as she faced the prisoners and their tormentor, but before she could move, a strong hand had taken the flask from her. "In the name of God, then," Jonathan said.

"I forbid it!" But the big man strode past Clandennon without so much as a backward glance.

"Would you arrest me for following the teachings of Christ?" the deep voice was openly mocking. "Have you forgotten your scripture, sir? Personally, I'd give a drink to a dog, if he were thirsty, or suffering as this man is suffering."

Clandennon's face flamed crimson and then paled to the color of putty. "You have no authorization to flout my orders," he said in a deadly whisper. "You will answer for this."

Jonathan ignored him. He was kneeling in front of the fallen man, holding the spout of the waterflask to his lips. As the man drank eagerly, Damaris began to tear strips of the blanket on which Guy St. Cyr lay. Then, the improvised bandage in hand, she hurried toward the prisoners. No one stopped her as she knelt down to bind Colonel Reisling's forehead.

He smiled into her white face and murmured his thanks. "It's almost worth a scratch or two to be tended by so lovely a lady. Being a prisoner has its compensations."

"I wouldn't count on it, friend." There was a wry twist to Jonathan's lips as he helped the other bound men quench their thirst. "It's a long walk to London. Perhaps you won't finish it."

"You roundheads would say that that was in God's hand." How could the man joke at a time like this? But Jonathan was smiling in grim approval of the man's courage. She set about binding the worst of the prisoners' wounds, and as she worked she felt the silver-gray gaze upon her. But when he spoke it was not to her but to Clandennon.

"I am a soldier, sir, and in battle I have killed many and have taken many prisoners. But I do not believe in mistreating men whose hands are bound." Clandennon said nothing. "There's no sport for me in cruelty, my friend."

"Take your horse and go—both of you." Damaris did not need to look up to see the cold blaze of fury in Clandennon's thin face.

Hurriedly she finished her ministrations, then

gathered up the still-damp blanket and quilt. Jonathan aided her in settling her father on his uncomfortable bed before mounting his horse and sweeping off his hat with courtly grace. "Clandennon, I hope you and your charges reach London safely."

"We'll meet again, Jonathan Hartwell."

The hoarse tone quivered with menace, and Damaris caught her lower lip in her teeth as they moved away from the checkpoint. "You've made an enemy of that man, and it was my fault. But those prisoners were so desperate."

"Some men are born cruel." Again, distaste filled his deep voice. "I wouldn't be surprised if Clandennon learned his lessons at Drogheda."

She had heard of the atrocities committed by Cromwell's forces in Ireland, and she suppressed a shudder. And not only because of Clandennon. It reminded her that even though Jonathan Hartwell was not cut from the same cloth as Clandennon, he was still a roundhead officer. Some sixth sense made her glance up at him, and she saw that he was watching her with keen interest, and she hastily schooled her features to calm.

"I suppose sometimes terrible things are necessary," she forced herself to say.

They were both silent as they followed the river road for the next hour. She had thought that Jonathan would ride on ahead once they had cleared the village and left Clandennon behind, but though he could have ridden on ahead more than once, he showed no sign of wanting to leave their company. It worried her. Supposing he accompanied them all the way to Stourbridge, she asked herself. She did not want to lodge in the town, and she could not let him know about the Kirkes. To do so would put those good friends in danger.

She tried to get the colonel's advice, but he was sunk deep in gloom. "I should have died before I cursed my king," he told her miserably. "In front of Colonel Reisling and those others, I cursed him. I was afraid that if we stayed there longer I would be recognized and that the secrets I carry for the king would be lost, but that's no excuse."

Her heart bled for him and for his pain. "If you had fallen into Clandennon's hands you would have been treated like those poor prisoners. You would have died."

"I should have done so. His Majesty always said that a man can only lose his life once. Now I am dishonored and unworthy of serving him."

She blinked tears from her eyes. "Don't talk like that, Colonel, sir," she said as lightly as she could. "Soon we will be with Aline and Robin, and you will have a soft bed to lie upon." But when she stopped to give him water, she noted that he was burning with fever and shivering in his still damp clothes. He looked at her with vacant, rheumy eyes.

"Where is my daughter, lady?" he whimpered. "Is she coming with Colonel Reisling's regiment?"

Delirious—worse, babbling. She watched distraught as his fluttering eyelids shuttered his eyes. If he spoke like this when Jonathan Hartwell was by—she was grateful that he had ridden on ahead and could not hear, but now she thought she heard the hoofbeats returning. Desperate to keep him at a distance from the cart and from the feverish man who slept there, she left the cart and walked down the road to meet him.

The road had narrowed into a lane shaded by tall trees, and the afternoon sunshine lay dappled over the green grass and early autumn flowers that bordered it. A bird called somewhere nearby; its mate answered. September warmth lay drowsily upon the countryside and offered a sense of peace. She wanted more than anything to sit down by the roadside and rest—to ease her cramped legs and aching neck and back and let the blood flow into her fingers and arms, painful from the continued pressure of driving the cart. Could she, for a moment?

She hesitated, and then left the road and walked a few steps into the meadow. The sweet, honeyed scent of grass and flowers rose about her in the warm sunshine, and she closed her eyes. But the hoofbeats were louder now, and reality had to be faced. "I must think of some excuse to part from him," she told herself.

He came almost on the heels of that thought, turning a corner in the narrow road and bending low to avoid the low-hanging branches of a giant elm. With the sun at his back he looked to be a figure carved out of jet or onyx, and as hard. The great wedge of his shoulders seemed to cut off the light as he rode toward her, and her sense of desperation mounted.

Then, unexpectedly, he smiled. "You look to be enjoying yourself," he said.

She squared her shoulders and lifted her head so that the sunlight gave a golden sheen to her pale cheeks, and he found himself catching his breath at her beauty. A ray of sunshine caught the fiery highlights in her magnificent hair and glittered against her lovely dark eyes. But the expression in the eyes was wrong.

"Is something the matter?" He urged his horse to a faster pace and saw her shake her head as he came level with her. "Is it your father?"

She dropped her eyes from his and he saw her catch her lower lip in her teeth in a gesture that invited kissing. But dalliance wasn't on her mind. "I needed to stretch for a moment," she murmured.

He dismounted, tossing the reins over the back of the horse. "Are you very sore?" His voice had a different note in it, one she remembered. And feared. Even now, even here, something within her was stirring awake at the concern in his deep tones, the softening of his gray gaze. "Turn around," he commanded.

Before she could protest, he had caught her by the shoulders and was turning her so that her back was to him. Then the strong hands slid up toward her neck, pressing skillfully into the aching muscles. She cried out with pain that was also half pleasure, as he kneaded out cramped nerves in neck and shoulder. "Isn't that better?"

"Y-yes." Her pulse had begun to leap and fall, her breath was unsteady. She needed to pull herself away from the spell of his touch, for spell it must be. She tried for a deep steadying breath and drew in the fragrance of this quiet, sunlit place and of him, his nearness. She realized that his hands had moved to her arms. Involuntarily, she felt herself leaning backward, tilting her head so that it rested against the hard-muscled chest. Her eyes closed under the ministrations of his fingers.

"You're purring like a kitten." His voice was amused. Her eyes flew open then and he said, "In this light your eyes look like black gold, your hair like flame."

"You make me sound very strange," she murmured.

"Strange, and wondrous beautiful. There's enchantment in your lips when you smile and show that dimple. A man could barter his soul to hold you in his arms."

She realized that she was in his arms, that her full weight leaned back against him. Now he drew his arms across her waist under her breasts, pulling her even closer so that her back was pressed against his chest, her hips against his muscled thighs. Into her mind flashed a fleeting picture of how she had seen him earlier today—his soaked clothing revealing every muscle and sinew of his powerful body. Now, she felt that body against her.

His arms loosed her and hands moved down to stroke the curve of her hips. Moved up over her ribs, over her breasts. Erotic fire spread from his touch, spiraling through her, recalling the sweet madness of last night. She arched back against him as his mouth came down to join hers to his in a kiss, her lips parting under his. Her arms went upward and circled his neck, drawing him closer. Her breasts pressed against his seeking palms.

He turned her around to face him and then he kissed her, again, and yet again, with swift, passionate kisses. "Damaris." Her name was sweet on his lips and she murmured her response to that sweetness as he bent to trail liquid heat to her throat. Then lower, pushing down the thin cloth that covered her shoulders, the rounded breasts. Dizzying pleasure filled her as his mouth caressed her bare flesh, grazed the rounded slopes and then bent lower, circling but not yet touching the exposed nipples. She pressed closer to him, forgetful of all save his mind-drugging hands and mouth.

She nearly cried out as his open mouth covered the pale bud of her breast, his tongue circling, his lips closing with tender pressure over the taut peak. Surely, warm wine rippled through her veins instead of blood? Or honey— honey warmed by the sun and ready to savor, to suck. She registered his tender-rough hands as they moved over her hips and down the backs of her legs. One big hand flattened itself against her hips and lifted her against him so that she could feel against her soft womanhood the hard power of his desire. And then, still holding her thus, he eased them down onto the fragrant grass.

"Jonathan." She had called out to him in her heart back at the river, and now her voice was soft against his name. The tremble in the sweet, low voice fanned his desire, and he bent to draw again the honey from her breasts while his hands found the cool silk of her skin under her still-damp clothes.

She pushed her own hands against his broad back under his doublet and tugged at the hem of his shirt. Her palms registered the feel of his skin—smoothly muscled under her fingertips. And the strength of those muscles was sweetness—like his mouth. A yearning grew within her to hold him against her without the barrier of clothing.

His mouth left her breasts and found her lips again, and all thought ceased as his tongue explored the inner satin of her mouth. He nibbled her lower lip and kissed it again. She drew breath from his lungs. Their tongues touched, warred, loved.

"Dear one," he whispered, and while holding her so close that the buttons of his shirt pressed into her soft skin, he lowered her down against the meadow grass. She smiled up at him tremulously, and he kissed her mouth and her eyes and the sweet upthrust peaks of her breasts and smoothed back the tumbling glory of her hair. Want of her was sweeping through him like flame, and with it an odd tenderness that made his kisses both gentle and rough. She welcomed his caresses, nestled further into her soft and fragrant bed. It was cool against her back, while the fragrance of summer and of Jonathan enfolded her and became all the world that she ever wanted. She shivered with a rapture almost too strong to bear.

Wanting to feel him even closer, she drew her hands up under his shirt to the sockets of his arms, then over his chest, baring it against her so that now his flesh met hers. The thick, crisp fur teased her nipples, and she moved against him. She loved the feel of his tough strength against her softness. Wanted more . . .

There was a noise beside them, barely perceived on the periphery of her consciousness. Somewhere near them, Jonathan's horse snorted as it grazed. Then it threw up its head to whinny. The loudness of the sound surprised her, and she felt him tense. He looked up and around him, and then he shook his head and touched her lips with his again. "There's no one here, my heart," he murmured.

But as her eyelashes fluttered down over her eyes again, there was another sound—a far off, answering neigh. The carthorse was replying to Jonathan's. The carthorse . . .

"My father." How could she have forgotten even for a moment? Damaris's eyes fluttered open, and she put her hands against Jonathan's chest. He did not release her. "Please," she begged.

Gray eyes narrowed for an instant, and she saw the hardening of his strong features. For a heartbeat's time she did not think he would let her go. And what then? There was no way she could fight him—even if she wanted to. Then his arms loosened, and he half turned away.

Hastily, she righted her clothes and turned to hurry back down the narrow road. Frantic with self-reproach, she reached the cart at a run and bent over her father. He slept, still feverish, his lips moving as he mumbled of Worcester and betrayal.

"Damaris."

She jerked around to see Jonathan close behind her. He was leading his horse, and the expression on his face was harsh. For a moment she was terrified that he had heard the colonel's mutterings, but if he had he gave no sign of it. Instead, he spoke abruptly, almost in command.

"There's a crossing a mile or so away from here, and the left fork will take you toward Stourbirdge. I am going the other way, so I will take my leave here. I was coming back to tell you, when—when other thoughts occupied us both."

Her cheeks felt hot at the memory, but she managed to meet his eyes steadily. "I understand. I'll do as you say."

He nodded briefly, with none of his customary grace, and then he mounted his horse in that same silence. She was silent also as she watched him canter away, and she told herself that she was grateful that he was leaving. But when his powerful form dwindled into the distance and was hidden by the trees that shaded the road, she felt an inexplicable sense of loss.

The sun was setting two hours later when she turned off the road onto a smaller pathway that led across a copse of woods. "Not long now," she said cheerfully, as if the feverish man in the cart could hear her. "Not long, Father."

She was grateful that she had come to Kirke Hall with her father more than once in happier times and knew the way, and even more grateful when, after two or three miles through the woods, she drove horse and cart into a clearing and saw Kirke Hall's high corner turrets before her. She had never seen anything so beautiful, and the scent of apples from the fruit orchards that ringed the house had never smelled so sweet. Beyond the orchards were Aline's flower gardens, and the summerhouse that Robin's grandfather had built for his bride when they had first come to Kirke Hall. "It's like coming home," Damaris whispered.

The colonel stirred and sighed in his delirium. His condition had worsened as they rode, and Damaris's pleasure yielded again to the raging anxiety that filled her. That, and a sense of guilt. If she hadn't gone to meet Jonathan Hartwell—but she knew well that that delay had harmed her more than it had harmed the colonel. He was suffering from what he took to be disloyalty and dishonor. As was she.

She bit her lip at the thought of how easily she

had gone into her enemy's arms and then pushed that aside. He was gone—and now she was at Kirke Hall. Just let Robin and Aline receive us kindly, she prayed as the cart rattled down the bumpy road to the door of the big house. Let them be willing to take us in.

Servants were clustered in the doorway by the time she drew up to the door, and they gawked at her as she got wearily down from the cart. As she began to explain the situation to them, a round-faced, balding, middle-aged man pushed impatiently through the servants and hurried down toward her, arms outstretched.

"Damaris St. Cyr!" he exclaimed. "By all that's wonderful, it's you!"

He caught her in a hug, and she hugged back, thankful beyond tears for this reception. "Robin, we are fugitives, my father and I . . ." she told him. "We need your help."

A groan from the cart brought an exclamation from Robin Kirke. "Good lord, what has happened to my poor old friend?" He peered closer at Damaris and lowered his voice. "The battle at Worcester?" Then, as she nodded, "How did you escape the roundheads, through all those miles from the battle? But you can tell the tale later." Raising his voice, he shouted to the gaping servants. "You, Peter, and you Ned—hurry and get the colonel to the room west of the hall. And you, Helen, stop your gawking and ask Mrs. Gurney to inform the mistress that she has guests."

"Our thanks." Relief made her knees buckle

under her, and she hung onto the portly shoulder for a moment. "But, Robin, we bring danger to you . . . if you or Aline wish us to move on, we will go. Only let my father rest the night."

"Nonsense. He will rest and heal here. The roundheads won't trouble us," Robin Kirke dropped his voice as he led Damaris into his house. "They think that because I am a man of peace and tend to my orchards and my affairs, that I am no royalist. They do not know how much I pray for the day when His Majesty returns to England."

It was stoutly said, but Damaris persisted. Robin might not know the dangers that beset them, but she could still remember every detail of those dangers. "But, Aline . . ."

"She'll be grateful to see you." Beaming, Robin drew her down the hallway and threw open a door, and a pleasant-faced woman of about thirty-five rose from a chair by the window. Her movements were clumsy, and Damaris saw why. She was heavy with child.

Laughing at her surprise, Aline Kirke came forward to greet her. "Is it not wonderful? After all these years, when we'd almost despaired of having a babe, I have been blessed." She hugged Damaris and added, "Welcome, dear child. I have been fretting, for I become increasingly clumsy and useless as I grow heavier, and I had been wondering which friend I should send for when my time came. Now here you are." Damaris began to explain, but Aline cut short such explanations. "I know. We will get a discrete physician for our dear friend Guy to-night, do not fear. And you may rest here for as long as you like."

"But you don't know the risk . . ." Damaris thought of Clandennon and shivered even in Aline's comfortable arms.

The older woman hushed her again. "Of course we know the risk, but we have always been peaceful people, and not even the round-heads have bothered us. Now sit down, dear one, while Mrs. Gurney prepares a room for you."

But Damaris could not rest until the colonel had been attended to. Robin guided her through the house, very proud and pleased to show her the improvements and additions they had made. Though Kirke Hall had been built at the time of the Tudors, it was constructed in the modern style with a small central hall and entryways from either side. These entryways led both to the Kirkes' central chamber upstairs and here on this floor to comfortable rooms that had been set aside for guests.

The room west of the hall where the colonel had been taken actually boasted a huge bed with scarlet and gold hangings and posts carved with a design of leaves and vines. On it Guy St. Cyr seemed a small and shrunken figure, and he mumbled deliriously as Damaris and Mrs. Gurney, the housekeeper, removed the damp, travel-worn clothes and replaced them with bed-clothes of fine linen. Damaris wished also to change his bandages, but Robin demurred, saying that it might be better to wait until the doctor he had sent for arrived.

"And you must bathe and rest, Damaris," he told her kindly. "Mrs. Gurney will sit with your father, never fear. It will do him no good for you to become ill yourself."

At last satisfied that the colonel was as comfortable as possible, she let herself be shown to one of the two rooms adjoining the sickroom. This room was smaller and less grand, but even so garlands of flowers, curved snakes, and baskets of fruit had been carved into the chairs and chests, while from the open window the fresh scent of real flowers from Aline's flower gardens filled the air.

Gratefully, wearily, Damaris laid aside her hat and the heavy weight of Jonathan's pistol, tucking this last out of sight in one of the carved wooden chests. Then she went to the window and leaned against the sill, and for one bittersweet moment it was as if she were again drawing in the scent of her mother's rose garden. Then a deeper breath told her that the air had become heavier than when she and her father arrived at Kirke Hall. The wind was moist, and in the somber twilight she could see the flicker of faraway lightning. A September storm was coming, she thought, and breathed a prayer of gratitude that she had found refuge in time.

Thunder had begun to roll in the distance by the time she had bathed in the waist-deep tub which servants brought into the room, and as she changed into one of Aline's dresses and combed out her hair, lightning forked across the lamplit room. In the sudden flare the red-gold tresses flamed like silken fire, and before she could check memory, she remembered a deep voice that spoke of the sun turning her hair to flame. Her hand clenched tight about the comb. Some things were better forgotten, she told herself resolutely.

She had scarcely finished brushing out her hair when Mrs. Gurney came to say that the doctor had arrived. The physician was tall and gray-haired and had an air of command which made his reaction to the exposed wound all the more ominous. "It's not good, mistress," he told her bluntly. "This man should never have traveled with such a wound. His strength is nearly exhausted, and the jolting of the cart has caused fever. You have kept the wound clean, I see, but he has needed medical help long before this."

He made it sound like an accusation. "Please, can't you do something for him?" Damaris begged, and the doctor said solemnly that he would bleed the colonel to purge the evil humors of his blood.

"That will help the fever. I also will prescribe a salve of herbs, neat's foot's oil and garlic. The rest is up to God."

Damaris assisted the doctor as he worked and would have sat at the colonel's side after he had gone had not Aline insisted she come down to dinner. "A servant will stay with your father and call you if he wakes or if there is any change in his condition," she insisted. "As Robin says, all you can do for your father now is worry—and that he would not wish."

She would not take no for an answer, and Damaris reluctantly went with her down to the central hall, where food was piled on the great oaken table. She had thought herself unable to eat at all, but now she found that she was famished and vaguely remembered that she had not eaten since that morning. Aline urged her to try more of the boiled capon and the collop of beef, urging her to taste the marrow pie with its alternating layers of artichokes, currants and potatoes.

"And do not forget drink," Robin added genially. "This is bastard malmsey, sweeter than most and fatter. You need to put color into those cheeks, Damaris, though I don't doubt that what you saw on the road was enough to make a strong man pale."

She told them, then, of Bridgenorth and her meeting with Jonathan Hartwell, of Clandennon and the river. The Kirkes listened so intently that the meal cooled on their plates. Finally, Robin shook his head. "I had thought you had been in one or two tight places, but I hadn't dreamed you were in such danger." He shook his head again sadly. "Poor England, divided so radically between royalist and Puritan! I've heard it said that Puritans are by and large not bad folk, but I for one will never rest till Cromwell's yoke is off our back. He condemns beauty because he feels that earthly beauty is sin, he is harsh with laws and taxes, and he cruelly persecutes all who follow a different creed from his strict Calvinism. You know the stories about Drogheda . . ."

Damaris glanced toward Aline. "I've heard."

Leaning across the table, the round-cheeked man spoke in a low tone. "It's said that thousands of Irish Catholics were put to the sword in Drogheda, and that Cromwell gave orders to fire a church so that the people inside were burned to death. And the Irish prisoners were sold into slavery to toil in places like Barbados. He did all this in the name of God."

A fork of lightning illuminated the room for a moment and then was followed by a boom of thunder. Damaris shivered. Robin's words had recalled Clandennon's cruel smile too vividly. "Some men are naturally cruel . . ." she murmured, then stopped in confusion as she realized she had echoed Jonathan's words.

"Ah, but he was not like that, was he?" Aline put in. She smiled at Damaris and added, "I mean the captain that saved you so many times. What a shame that you're on opposite sides, my dear. He'd have made a gallant lover."

Robin looked scandalized. "Wife, what are you saying? Don't pay attention," he added to Damaris. "Her condition makes her lightheaded sometimes."

"Nonsense," Aline said spiritedly. She lifted a cup of bastard malmsey and sipped on it. "Damaris is over twenty, and she needs to find a good man and settle down. It's true, my dear," she continued. "I know that you are devoted to Guy, but I must say that your father hasn't done well for you. Instead of settling a dowry on you so that you could marry a nice country squire or some suitable gentleman, what does he do? He sells that little home of yours in York to raise money for Charles II . . ."

"Really, Aline!" Robin was truly embarrassed. "It's none of our business."

"But of course it is. Damaris's dear mother is dead, and we are old friends to Guy. Besides, this horrible civil war can't last forever, and everyone will soon be getting on with their everyday lives." Aline looked fondly at Damaris. "It's a shame that you have no fortune or a peerage to tempt a nobleman, but we must find a gentleman for you to marry. What you need is a good husband and a family before it's too late."

Damaris chuckled at Aline's firm words. "You make me sound as if I'm over fifty," she protested. Relief at being with friends in a comfortable, hospitable house was making her light-headed, too. She was also suddenly and unaccountably weary, and at her hosts' urging, she left the table to go to her room.

"I insist that you go to your chamber and sleep," Aline urged her, but instead of doing so Damaris went across the hall into the colonel's large room and relieved the servant who watched by her father's bedside. Settling herself into a comfortable wing chair there, she readied herself to watch. She resolved to stay awake until she could see whether the doctor's salve did any good, but her eyelids were heavy. Dimly, she heard a soft drumming on the eaves and thought, the storm's upon us. It's raining hard. Then she slept.

For awhile her sleep was mercifully deep and dreamless. Then without warning she was catapulted into nightmare. She thought she was swimming in the river again, swimming with her hair billowing about her, and her clothes dragging her down. She could not reach the cart which was whirling downriver and she shrieked for Jonathan. But he did not come. Instead, she saw the torn face of Colonel Reisling as she had seen him earlier that day. "Danger," he croaked. "Danger is near to you." And then there was the sound of thunder . . .

She came awake trembling and sobbing, and it took her a full moment to realize that the thundering sounds were not a part of her dream. Someone was hammering on the outer door of Kirke Hall. The colonel murmured fitfully in his sleep. "The roundheads. Damaris, I must reach the king and tell him what I know . . ."

Roundheads. Danger. Still half-dazed with sleep she got to her feet. As she did so the pounding on the door intensified, and simultaneously the door of the sickroom swung open.

Robin Kirke stood framed there, his round face no longer complacent but very worried and frightened.

"God help us, Damaris," he stammered, "there're roundheads at my door. What am I going to do?"

Chapter Six

"ROUNDHEADS!" AS SHE STARED AT HIM, HER terror increased.

His round cheeks quivered with dismay. "I care not for myself," he mumbled, "but for Aline and the babe—" Interrupted by more blows on the outer door, he looked pitifully at Damaris.

"If we're recognized, I'll swear that I lied to you and that you never knew you harbored fugitives." Lightning sizzled against the dark and mingled with the thunder that followed. Through it all the knocking was resumed. She said, "Robin, you must let them in. They're the masters of the land now that we have no king."

Wordless, Robin left the colonel's room, and Damaris went with him as far as the entry to the central hall where her host begged her to remain. "Perhaps they just want shelter from the storm," he reasoned. "I pray they'll go away without ever knowing you and your father are here."

He left her forming desperate thoughts; there was no way she could get her father away. If she moved him now, he wouldn't survive, but if she didn't, the roundheads would get him. She remembered Clandennon's smile and thought that it was better to be dead than under such a man's power.

There was a squeal of hinges as the great door of Kirke Hall was opened, and now the sound of rain grew louder, and the sour scent of sodden earth intensified. From where she stood she could hear Robin say bravely, "This is Kirke Hall and I am Robin Kirke, its master. Why do you come to my door this night?"

The reply was lost in a blast of thunder, and while it rolled jaggedly across the sky she felt a touch on her shoulder. A very pale Aline stood beside her and they both heard Robin say, "You must stay with us, of course. No one should be without lodging on a foul night like this."

Aline leaned closer. "How many?" she whispered.

Damaris shook her head and spoke with a conviction she didn't feel. "Don't worry. I've outwitted them before, and I will again. They won't hurt you or Robin or the baby, Aline."

"Hush," the older woman whispered, "they're coming."

Damaris shrank back into the shadows at the approaching footsteps, and then a tall man followed Robin into the central hall. He was dripping with rain from his hat to his boots, and in spite of the weather he wore no cloak. "Only one man," Aline murmured, relieved.

The man removed his dripping hat, and his profile caught the light. Damaris's hands flew to her lips to stifle her gasp, but alert gray eyes swung to the dim entryway. "Who's there?"

There was a grim note in his deep voice, a hand rested on the pommel of his sword. Heart hammering, she stepped forward into the light and met the incredulous stare. "You!" Jonathan Hartwell exclaimed.

She stood speechless, noting the narrowing of his eyes. She did not know that he thought her more beautiful than any woman he had known. He had seen her harried, seen her battle bravely against fear and danger, watched the soft beauty come alive in her face. But tonight, framed against sputtering lamplight in a borrowed dress, she looked different. And it was not the modish dress with its tapered waist and full skirt, the exposure of her white throat and the beginning swell of her breasts framed by creamy lace that held him but her face—huge black eyes, soft mouth, courage and vulnerability both reaching out to him across the dim-lit hall.

"Jonathan." Her whisper reached him where he stood, and for a moment he forgot the reason he had lashed his horse through wind and rain to reach this haven. He forgot the times in which they lived and his mission, and he took a step toward her.

"Damaris, do you know this gentleman?" Robin asked.

They both started, and then Damaris's long eyelashes veiled her eyes as she nodded. "We were companions on the road. Captain Hartwell is the officer I spoke to you about, but I never thought to meet him here when we—when we refuged here."

"The storm blew me here." He took his eyes away from her with effort and faced the round-faced, agitated little man beside him. "Master Kirke, I apologize to you and your good wife for hammering on the door and frightening you as I did. But I've ridden far today and my horse was exhausted. We'd hoped to ask for a dry corner to sleep in tonight."

Robin's voice was firm again. "We can do much better than that, Captain. Kirke Hall welcomes any friendly stranger. We'll get you dry clothes as well as something to eat." He turned to a waiting servant. "Conduct our guest to the third room in the west wing."

Damaris watched the tall captain bow his thanks and wished that her pulse would resume its normal beat. It was simply the shock of seeing him here, she told herself—that and the fact that his powerful stature dwarfed everyone about him in the central hall.

"Come, Damaris." She felt Aline's hand in hers, and she held it tightly as they slipped away down the hall and up a flight of stairs to the central chamber. As they climbed, Aline murmured, "He's come here looking for you. Why else would he come this way? You said that he was on orders from Cromwell himself and that he parted with you on the river road. Why would he still be in these parts if he wasn't following you?"

She drew away as she spoke and began to rummage through a wooden chest by the great bed in the central chamber. Damaris watched her friend fearfully. "You mean that he suspects we are not mere merchants," she murmured.

"I mean that he's interested in you." Aline turned to face her younger friend and spoke earnestly. "Didn't you see the way his face changed when he saw you? Believe me, I know the look a man gets when he wants a woman."

"I don't believe you." Damaris turned away to stare blindly at the sheeting rain outside the window. She, too, had seen the look in his eyes and she knew her own body's response to his nearness.

"Look, don't you see that it is God's mercy that this is so? What a man desires he won't destroy —nor will he betray you and your father if he wants to be your lover. You have only to keep him interested until he rides away, and you'll be safe."

And the Kirkes would be safe, too. The logic of what Aline was saying could not be disputed, and Damaris clenched her hands tightly against her sides to stop the sudden shake in her body.

"Take these to him now." Aline was holding out some articles of men's clothing, a shirt, breeches, hose, a doublet of fine gray velvet.

"Robin's clothes would never fit a man like the captain, but these belonged to my father who was a tall, well built man. They should serve." Her eyes met Damaris's directly. Remember that all our lives hang on your ability to keep the captain dangling, that gaze said.

What right did she have to protest? She had brought her father and danger into this small, peaceful household, and she had sworn to keep harm from her hosts. Yet, she almost shook her head and pushed the garments away. "You're wrong," she murmured, "He's a Puritan . . ."

"Puritans are men too, aren't they?" Aline almost smiled. "And I'd say that this captain of yours is all man," she added.

Holding the clothing to her, Damaris walked down the stairs and then hesitated before crossing the hall toward the three guest rooms. Her heart beat fiercely as she stood before the door of the chamber adjoining hers, and she thought—I cannot do this. She started to turn away and then remembered how her father had murmured about roundheads in his sleep. She couldn't let any harm come to him.

She knocked on the captain's door and heard the deep voice bid her enter. She obeyed before she could lose her nerve, but her courage faltered when she realized that the man was half naked. Lamplight glinted gold on his bare torso, turning the dark mat of his chest fur to shadow against the broad, muscled chest and the flat, hard belly. Raindrops still flecked his powerful arms and the wedge of his shoulders as he braced himself against his bed to draw off his boots. Intent on what he did, he did not see or notice her as he said, "Come over here and help me with these damned boots, will you?"

She hesitated a moment and then crossed the room toward him. Robin had lost no time in seeing to the comforts of his new uninvited guest. A fire against the damp had been laid in the grate and a low table by the big bed held a tray of mulled wine and pewter goblets. As she came nearer, he moved so that his side was to her, and she saw the jagged scar of an old wound across his lower ribs. Above this was a new and seeping line of red.

"You're hurt," she exclaimed.

He looked up instantly at the sound of her voice, and his eyes widened in surprise. "Good Lord, Damaris. I thought you were that servant fellow come again to help me."

Hastily she held out the clothes she carried. "Aline Kirke sends these clothes to you," she began. "They belonged to her father and should fit you."

She started to put them down on a chest near the door, but he came to her and took them from her. Their hands touched in the transaction, and she pulled her fingers loose from that remembered clasp and rubbed them against each other as if to erase the new awakened memory in her blood. "Thank Mistress Kirke for her father's clothes," he was saying. "And, speaking of fathers, how is yours?"

"Asleep. I should be with him now . . ." She

stepped backward toward the door, but he stopped her.

"If he is asleep he can spare you for a moment. Stay and have a glass of mulled sack with me, Damaris, and tell me why you are here and not in Stourbridge Town as I thought."

She hesitated a moment too long. He had already divested himself of his boots and now strode lithely barefoot across the room to pour hot sweet wine into the pewter goblets. One he extended to her, and gingerly she took it. He raised his cup to her and drank, throwing back his head as he did so and she was again aware of the cut on his side. Where had he got that? Her mind shrank away from its own question, and she couldn't meet the quicksilver of his eyes.

"I thought that you would be miles away," she said for want of something better to say. "Did your mission bring you close to Kirke Hall?"

He seemed to hesitate but then shrugged broad shoulders. "There was a rumor of royalists skulking in the woods nearby, and my aid was required." One dark eyebrow slanted up drily. "There are more followers of Stuart than I thought possible hiding in the trees. One gave me this scratch to remember him by, but it did him little good in the end."

"And was all this in the name of your mission for the Lord Protector?" She was careful to keep all feeling from her voice, but against all efforts her mulled ale shook in her hand. "Was this why you tarried to seek out roundheads?"

"As I told you before when we spoke of this, my

special duties are known only to me and to my chief. That is all I can tell you, flattering though your curiosity be." Thunder, more distant now, groaned in the sky, and when she looked up she saw unmistakable speculation in his eyes.

"I see," she managed to say.

"Do you?" he murmured. He came closer and through the hammerblows of her heart she knew that Aline had been right. He wanted her. Whatever his mission was, he was dangerous. The sword cut he dismissed so easily proved that. If such a man became suspicious, nothing would distract him except—except perhaps herself.

She only needed to stand up to be in his arms. The knowledge made her feel lightheaded, and she clung so tightly to her pewter goblet that the warm wine sloshed out in a crimson puddle onto her lap. He took the goblet from her then and knelt down before her to look into her face. "What's the matter, dear one?" he asked her.

The unexpected tenderness in his tone was her undoing. If he had pulled her roughly to him she would have gone to him resolute, inwardly unyielding. Now, she felt the stiffness go from her back and her shoulders, and something deep and elemental within her yearned toward the hardness and the remembered strength of him. He caught her hands in one of his and looked into the downcast face, saw how the lamplight played tricks with her hair and shadowed the uncertain dimple in her chin, spilled dark gold into her eyes when she finally looked at him. The high young bosom rose and fell, recalling the cool sweetness of her breasts in his hands. The subtle scent of her, clean lavender and sunlight, drew him closer as did the look in her lovely face.

As he reached for her, she leaned forward into his arms. She did not know who had moved first, nor did it matter. They held each other, warm soft breasts crushed against the hard wall of his chest, her soft cheek against his tender-rough one. He said her name, slowly, almost devoutly, and she turned her lips to meet his.

Their mouths touched with a passion that was gentled by tenderness. His name trembled on her lips, was lost as his insistent tongue demanded the surrender of her mouth. Her eyelids veiled her eyes as she obeyed his demand, welcoming the swift invasion of his tongue. She ran her hands over the bare shoulders, registering the rough silk of his skin, the powerful bunch of hard muscle, the lean strength of his back. In response he stood up and drew her out of her chair and cradled her against him. His hands roved over her as if re-establishing possession of her slender shoulders, the curve of her breasts, her waist, her hips. Then, impatiently, he pushed down the fabric of her bodice to bare her breasts to his lips.

She caught his dark head and held it against her as he first pressed his cheek between the proud valley of her breasts, then turned to kiss the high inner curves. "Sweet," she heard him murmur, and she pressed against him, impatient for more caresses. But when his lips teased the taut pale buds, she protested softly. "Oh, Jonathan, please . . ."

"You please me, my love. Before God, you please me past all reason." The words were formed deep in his throat, and she caught her breath as his mouth closed about her nipple, his tongue adoring, enticing, rubbing against the distended bud. Then, with sure, swift movements he began to unhook the back buttons of her dress so that it sank to the floor. Her shift followed. Now he smoothed his palms over the long, silken slenderness of her legs, stroking upward over her softly rounded hips and then caressing between her thighs.

A shudder spasmed through her as his fingers smoothed and traced erotic patterns over the silk of her inner thighs and trespassed upward with a delicate, rubbing movement. Again the touch tormented her with pleasure that was more than pain. She found her hips moving, thrusting forward against his hand, against his hardness, instinctively mimicking the dance of love. And instinct also made her hands rove downward, tugging at the fastening of his breeches, smoothing the lean tension of his belly and following the crisp line of his body fur down until she felt his arms tighten around her and heard his deep male growl of pleasure.

She curved her hand about the strength of him and felt its heat pulsate in her hand and through her own blood. She stroked softly along implacable hardness and caressed the rock-hard tension of his thighs. She wanted him. She wanted to cradle his hardness, sheath his demanding flesh in herself. She tugged at his breeches, pressed herself against him. Only the gossamer-thin underclothing she wore now separated them, and through them she felt his heat and her own answering want.

His lips left her breasts and sought her mouth again as he lifted her up and against him and into his embrace. Then, wordlessly, he caught her up and laid her on the big bed. She felt the cool sheets under her nakedness and shivered at this coolness as well as at the sensations that were imploding within her. She wanted to draw him to her but he held back. "Wait, my love," he told her.

With swift and economic movements he loosened his breeches and drew them off, and for a moment stood naked in the golden lamplight before he came to sit beside her on the bed. He kissed her mouth, her temples, the dimple in her chin, her breasts. Then he bent in further adoration, caressing the tender silk of her thighs and moving his mouth upward, he sought with lips and tongue the honey of her womanhood. She was shattering with pleasure, turning molten, liquid. Again she murmured his name.

"Oh, Jonathan, come to me. I feel as if I'm breaking apart, shattering . . ."

Supporting himself on his elbows, he knelt between her thighs, and she registered the sweet weight of him. He kissed her again, and his hands were everywhere, stroking, loving.

She closed her eyes and let herself be swept away in the molten heat of her passion, as he lifted her hips toward him.

It was then that she heard the sound. She did not want to hear it and at first it was all but lost in the frenzied beat of her blood. But then it came again, soft but damning in its insistence. "Damaris," a thin, weak voice was calling.

He heard it, too. His arms loosened about her, and she gave a little gasp as sanity rushed back. And with sanity came shame that she had come to offer her mouth and her arms for Jonathan's silence.

Wordlessly, not meeting his eyes she twisted away from him, she pulled her clothes to rights as best she could. He didn't stop her but sat up on the bed with the gold of the lamp bathing his proud nakedness. As he watched her as she drew on her clothes and smoothed her tumbled hair, desire for her was like a deep, aching throb in his body and when she stopped uncertainly at the doorway and half turned back to him, the look in her eyes made him want to stride across the room and take her back into his arms. He wanted nothing more than to carry her to the bed and pull away her clothes and find release in her lovely body, and yet a part of him also wanted to hold her close and kiss quiet the trouble he saw in her face and protect her from all ill.

Christ, he thought, what ails me? And out of his mental turmoil he spoke abruptly, even coldly. "I see that you have other business afoot, and so I give you good-night."

She winced at his hard tone, but she echoed, "Yes, good-night," and the cold doorknob dug into her palm as she pulled open the heavy wooden door and walked into the cool of the hallway. Every fiber in her being urged her to return to him, to throw herself back into those powerful arms that could bring her such incredible pleasure.

And incredible peril. She had been willing to barter her body for the safety of her dear ones, but not her heart. As Damaris closed Jonathan's door behind her she knew she was in danger of falling in love with her enemy.

Chapter Seven

"FATHER, PLEASE, TRY TO DRINK A LITTLE OF THE soup," Damaris coaxed. "I made it myself, and it's the beef broth you like so much. Please, dear one."

He tried gallantly, and that made it harder to bear when he could not swallow. He tried to smile. "It's not the cook who's at fault but the patient," he told her, and her heart caught on jagged pain at the weakness in his voice.

He had been sinking steadily for the last two days and at last she had to admit that this was so and accept what was inevitable. She had not believed the doctor yesterday when he shook his graying head; she had refused to leave her father's side even for a moment except to brew this soup, dozing here in the high wing-backed chair by his bed and waking to every tortured movement he made. When he had awakened clear in his mind and without a trace of delirium today, she had taken it as a sign that he might be well again. But now she had to admit that the old soldier was slipping away from her.

She turned away from him and closed her eyes to hold back the tears. Fiercely she told herself that tears were worse than useless, that she must fight death for him somehow. Death was a terrible adversary, but she would face him and best him.

"Daughter, you mustn't grieve." The labored voice behind her brought tears even closer. "You did more than ten strong men could do. But even you cannot change the appointed end of a man's life." He began to cough again, and as she turned to try and ease the racking coughs, she heard the sickroom door open. Thinking it was one of the servants or old Mrs. Gurney, she spoke without looking.

"If you please—if you can hand me the posset of lemon and boiled honey for his cough," she began.

"Here it is."

The cup of medicine was placed in her hand, but the deep voice beside her nearly made her drop it. She had known that Jonathan was still a guest at Kirke Hall these past forty-eight hours, but she had done her best to ignore his continued presence. She had told herself that it was because of the continued foul weather that he stayed, that he preferred to wait out at Kirke Hall the heavy rains which had lasted through the last two days. Or perhaps he was playing some waiting game with royalist fugitives in the area. She had vowed to herself that nothing Jonathan Hartwell did mattered to her, and yet now that he was near she couldn't help the treacherous leap of her pulse.

Ignoring his presence, she began spooning the medicine bit by bit into her father's mouth, and Jonathan came around the other side of the bed and supported the old man. Though she resented his presence here in the sickroom where she was most vulnerable, she had to admit that he handled the patient with a surprising skill and gentleness. When the colonel's coughs had subsided, he eased the wounded man competently back on his bed.

Guy St. Cyr blinked up at him. "Captain—I'm relieved to see you're still here. My daughter has need of a protector."

He is no protector, she wanted to cry, and you know it! But the old man held Jonathan's gray eyes with his own. "My daughter is so young and so brave. She has endured too much already. She will not sleep or even eat because of me. She will make herself ill, Captain—cannot you persuade her to rest?"

The old eyes were closing as he spoke, and he was slipping away into sleep again. Sleep—or death. As terror filled her, Jonathan's quiet voice took that fear away. "He's only sleeping, Damaris, and you should, too."

"You think I can rest while he's sick like this?" she cried at him.

"Especially while he's sick. You need your strength and skill to help him."

"No," she said. "I can't bear to leave him."

He left the colonel's side and came up to her. "Damaris, look at me." She did not want to obey, but her eyes rose slowly to meet his concerned gaze, and she felt a sudden ache that had nothing to do with her father's condition as he added, "You are exhausted, girl."

With his thumb he lightly outlined the shadows below her eyes, then stroked downward over her tense cheek. "Do you think you can aid your father by turning yourself into a ghost? It must pain him to see you so weary."

She found that she had clasped her arms about herself in a despairing gesture. "But he needs me here," she whispered. "Aline is too big with child to help much, and Mrs. Gurney doesn't know how to nurse so sick a man. None of the servants understand his pain . . ."

"But I do." She stared at him and he smiled a little at her surprise. "I told you I nursed men on the battlefield before." He pushed the winged chair into a darker corner of the room. "Sleep there, and I will wake you if his condition changes or if he asks for you."

Again she felt the strange, compelling trust she had always had in this man. She was too tired to question her own wisdom, and still, she hesitated. "You promise? On your honor, you swear?"

His fine lips twisted drily, his eyes held an odd, shadowed look. "On the rags of my honor, yes, I swear," he said.

Strange words—but now she was suddenly too weary even to thank him, too tired to do more than sink into the chair and lean into its comfortable softness before closing her eyes. As she plunged many miles down into exhausted sleep she found herself thinking that this Puritan officer was a man that soldiers would follow without question, and follow with love and trust.

She slept deeply, soddenly for a while, and then surfaced to a groggy awareness that the colonel still slept and that Jonathan sat beside him in one of the straight-backed wooden chairs. The sight was reassuring, and she slept again. When at last she came more fully awake she saw that a dull, reddish glow filled the chamber, and for a moment she thought of fire. She struggled awake and looked around her in disoriented panic.

"It's sunset," she heard Jonathan's deep voice say, and the panic ebbed away. "The rain has finally ended." He forestalled her next question by adding, "He's still asleep. He awoke an hour or so ago and had some water and slept again."

She got to her feet realizing how refreshed she felt, but it was clear when she went to the old man's bedside that he was no better. He looked even paler than before, and his breathing was more labored. He is dying, she thought, and could not bear the thought.

"While you were asleep Mistress Kirke came

in to say that the doctor will come again this evening," Jonathan was saying.

"Thank you." She knew from the compassion in his voice that he, too, knew what the doctor would say, and abruptly, she turned away from both the bed and Jonathan. "I'm all right, now. Please—you must be in need of rest and refreshment yourself after that long vigil."

As he sometimes did, he seemed to read her thought. "I'll leave you with him, then, but if you need my help, you have only to ask." He hesitated a moment and then added, "I will gladly serve you in any way I can."

When he had gone she went to a basin on a sidetable and washed her face in cold water, splashing her hot features and swollen eyelids again and again until her mind was sharp and clear again, all thought of sleep gone. Then she sat beside her father hour upon hour dreading the doctor's coming, and yet hoping for a miracle. When he did come, however, his words were the ones she feared.

"All flesh is mortal, mistress," he said. And then he added, "He will be dead within the next day."

She had known what he must say, but the blunt words tore at her heart. Aline, who had come in with the doctor, asked, "Isn't there something else you can do for him?"

"I have done everything that can be done," he stated. "I have given him medicine made from black cherry water and the crushed particles of human skull. I have tried an emetic made of an infusion of metals in wine. And I have bled and poulticed him . . ." He shook his head again. "No, I am sorry. There are some matters beyond my skills."

When he left Aline said, "Damaris, you are as white as paper. Do you feel faint?"

"No." Her own voice seemed to be coming from a long, long distance away as if she stood at the bottom of a well.

"Poor Guy." Aline enfolded her in her arms and wept, but Damaris couldn't cry. It was as if the tears had been frozen to an ice which invaded her entire body. Not only couldn't she cry, she could hardly breathe. There seemed to be an immense and crushing weight on her chest and a ringing in her ears as she looked down at the haggard old man on the big bed.

That wasn't Guy St. Cyr. It couldn't be the loving father who had comforted her after her mother's death nor the brave warrior who had been Charles I's man. And surely, this could not be the aging but stalwart companion with whom she had lived happily in York until Charles II recalled him to action. Small memories tugged at her mind: a May morning when he first taught her how to ride, his face when he spoke of her mother, the way he always laughed at foolish jokes and loved to talk about old campaigns with his cronies. And when she thought of the dreams they had spun together of a peaceful England, and the way his face lit up when he spoke of her marriage someday, and grandsons to dance upon his knee . . .

She could no longer bear to be here in the sickroom. She needed desperately to be out in the air under the sky where the memories would not tear at her heart. Aline understood.

"Go, dear. I will sit here and watch. Believe me, I will not take my eyes away from Guy," she assured the younger woman.

She went numbly, hardly aware of walking. The compassionate murmurs of the servants and the housekeeper fell about her like sod on a new-closed coffin until she found herself in Aline's flower garden. And even here, sorrow followed her. The scent of dying summer reached out to her and mocked her as did the busy chirp of autumn crickets under the pale moon. Soon the last of the autumn flowers would fade, and the world go down into winter darkness. There was no hope. She began to walk between the flowers, her skirts brushing against the wet, heavy-headed flowers, and as she walked she remembered a night many years ago when she and her mother had laughed and picked flowers and felt that nothing could ever harm them. A bruising loneliness filled her.

It was then that she heard the footsteps. They came from a short distance up ahead, and looking up she saw Jonathan. It was unmistakably he, and she sensed that he was deep in thought, but he seemed to intuit her presence and for a long moment their eyes met. Then he asked, "The doctor came, then?" She nodded, and he said, "All men have to die sometime, dear one."

The small endearment tore at the remnants of

her self control. "Not like this," she cried, "dragged across England in a cart in the heat and through the river—oh, God, the river. If I had been more careful, he wouldn't have gotten so sick."

"He was the one who wanted to get home to Portsmouth, remember. You did the best you could," he told her. "Don't blame yourself."

She felt the tears sliding down her cheeks and gasped with the pain of shedding them. You don't understand, you don't know, she wanted to cry, but now the dammed-up tears were flowing and there was no stopping them. Not to cry had been bad—to cry was worse. It seemed as if each sob would tear her heart loose from her body. Dimly, she realized that he was holding her in his arms and that she wept against him, and she clung to him in inarticulate grief as his strength enfolded her.

Moonlight silvered and pooled about them like quiet water as he held her, and she heard him say, "My brave Damaris—hush. You must not tear yourself to pieces like this." Gently he rocked her and she burrowed closer to the hard comfort of him, felt his lips against her hair. "My dear one," he called her. "My heart."

Her hair had come loose and was streaming down her shoulders. He stroked the bright waterfall of silk and kissed her forehead and her temples as he murmured his words of comfort, and as her despair gentled with her tears, she felt a different awareness stir into life. She had come to his arms for comfort, but now she wanted more, and under her thin clothes her body felt suddenly afire. A surge of passion swept through her, a feeling so intense that it shook her to her deepest core. The breasts pressed tight against him seemed swollen with remembered need.

And he was likewise shaken. She knew it from the way his arms tensed suddenly about her, from the way he bent to kiss her. His tongue circled the periphery of her soft, parted mouth and then invaded its willing recesses. His arms loosened about her and his hands began to move lightly down her arms, so that this erotic shadow-touch seemed to awaken all her senses to fever pitch. She drew in his scent, his breath, the taste and texture and nearness of him as their mouths strove for more closeness and his tongue mimicked another loving invasion.

Then suddenly she felt him pull away. His mouth left hers, and he lifted his hands to break the hold of her arms. "No," he told her, and still holding her hands tight in his, he kissed the knuckles of each and let both go.

"I was looking for you." Stepping back he spoke quietly. "It will soon be dawn, and as I must leave with the first light, I wanted to say good-bye."

Uncertain, lost in the welter of her emotions, she could only look up at him, his words adding to her confusion.

"You're leaving," she repeated, and he nodded.

"You must have wondered why I stayed here

so long. There's been a man I have been stalking, and now he's played his hand and I must make my move." Don't tell me more, she wanted to cry, but he made it worse. "I could not tell this to anyone, but you are loyal to our cause."

She nodded dully, wondering what he would think if she told him everything—her subterfuge from the first moment of meeting at the Silver Dragon till now. Suddenly she wanted to tell him, to have done with falsehoods and half truths, but she knew she could never tell him, never explain.

He made it worse. "You are brave, Damaris, and I honor you for it." He seemed to be about to say more, then added, "I don't want to leave you or your father now, but I must. I cannot let my concern for you keep me from my duty any longer. You still have the pistol I gave you in Burrey, do you not?"

She nodded, and he frowned down at her, wondering what it was about this woman that continually upset his balance and his sense of duty. That duty was very clear, and yet here in the moon-drenched garden the only thought in his mind was worry because she seemed too fragile for her burdens. He wanted desperately to take her back into his arms, and yet to do so was great folly.

"Good-bye, then," he began, but before he could continue there was a sudden outcry from the house. Old Mrs. Gurney came hurrying out of the door, calling distractedly for Damaris.

"Mistress, it's your father. The madam says to come quickly. To hurry . . ."

Damaris's heart turned to stone. He's gone, she thought. Bunching her skirt in her hands she skimmed through the garden and into the house. But when she burst into the sickroom, she saw that the old man was actually smiling. Aline stood by the foot of the bed, her eyes bright with tears.

"Daughter." His voice sounded actually stronger, and into Damaris's heart leaped a wild hope such as she had not dared hold before. "Daughter, I've been a sore trial to you."

Half laughing and half crying, she hurried to the bed and sank down beside it. "But you look so much better, Father . . ."

Behind her, she heard the door close softly and when she glanced around, Aline was no longer there. "She is a good woman," the old man was saying. "She left because she knew I must speak to you. There isn't much time. I'm dying, Damaris."

He silenced her protests and drew a breath that was almost a gasp. "I cannot believe in my heart that our king has been taken. Surely he will get away to France, and you too must make your escape. When in France, you will be greeted by English royalists who have found refuge there, including the widow of my old comrade, Lord Blount. Lady Blount and her son will give you refuge and help you reach the king." He caught her hand in his weak one, drew her closer. "Now listen carefully, child. While I lay wounded and barely conscious during the battle of Worcester, I learned the reason for our betrayal. The king knows that Lord Leslie betrayed him. He doesn't know that the duke of Deerforth also played him false."

Damaris knew very little about matters of the court, but her father had often told her that Charles II numbered the duke of Deerforth among his dearest and most trusted friends.

"Deerforth struck a bargain with Cromwell. The men under his command didn't deploy themselves as they should have, and that is why we were cut to pieces. Had it not been for Deerforth, Worcester might have been won. And he wasn't the only traitor."

She listened in horror as her father spoke names she recognized, names of high-ranking soldiers and of peers. She felt sick as the feeble voice continued to speak.

"I learned of this treachery while I lay bleeding at Worcester, Damaris. The traitors spoke freely over my head, thinking me dead." He drew painful breath again and added, "His Majesty can use the knowledge to his advantage when the restoration comes. But Cromwell's men must not know you have this information; they will kill you for it—and then they will use it to harm the king. Daughter, promise me . . ."

"I promise," she replied dully, but it was only to ease his mind. She had no idea how to escape to France—no desire to do so, even. As if reading her thought, the old colonel motioned her closer.

"It won't be easy, but you are a brave girl. And—and Captain Hartwell will help you."

She stared. "Father, he's a roundhead."

"I've known many men and I know something about human nature. Jonathan Hartwell is an enemy, maybe, but he is also a man to trust." He added softly, "I asked Aline to fetch him, for I wanted to speak to him before—I went."

The door opened now and Aline and Robin, followed by Jonathan, came into the sick room. The old man's eyes sought the tall captain.

"I'm here, Master Langley," Jonathan said.

"My daughter will be alone, now. I know you—are under orders, but—somehow, I beg of you, see that she is safe in Portsmouth."

It was clear that Jonathan was at a loss. He frowned, wordless, and as he hesitated Damaris could hear the busy chirping of birds under the sickroom window. Dawn was coming, the dawn in which the tall captain was to have ridden away. She could see the first faint dove-gray streaks in the sky as Jonathan drew a deep breath that seemed like a sigh. "I'll do my best," he said.

St. Cyr's eyes opened and fixed themselves on Jonathan's. "Your oath, man?" he asked, and now he sounded like no merchant but an officer used to command. "Your sacred word?"

Before Jonathan could respond, there was the sound of hurrying feet outside in the hallway and the door was pulled open by the housekeeper. "Master," she began in an agitated voice, "Ned just came hurrying in from the orchards with news. He says there are several Common-wealth soldiers coming this way. They told him that they were the men of a Captain Clandennon, and that they were on the trail of runaway royalists known to have come this way."

Damaris forced a calm she didn't feel. "Did they mention any names to Ned, Mrs. Gurney?"

The housekeeper took a gulping breath and stared back with round, frightened eyes. "They said as they were looking for Colonel St. Cyr."

Chapter Eight

"WHY WOULD THEY SEEK A ROYALIST COLONEL here?" Jonathan sounded astonished.

No one answered. Damaris sank down on her knees beside her father who whispered, "Your word, Captain? You'll see to it that Damaris is safe?"

Robin interrupted. "Captain, perhaps you can speak to these soldiers, tell them that there's no royalist hiding here."

Jonathan nodded. "I'll go at once." He then looked down at the man on the bed, and his voice softened. "There may not be any such thing as safety in these times, but I'll do my best to see your daughter in good hands. On that you have my word, so content you."

As he left the room with Robin, Aline moaned, "We're lost, all of us."

The dying man ignored her. "He promised to guard you, and he will," he told Damaris. "Get to the king, my child. Some day there will again be another golden day for England . . ."

"Yes." She remained kneeling beside him without words, almost without thought, but she knew when it was over and she didn't need Aline's sob to tell her he was gone. She could not find it in her heart to wish him back to pain and sure imprisonment, but her sense of loss was too heavy even for tears. She remained slumped on her knees beside the bed until Aline gave her shoulder a small and urgent shake.

"They mustn't find him here, Damaris. While the captain keeps those soldiers occupied, we must hide your father's body in the orchard. Then, at night we'll bury him in our family churchyard."

Damaris got wearily to her feet. "As you wish," she began, when there were sounds of hoofbeats under the window. Aline looked out and put a hand to her throat.

"They're here. We're too late."

The words echoed against Damaris's numbed mind as she heard Clandennon's familiar rasping voice mingling with Jonathan's deep tones. As if in a dream she listened to the squeak of the main door, the tramp of boots in the central hall, and then those heavy steps coming closer.

"What shall we do?" Damaris saw her friend put protective hands about her unborn child and the helpless gesture pierced her stupor. Cromwell's harsh laws about aiding escaping royalists were plain, and if she didn't do something now, her good friends would suffer terribly. For a moment she thought of running to her chamber and finding the pistol Jonathan had given her, using it on Clandennon. But she saw the folly of that at once.

"Don't say a word—let me do the talking," she said. She squared her slender shoulders as the heavy steps halted in front of the sickroom door, lifted her chin with a defiance she didn't feel. "Remember—you took us in because you thought we were a sick merchant and his daughter. You are innocent of any wrongdoing."

Her words ended in an urgent rush as the door creaked ajar. Clandennon, flanked by one of his men at arms, stood in the opening. "Mistress, we meet again," Clandennon said. He wet his upper lip with his pointed tongue and added, "I've come for your father."

"He's dead," she said, and saw the incredulous anger in those feline green eyes.

"May he rest in hell." Impossible to describe the venom in those words. Then, Clandennon added, "I hope St. Cyr knows that I have his daughter."

"St. Cyr!" She hadn't seen Jonathan standing in the shadows behind the thin officer and his man. "Are you mad, Clandennon? This girl is . . ."

"Damaris St. Cyr. And the old man dead on that bed is her father, the colonel whom we sought." His rasping voice barked into furious command. "Answer, woman, and tell the truth!"

She felt black dots dancing before her eyes. She could not take her gaze away from Jonathan's. She felt locked into the stunned shock she saw there, a shock that was replaced almost at once by dawning realization and anger. Please, she begged him silently, understand. I did what I had to do to save Father. I didn't want to lie to you, but I had to—don't you see?

"Answer, damn you!" roared Clandennon.

"I am Damaris St. Cyr." Could it be she who spoke so calmly? "My father was an officer in the army of the king."

"You mean, the son of Stuart," he jeered.

She drew herself up and matched him look for look. "He served Charles I who was brutally murdered by your master and the courts. Now, we both serve Charles II who will return some day to . . ."

Before she could complete her sentence, Clandennon had slapped her across the mouth. She tasted blood from her cut lip and saw Clandennon's hand go back again. Then there was a blur of motion and Jonathan caught him around the throat and hurled him against the wall. She heard the dull thud and the man's gasped curse.

"Let me go. Are you mad, Hartwell?"

"You're brave with prisoners and women, Captain." The savagery in the deep voice was more frightening because it was controlled. "Perhaps you'd like to try your sword on me?"

There was a deathly silence. In the hallway, Clandennon's man at arms and Robin Kirke hovered in dumbstruck silence. Aline gave a little scream and took a step toward Damaris. She shook her head. No. Safer to leave me be.

"I would remind you," Jonathan was saying with the same cold driving rage in his voice, "that we are both under the Lord Protector's orders. This is not Ireland, not Drogheda. You won't find any men to burn or women to rape and torture here."

The hatred in Clandennon's twisted face was almost demonic as he struggled for control. Finally, he said, "We are on the same side, Hartwell. I have no quarrel with you." He tried to push the big man away, but Jonathan did not budge. "There is enough trouble without our fighting each other. Reisling and his friends escaped me two nights ago."

"Escaped!" Surprised, Jonathan released his fellow officer. "How, escaped when you had them trussed up like market-going chickens?"

Clandennon massaged his neck and glared first at Jonathan and then at Damaris. "The devil their master must have helped them. We had taken them to Burrey and they were well guarded. During the night, a storm raged up and under its cover a gang of ruffians attacked and overpowered the guard, turned the prisoners loose. We searched every inch of Burrey, but there was no sign of them. It's my feeling that they've headed for the coast."

"That's grievous news," Jonathan said somberly.

"There's worse. The rumor that Charles Stuart was captured was false. He is either still at large in England or has gone overseas."

"Thank God!" Damaris exclaimed. Both men turned to her and she added, "In his heart my father never believed that the king had been taken."

Clandennon took a few steps into the room and stared bitterly at the still figure on the bed. "When I first saw him I knew in my bones that he was no merchant. I had never seen St. Cyr face to face, but the description of him haunted me. But you vouched for them, Hartwell. How came they to trick you who are an officer on the Lord Protector's business?"

"Because I was a fool." The bitterness in the deep voice hurt. She sensed that he was looking at her, but she could not bear to meet his eyes.

"Well, it does not matter. The Lord will destroy all those who commit abominations. Yea, for they shall be brought forth to the day of wrath." She shivered at the harsh, fanatical intonation of those words. "You tremble, Damaris? You have good cause. As St. Cyr's daughter, you are my prisoner to interrogate and to release or imprison as I choose. To begin with, answer me this: how came an old warhorse like your father to join the son of Stuart? Is this not treason? Was he not too full of years to sell all he had and follow the man of blood?"

In spite of grief and fear she could still smile. "It's not treason to love one's country. Father was always a king's man, and when he knew the king was in Scotland and needed him, he rode out to join him." Her voice turned soft, remembering. "He told me later that he rode back into England with His Majesty along the moorlands by Shap Fell and looked at Derbyshire beckoning to them from above. It was a beautiful summer's day, and he felt all of England welcomed them."

Aline made an involuntary movement toward her, and Clandennon's keen eye swung toward her. "How came you to give this woman and her father shelter?" he demanded roughly.

"They knew nothing—I lied to them also." Boldly, Damaris took the only route she could to clear her friends of complicity. "These people thought us a family of merchants and were charitable enough to take us in." Clandennon did not look convinced, and so she added with desperate scorn, "If I could lie so well to a roundhead officer, don't you think I could hoodwink a simple country couple?"

Robin followed her lead. "We had no idea they were royalists, Captain, sir. This I swear. The old man seemed sick, and the girl begged so prettily . . ."

"Aye, no doubt it was prettily done. You were made fools of—and she also made a fool of Captain Hartwell." Clandennon seemed to relish that thought. "I saw you that day by the river, mistress. You with your wanton smiles and the way you flaunted your body. . . . Hartwell, it's you who didn't heed your scripture this time. 'Better is the sight of the eyes than the wandering of desire.'"

She saw a muscle twitch in Jonathan's hard cheek, but before he could speak one of Clandennon's men appeared holding the pistol he had given Damaris in Burrey. "Sir, we found this in the St. Cyr woman's chamber," the man said.

Green eyes glowed with unholy pleasure. "Certes, Hartwell, see you the danger you ran? You could have been killed by a royalist bullet when you least expected it." He took the pistol from his man and proffered it to Jonathan. "Perhaps you'd like it as a souvenir of a romantic adventure," he said mockingly.

Jonathan took the weapon without comment, and Clandennon turned to his man again. "Take the Kirkes to the central hall. I will interrogate them there. As for St. Cyr's daughter, take her to her room and bar the door. None may enter without express orders."

Oddly enough, she felt little fear. Her fear had been for what the roundheads could do to her father, and now he was beyond their malice. And if she had saved Aline and Robin by her lies, she could face whatever came. Only . . .

She heard Jonathan move behind her and that small sound forced her to look back at him. He was watching her with an expression that filled her with shame. I don't owe him any explanation, she told herself, I only did what I had to do. He's my enemy, and it is said that all is fair in war.

And in love. The words sprang unbidden into her mind as did memories. They were so strong, so compelling, that for a moment the room and everyone in it ceased to exist and they were alone again on the green and gold river road, in the garden moonlight. She almost said his name aloud, but stopped herself in time.

He saw her lips shape his name. He saw how her face changed, softened, the dark eyes widening, the mouth going tender. She had lied to him, and made a fool of him, and yet when she looked like that he found himself taking a step toward her. Then Clandennon laughed, and the mood shattered.

"See, Captain. She's still trying her harlot's tricks on you," he crowed. "She'd barter her white body for her safety, all right. I know her kind."

The loathing in the big man's eyes felt like a sword thrust into her heart. That look was her punishment, her damnation. It didn't seem to matter now that she had been willing to do his will for her father's sake. It only mattered that she had acted with dishonor and earned Jonathan's contempt.

Head down, she meekly followed the guard from the room.

Clandennon used Kirke Hall to quarter his men. Damaris could hear their heavy stamp in the hall, the creak of their boots and the thump of their swords hitting the wall as they swaggered by her room. She heard them commanding the frightened servants who hurried to get them food and drink while their chief interrogated the Kirkes in their own central hall.

She did not know how the interrogation was going, for no one paid any attention to her or even came near her. The middle-aged soldier who guarded her would not speak to her or answer the questions she put to him through the heavy oak of the closed door. At noon, when he thrust a platter of bread and cold meat and a cup of water roughly into the chamber, she managed to frame one question: "What is happening to the Kirkes? Of your kind mercy, tell me. Please . . ."

"The two captains be judging the matter now," the guard told her grudgingly before he slammed shut the heavy oak. Two captains, she thought. Then Jonathan had not ridden away.

She drank the water gratefully but could not eat. She paced the chamber ceaselessly as she worried about the fate of her hosts. And there was another concern—now that she knew Charles II was safe, she must somehow carry out her father's request. But how could she get to France when Clandennon had her prisoner? And supposing they wrung the information out of her, what then?

The afternoon turned to dusky gold about her and evening came. From her window she could see birds winging homeward. She watched them with a yearning loneliness and as the shadows deepened and the night air grew cool, she leaned against her window and wished for some chance for freedom. If only she could lower herself from the window and escape into the coming darkness—but Clandennon had stationed a guard under her window, too. She could hear him clanking to and fro as the last of the daylight died away.

How long she remained in the darkness she did not know, but after some time she heard footsteps coming down the hallway and saw a bright line of light under the sill of her door. The guard was being relieved, she thought, and then she heard Jonathan say, "It's all right. I've come to speak to the prisoner."

At the sound of his voice her heart began to hammer, and she became very still, listening. She could hear the guard at her door demurring. "Sir, I'm not sure. Captain Clandennon's orders were to let no one in."

"Do you question my authority, sirrah?" The guard must have moved aside rapidly for he then added, "Walk down the hallway and see that we are not disturbed. I must speak to the prisoner alone."

"Yes, sir." The door creaked open, and a tongue of light spilled onto the floor and danced against the walls. She blinked against it as he came in and set the lamp down on the table by the bed.

Then he spoke. "I trust your imprisonment so far has been quite comfortable, Mistress St. Cyr?"

The biting mockery in his tone must be reflected in his eyes, she knew, but as he stood behind the sputtering lamp, his face remained in shadow. She could not have expected anything from him but this contempt, and yet it wounded her.

"You're very silent. Don't you want to know what is going to happen to the Kirkes?" His words were almost a jeer, and anger took the place of pain. She was grateful for that anger, and for the pride that allowed her to lift her chin and face him.

"Are you going to tell me?" she demanded.

"After some time, my colleague Clandennon and I decided that the Kirkes were your dupes. Poor fools, they did not know what they did when they harbored enemies to the Commonwealth. They will be fined, but otherwise let alone."

"Fined—for charity. How just Oliver Cromwell is," she snapped.

"Softly, my lady. You should be asking for mercy, not justice. You stand accused of aiding enemies of the Commonwealth yourself, and you will accompany Clandennon to London where you will stand trial for that crime." He paused to let her digest this, and then he added, "Then, there is the matter of your father's body. Clandennon was all for spitting the old man's head on a pike and leaving it at a crossroads to show what befalls traitors."

She gave a horrified cry and turned away, covering her mouth with both hands. She must not give him the satisfaction of seeing her fall apart. But he was still speaking. "I argued against that. We do not make war on dead men. Your father will be buried tomorrow at dawn by Clandennon's military chaplain."

Gratitude welled through her, and her knees felt weak to buckling. Then, another thought came. "Captain Hartwell, I'm more thankful than I can say. But—but we are not Puritans. Cannot my father be buried by a minister of our own church?"

He gave an exclamation of disgust. "Do you think that would matter to him?" he demanded. "He's dead, woman. You would do well to worry about yourself. Don't think that you can get around Clandennon with your soft and womanly charms, either. He will not be moved by your black eyes and your lovely, soft mouth, or your warm, white body."

Anger shook in his voice, and with it something like pain, and she responded to this. "I had to lie to you," she said in a low, unhappy voice. "I had to try and save my father, Jonathan."

He stepped into the direct light of the lamp, and his eyes were hard. "If that was all you did, I could understand. It was how you lied that turns my stomach." He gave a short bark of laughter that was as hard as his eyes. "Do you know that because of you I have put aside my sacred duty? But of course you knew. No doubt you laughed at how easily you tricked me into offering you protection." He shook his head as he added, "How well you played me for a fool, Damaris."

"That's not true . . ." she began and he came across the room, striding swiftly to take her by the arms. His fingers bit cruelly into her forearms and his eyes had narrowed to dangerous silver slits. Even so, she said, "I didn't laugh, Jonathan."

"Why not? Or was the task of seducing me too distasteful for you?" The grip loosened on her arms, and she drew away from him and rubbed their hurts. "You did not make it appear so. That night you brought dry clothes to my room your eyes reflected black gold, and the lamplight on your hair was like fire."

She caught her breath as she heard the change in his voice and something deep within her responded. She wanted to say, I'm alone and afraid, Jonathan, hold me—but instead she merely shook her head. "I wasn't acting." Whatever else he believed about her, he must not think this, that she had taken his kisses and sneered behind his back. "Do you not see that I had my own duty, too, and that you were my enemy? Even so, I came to trust you." She almost added, "To love you," but his laughter stilled the words.

"You are very good at what you do, Damaris. Perhaps it is because you have practiced this scene many times with other men. St. Cyr was not rich or titled, and perhaps you have been in positions before where your wits and your tricks served you well."

His contempt hurt worse than anything else she had endured. And with that hurt came black loneliness. She turned her back on him. "Please —go away."

"Not before I tell you how I feel about you— mistress." His hands clamped down onto her shoulders, whirled her around to face him. "Was coming to me and offering your body your idea entirely? I cannot believe it was your father's. No matter what else he was, the old man was a gallant soldier and a man of honor. It isn't his fault that his daughter acted the whore."

She saw his intention in the smouldering gray of his eyes and struggled in his grip. She kicked out at him impotently as he crushed her to him. The harshness of his face made him seem a stranger, implacable as Clandennon and as cruel. "Let me go," she cried. "I'll scream . . ."

Softly, he laughed. "Go ahead. Do you think the guards will come running? But let me first give you something to scream about, my beautiful liar."

His mouth came down on hers, hard and bruising. Where before it had been tender, a lover's mouth, this time the kiss was meant to insult, to degrade. She tried to twist her head away but one hand clamped against the back of her head, the iron fingers pressing through the silky waves of her hair to her skull and anchoring it where he willed. The other hand swept down over her back, spanned her buttocks and lifted her hard against his chest and his lean, taut belly, held her there impaled against his man's desire.

"This was what you offered me that night." He laughed deep in his throat, a jeering, biting laugh as his lips came down on hers again. She twisted her bruised mouth free and cried out, but again he silenced her with his mouth. Still holding her, he moved across the small room and flung her down against the soft cushions of her bed. She tried to jump up and roll off, but he planted an arm on either side of her, imprisoning her in steel.

"Why leave? The fun's just starting."

One practiced flip and her dress was pulled up over her hips. As she struggled, her bodice was pulled down, exposing her breasts to his searching hands. "No," she moaned.

"But this is what you came to exchange for my protection. Perhaps you can still bargain for it, Damaris. Why not chance it?" He spoke between swift, painful kisses. "It was well planned. How could I refuse the grieving daughter?" He kissed her again, and his hands roved over her breasts then downward over her legs, between them. She struggled against him and against the fact that even here, even now, his touch excited her, filled her with black madness. But she would rather die than submit like this. She would rather die . . .

She gave a sound that was half sob, half protest. He did not heed her. The hunger in those hard eyes was purely, elementally male. Deep in his throat he made a sound that was both laugh and growl, and she knew she was lost for she wanted him. Even now, like this. And knowing this with every drop of her raging blood, she could no longer fight the hardness of his mouth, the driving, marauding tongue, and under his demand she felt her own lips tremble and soften. Her tense body went limp in his arms.

"Jonathan." She did not know she spoke the name, but he felt the tremor of sound against his harsh and angry mouth. It reached deep into him, touching all he had felt and still felt for this woman. Shaken, unwilling to feel anything but fury at what she had done, he fought against the rising tide of the familiar tenderness which mingled with desire. And lost. He drew a little away from her and looked down at her and saw that she was pale, and that while her eyelids fluttered shut over her dark eyes, her kiss-bruised mouth was soft for him. And in the golden glow of lamplight, the taut, pale peaks of her breasts invited his kiss.

She felt the change in him as he bent to kiss the tender peaks. She murmured with remembered pleasure at the touch of the delicately questing tongue, the knowing lips, the sweet tug of his suckling mouth. Touching, licking, stroking, he evoked a madness that she could not bear. Murmuring his name again, she lifted her arms and locked them about his neck, holding his dark head against her.

But his mouth would not stay where it was. He

kissed her lips again, her temples, her chin with swift, passionate kisses, and then bent lower, trailing a line of fire across her ribs, the concavity of her belly, the gentle rise that led to the joining of her thighs. Hooking his thumbs into the delicate fabric of her undergarments, he drew them down and over her hips, then slid his palms under her to raise her hips a little. Feather-light, his mouth touched the inner satin of her thighs, moved upward.

Spasming through her, shaking her to the root of her existence, the ecstasy was so sharp that it was pain . . . she could barely endure the touch of his lips and the stroking of his tongue, could not bare to pull away. But he had moved away. Why? She whispered his name, trying to draw him to her again.

"No," he said. She looked up him as he leaned above her. His shirt had opened to the waist and the dark, furred chest was hard with tension. His face, too, was like stone. "I'll not play this game a second time," he gritted.

At first she didn't realize what he was saying, but when realization came, shame as great and as powerful as ecstasy filled her. He got up from the bed and loomed above her and she cried, "It was you. You who began . . ."

Without word he turned his back to her. She saw the heaving of the muscles of his back, the tense line of his shoulders, saw how his hands clenched hard against his sides. Suddenly and without warning, he slammed his clenched fist hard into the wall beside the bed.

"No, by Christ," he swore.

She watched him, feeling bruised. She ached, her nipples were tender from his kisses. Whore, he had named her, and now the word had meaning. He had tried to force her and instead of defending her honor she had wanted him. Still wanted him.

"Go away," she seethed at him. "Go away from me!"

He interrupted her, his voice controlled again, even calm. "Well, at least that business is over and done with, and I want you to understand another thing. I do not feel bound by my promise to your father. I gave my word to Master Langley, a merchant, not to a royalist colonel."

Strange how his scorn could still sting. She pulled the coverlet of the bed over her nakedness, hating him, hating herself. "Get out. I hope I will never see you again," she gritted.

With his hand on the doorknob he half turned to her. "As our friend Clandennon says," he told her, "that rests in the hand of God."

And then he left her.

Chapter Nine

"WE LEAVE KIRKE HALL WITHIN THE HOUR," Clandennon said. "See to it that you are ready to ride." When Damaris did not respond he added brutally, "We will ride to Long Marston whether or not you are ready, mistress."

Wordlessly she inclined her head. It was the first time she had seen Clandennon since her father's funeral, four mornings ago. Since that time she had been shut up in her room, barred from all human contact except for the guard who brought her food twice a day. The gruff middle-aged man said little to her, but she had the feeling that he pitied her. From conversations in the hallway outside her chamber she had learned that his name was Tam Linker, and from that same source she had heard enough to guess that they would ride to Long Marston.

Clandennon folded his bony arms across his thin chest and smiled at her. "You've been lonely no doubt, with your champion gone and no one to talk to. Well, you will not be lonely at Long Marston, Mistress St. Cyr. You'll have a lot of company there."

Loathing the man, she simply listened and refused to rise to his bait. This seemed to give him even more malicious pleasure for he took a few steps closer and leaned forward as if studying her. She had to fight an impulse not to shrink away from the scrutiny of those cat's eyes.

"Is there something else, Captain?" she demanded.

"You must remember whose prisoner you are, Damaris." His lips moved so softly on the words she could hardly hear them, but she could feel his hot breath. "The curse of the Lord is on the house of the wicked. He blesseth the habitation of the just. It is said that there is a place for the penitent in heaven. Pity for those who ask for mercy at the judgement seat."

He made her skin crawl, and she was relieved when he finally left her room. But when she could hear his footsteps echoing down the hall she shivered again. He was up to something, and whatever this was awaited her at Long Marston.

There was a perfunctory knock on the door, and her gruff guard entered. He was carrying an armful of clothes which he dumped on the bed.

"For the ride," he explained briefly. "The lady of the house sent them."

She examined the plain but serviceable riding habit, the small leather boots and the cloak against the mid-September chill. As she did so, she again detected a hint of sympathy in Tam Linker, and she said, "Can you tell me why we are going to Long Marston?"

He hesitated. "Captain's orders. A lot of our troops are gathering there, or so I hear." He paused and then added with even more reluctance, "There's to be a public execution of some kind."

So this was what Clandennon wished her to see. As she thought this, her questing fingers felt something rustle in a fold of the cloak. She glanced quickly up at Tam Linker, but though she was sure he'd heard, he squinted away from her.

"Best to dress fast, missy, we be starting soon," was all he said.

When he had gone, she read the note. It was in Aline's writing and contained only two lines: "You are so brave. God bless you." The short message comforted Damaris and healed some of the hurt that Jonathan had left when he rode away several nights ago. For a moment her treacherous mind held his image and then she pushed the thought away. She had trouble enough to face without thinking of him.

Half an hour later, dressed in her new traveling clothes, she was escorted out into the yard of Kirke Hall. Here her hands were bound before her on Clandennon's orders. She saw the pain in

Aline's and Robin's eyes as they watched help-lessly.

"Is that necessary, Captain?" Robin pro-tested. "The girl cannot ride with her hands bound . . ."

"You mean, she can't escape as easily," Clandennon snapped. "I'm not about to lose St. Cyr's precious daughter." He then assisted her to mount, and though the feel of the man's bony hands sickened her, she submitted without com-plaint. God help me, she thought, now I'm truly alone and in this man's power.

Clandennon gave the order to mount and ride, and Damaris picked up the reins as best as she could with her bound hands. Tam Linker had tied her wrists somewhat more loosely than his captain had ordered, but the rough rope still chafed her wrists as they rode away from Kirke Hall.

They rode through the heat of the day, and though her throat grew parched Clandennon's orders were that no one offer her drink. By late afternoon they wound through narrow trails that led into a wilderness of downs and ram-bling valleys, and Damaris's thirst intensified into acute pain. She could think of nothing else but water, and the chafing of her wrists, rubbed raw with the effort of keeping her horse in line with the others, accentuated her misery. Water, she thought longingly, and in her mind she saw cool goblets of icy water and fountains bubbling with crystal droplets. Then, the picture changed and she could see Jonathan kneeling to offer water to Colonel Reisling and the other royalists . . .

"Would you drink, mistress?"

Looking up, she realized that Clandennon had left his position at the head of the troops to draw closer to her. He held a flask of water in his hand, and as she watched he uncorked it and poured a stream of water down his own throat. She tried to ignore him, but she felt dizzy with want as the water spumed around his mouth and fell into the dust of the road.

She did not realize that her throat was making little convulsive movements until he laughed and wheeled his horse about to canter back to his leadership position. Then she heard Tam Linker, who rode beside her, mutter a curse. "Commanding officer or not, that one sickens me." He unbuckled his own container of water and placed it between her bound hands. "Here, missy, you drink fast when yon bastard ain't looking our way."

There had been nothing as good as this water, nothing as sweet as its cool trickle down her throat. She realized that helpless tears flowed down her cheeks as she swallowed again and again. Finally, Tam Linker stopped her. "You don't want to make yourself sick," he said, "but you'd know that, being the old colonel's daughter."

To her surprise this was said with a kind of grudging respect. "Did you know my father?"

"I did," Tam said. "Fought against him at

Marston Moor when King Charles the First was brought down. He were a good soldier, your father, and enemy or not I thought well of him. You had his spirit when you went to give water to those prisoners against Clandennon's orders." He met her eyes squarely. "I'm sorry you're in the mess you're in, and that's a fact."

Strange how words of kindness could give her more pain instead of comfort. As she murmured her thanks for the water, she thought of what Jonathan had said so many nights ago in Burrey about there being good people of England. It was a mistake, for immediately he seemed to be beside her, mounted on his great dark horse and smiling down at her with those wide silver-gray eyes.

"Pick up that pace, Mistress St. Cyr!" Clandennon's rasping voice was full of cruel pleasure as he urged her on, and Jonathan's image shattered in her mind. Jonathan didn't exist for her anymore. Only the reality of what awaited her at Long Marston existed. Damaris took a deep breath and rode on.

They reached Long Marston near sunset of that day and found the bustling town agog with noise and excitement. Urchins shouted and cheered the soldiers, and then seeing her bound hands hurled clumps of dirt at her as she passed. "Another of the dirty prisoners," one of them shrilled. "One more royalist bitch for the long rope . . ."

Tam Linker drew a whip from his saddlebag

and cracked it over the heads of the brats who ran away shouting insults at the soldiers. "Bloodthirsty little brats," he growled and shot a look at Damaris. "Any of them hit yer, missy?"

She shook her head. The children had been talking about the poor souls who would be executed tonight, of course. She wondered where the condemned prisoners were being held, and the answer to that came sooner than she expected as she saw before her what seemed to be a wall of people who milled about the town square. On the outskirts of this crowd, near a long, low-roofed building, squatted more than three-score men and women, obviously prisoners. They were yoked together and their hands were tied before them, and to her horror there were old people and even some children in the group. Some were weeping, some cursed their captors, others sat in a numb, apathetic despair.

"These prisoners are said to have helped royalists escape," Tam Linker told her. He spat, and she sensed that the scene before him was not at all to his liking. "It minds me of witch pricking in these parts when I was a boy. If you didn't like some old hag, all's you had to do was to inform against her to the witch hunter. He'd prick her to see if she bled or dunk her to see if she drowned, or hang her. . . . And it was all by good church-going Puritans following the word of God. It does make you wonder."

"You'll have a lot of company to look forward to—there is pity for those who ask for mercy at the judgement seat . . ." Clandennon's words came back to her now, and she felt sick.

"Are they going to hang all these people?" she whispered.

"Not all." It was not Tam who answered, but Clandennon's rasping, gloating voice. "Some will be taken to London to stand trial; others will be shipped out to Barbados as labor for the plantations." He leaned closer to add, "Some of these prisoners are valuable to the Commonwealth. They have information that is valuable, and they will be urged to speak and save the torturers much time and trouble. And finally, there are others who will die tonight to make a fitting spectacle for the crowd."

She spoke with a coolness she didn't feel. "The crowd is worthy of you."

"You are proud, Damaris, but remember that pride will fall into the dust." He leaned forward and placed a gloved hand on her bare arm. "Tell me that again when you have not eaten or drunk for several days and nights. Tell me that when you have been interrogated for hours. I will see you crawl for mercy, proud lady."

"You sicken me," she whispered. He didn't seem offended. He laughed and his hand tightened on her arm, pinching the skin cruelly.

"There is salvation for those who show a willing heart," he jeered at her.

A roar from the townspeople up ahead interrupted him. The dense mob had parted and now she could see that huge bonfires had been piled in the center of the square and that a gibbet with five dangling nooses had been erected there as well. The sight filled her with such horror that she was hardly aware that Tam Linker was guiding her horse toward the other prisoners. Here, Clandennon ordered her to dismount.

She could not get off her horse without help, so Tam Linker assisted her. As he set her down she heard him growl, "Don't pay attention to what he says. I heard Captain Hartwell insist that you be taken to Lunnon for trial. He won't harm you."

Jonathan—she put the thought of him away quickly as she looked about her at the other prisoners. Most of them looked back at her with dull curiosity, but some of them even seemed to resent the fact that she had arrived on a horse. "The lords and ladies still get special treatment," one man muttered belligerently. "They won't hang this one or burn her neither."

A growl of agreement rose, and as Damaris looked about her in bewilderment, someone tugged at her skirts. "Sit down, dearie, so they won't see you to grumble at," a tired old voice commanded.

Obediently she sank down into the narrow space beside an old woman. She was brown-skinned from the weather and narrow-eyed, and her hair was gray and sparse, but her smile was kind as she asked, "Who are you, child? Why are you here?" When Damaris told her, she formed the name two or three times and then shook her head. "St. Cyr—I have never heard the name.

But then, what did we know of lords and ladies? My man and I both till the soil, that is all."

"Is your husband here?" But the old woman shook her head.

"He died—and I thank God for't, dearie. But my three strong sons are here with me because they could not let a hungry man go past without food in his belly." She paused and then added sadly, "I've heard that my good boys will hang because of that."

"Oh, cruel . . ." Damaris cried, forgetting her own plight, and another woman chimed in.

"If it's cruelty you want, you'll get your bellyful here. Most of us have done nothing. Others of us have only given food or water to frightened or wounded men." She paused and then added, "Molly, at least ye and your sons done something. Ye helped *him* . . ."

She could not miss the emphasis on the word. Damaris's eyes flew up to the old woman's and saw the tremulous smile in them that confirmed her unspoken question. "Aye," the old lady said softly. "We did that."

Speaking in a whisper, Damaris asked, "You helped the king to get away?"

Again the shy happiness filled the old lady's eyes. "I did not know he were the king at first. He were very tall, and dark, and he had big black eyes, and a big ugly mouth, but he were kind, and he had a goodness about him. I gave him what food we had, and all the money we had, and my boys knelt down and kissed his hand." She caught her breath and wiped her eyes with the back of her hand as she added, "Before he went he said, 'Good dame, there is no reward for good hearts like yours, but I will remember. With all my heart, I will remember.'"

"It was the king. That's his favorite expression —'with all my heart,'" Damaris whispered. Tears shone in her own eyes.

Others were now listening to the conversation. "You know the king, then, mistress?" one woman asked wonderingly and another implored, "When is he coming back, our king? I heard he were taken . . ."

"He's not. By now he must be in France." She clasped her bound hands together and felt a joyful sense of release that she had not experienced for many weeks. She could see that same happiness shining back to her mirrored in the eyes of these simple folk. "He will come back to England to claim the land again and make it whole. I know it."

"It'll be too late for me." One of the men near her groaned. "I've not done anything wrong, but because I'm suspected of aiding royalists my neck will be stretched. Maybe I'll even die tonight. They say as they're going to choose their victims at random."

A silence fell upon them, and she wracked her mind for something to say, for them and for herself. Those condemned to die tonight, she thought, should take something bright with them into the dark. As a woman nearby began to sob, she spoke slowly.

"You asked me about the king. I only met him once. It was just before the battle of Worcester . . ."

She paused, and the people leaned closer on her words. "Tell us what happened," the old woman called Molly breathed.

"My father sold our small land holdings to help the king, and he then journeyed to Scotland to meet His Majesty who was mustering his troops there. Because I refused to let my aging father ride to war alone, I'd arranged to meet him in Worcester, and I was there when the king and his troops marched by. So were many other loyal royalists—I was only one among the many thousands of people who lined the street and cheered for King Charles the Second." A lump had formed in Damaris's throat and she spoke with difficulty. "Standing next to me was a poor country woman. She'd heard that the king was marching on to London, and she wanted very much to kneel before him and kiss his hand. His lords and generals would have sent her away, but he spoke to her kindly, and when she wanted to kneel for his blessing, he humbly asked her for her prayers instead. 'Mother,' he said, 'God will listen to you and the people of England. It is an England that we both love.'"

There was a little hush, and then old Molly sighed. "I am glad ye told me that story," she said quietly. "If my sons must die, I'm glad they're dying for such a king."

Just then there was a shout from the crowd and a troop of Commonwealth soldiers in their drab uniforms paraded to the center of the square. At their head strode several officers. They came to attention under the gibbet, and one of them stepped forward and raised his hands for silence.

"The time for judgement is at hand," he shouted. "Tonight you will witness how twenty-five traitors to the Commonwealth of England suffer and die within the hour for their pernicious crimes against the state." He added that these men would now be chosen from the assembled prisoners and led away to await their death.

There was a visible shrinking among the prisoners as roundhead guards approached them. For a long and horrible moment there was suspense, and then a man screamed as he was pointed out, seized and dragged aside. "Not me. Not me, I say," he wailed and slobbered. "I done nothing!"

Others were quickly chosen, and Damaris saw Molly moan with pain as three tall young country lads were pulled aside to swell the roster of doomed men. The last to be taken was the man who had sat beside Damaris and heard her story. He grew very pale, but as he was led away he turned back and tried to give her a smile that tore at her very heart.

She dropped her face into her bound hands and struggled with tears. Never had she felt so helpless or so without hope. From Clandennon there would be no escape, and he could make her talk, enjoy forcing a confession from her.

And if he knew her father's secrets, that would lessen her king's chances for a restoration. But what can I do, she mourned, and into her mind, her heart, a litany crept like a prayer. Only, it was not a prayer, it was deepest shame. What right did she have at this moment of despair to think of Jonathan Hartwell?

"Damaris St. Cyr."

She jerked up her head at the sound of her name and faced a stern roundhead guard. The man motioned her to get up and watched stonily as she clambered stiffly to her feet. "You're to come with me," he then said.

Were they going to hang her, too? But he simply led her away from the other prisoners. She thought she heard old Molly call a word after her as she walked away—"Remember!" She said the word to herself, and then she shivered. It was the word the murdered King Charles I had spoken from the block before his death.

She would remember this scene forever, whether that forever meant a minute or an hour or years of life. As she went with the guard she could feel the gritty dirt under her feet, smell the clean scent of wood in the wind. She saw the expanse of faces of the noisy, expectant crowd, saw the doomed prisoners being led aside and the pitiful faces of those who loved them. She saw the bright colors that the town's women wore, the flash of the dying sun against soldiers' weapons. She heard the laughing babble of the crowd mingle with hopeless weeping from the prisoners, and she had the confused feeling that here in this moment was all of life, all of its pain and its merriment too. Suddenly she was afraid of what was waiting for her, and deep within her heart she whispered Jonathan's name.

The guard called a halt and nodded for her to precede him up to a doorway in a nearby house. When she reached it, he knocked on the door and then nodded to her. "You're to go in."

She hung back. "Where have you brought me?" she asked.

"Colonel Brace's quarters." He jerked his head toward the doorknob, and she lifted her still bound wrists. Nodding, he then turned the doorknob and pushed open the door. "You're wanted for questioning."

Steeling herself, she stepped inside. The room was dark, for the sun had almost set, and no lamps had yet been lit in the room. As she stood near the door, her eyes blinking fast to try and acclimate to the dark, she heard a low laugh that raised the short hairs of her neck. Then, an unmistakable voice spoke.

"Welcome, Mistress St. Cyr. How do you like the company of your fellow traitors?" Clandennon said.

Chapter Ten

"WHY HAVE YOU BROUGHT ME HERE?" SHE DE-manded. She could make him out now, an angu-lar shadow near the window. She thought she heard him chuckle and there was the hiss of a lamp being lit.

"My kind fellow officer lent me this place so that we could have an excellent view of the hangings." Now that there was light she saw that they stood in a large room furnished rather plainly with chairs and a large desk. A portrait of Oliver Cromwell hung above the desk. Vari-ous military equipment, a sword, a dagger with a brass hilt, boots and a soldier's cloak had been placed upon a wing-backed chair by the window. "I'd like you to see how your fellow traitors meet their death," he continued. "Death by hanging isn't pleasant, Damaris. I'm hoping that the sight will convince you to help yourself by helping us."

"You'll have a long wait, Captain."

He shrugged and drew a knife from his belt and came toward her, and for a moment she thought that he meant to threaten her with it. Instead, he cut the ropes that bound her wrists. She couldn't bite back a cry as pressure eased and blood began to circulate freely and painfully.

"Poor hands." Before she could prevent him, he'd picked up one hand and kissed the ugly weal along the inner wrist. The moist touch of his mouth was revolting, and she snatched her hand away from him and rubbed it on her skirt. "An ugly mark, isn't it? A shame to put one around your lovely white neck."

The green light in his eyes told her he was enjoying himself and she struggled to remain calm. She had to deal carefully with this man. "I don't know how you think I could help you," she told him warily. "Anything I did, I did to help my father. I know nothing that could be of use to you."

"You're St. Cyr's only daughter, and I know that you and he were close. He must have told you all his military secrets." The last word was hissed almost in her ear, and she shrank back from him.

"Secrets! What would I know of such things?" she parried desperately.

Eyes narrowed, he watched her. "You know a great deal, or I'm a bad judge of character. St.

Cyr had time to tell you all that he knew would benefit Charles Stuart's son. I want this information, and I'll get it." There was no laughter in his eyes now—they burned with fanatical fire. "If you don't speak willingly, I will be forced to persuade you by other means."

The gloating in his face was unbearable, and she turned away from it to look through the window. The scene there was unendurable, too. There was a dense circle around the gibbet, and she could see the prisoners kneeling or sitting in the dirt, all waiting for the hangings to come. "You're Puritans. You say you are men of God— how can you be such hypocrites?" she burst out.

She had struck a nerve. Angrily he said, "They are men of blood. They have given aid to the enemy. The Church of God has His favor, and victory is ours through His might. God has made these vermin stubble for our swords. He will smile to see them hang."

"You're insane!" she whispered.

A hand clamped down on her shoulder, turning her to face him. His eyes were glittering like a cat's. "You're wrong to mock me, Damaris. Your fine lover isn't here to help you now, and you are in my hands. I had hoped to spare you, to pluck you from the flames. You are too fair to kill . . ."

The change in that rasping voice filled her with extreme horror. She tried to pull loose but the hand on her shoulder was like steel. She stepped backward, and impacted with the hard wall and window. "No," she begged, but his arms clamped around her shoulders, pulling her forward with irresistible force. She tried to scream, but the sound came out in a choking gasp. He was saying softly, "Did you struggle for Hartwell, too? I'm your master now, Damaris."

Sick and faint, she still glared at him. Never, she wanted to tell him, but the words wouldn't come. The gaunt face, the wet lips came closer, and she struggled again. He laughed deep in his throat and she realized that he was enjoying her pitiful defiance, liked to have her fight him. Calling on every ounce of strength and will she still possessed, she closed her eyes and went limp in his arms.

It was the right thing to do. For a moment, he still held her, and then with a curse he let her go. She sank unhindered to the floor, and she could hear him muttering about feeble, fainting women. She kept herself inert, tried to school the wild leaping of her pulse. What now, she wondered, and as the thought filled her mind she heard shouting from the town square. "Fire. Fire in the town . . ."

She could hear Clandennon flinging open the window, and a rush of chill twilight air filled the room as he called, "What fire? Where, you fools?"

Many voices informed him that fires were burning in several parts of the town, and both the soldiery and the townspeople were busy putting them out. "They just started for no reason, Captain," she heard a gruff voice say, and Clandennon swore again.

"Nothing starts for no reason. Guard those prisoners, or I'll flay you alive." He paused and then he added, "And you—yes, you, soldier! Guard this door and let no one pass. I want to see for myself what is going on."

Damaris lay still until she had heard his footsteps on the steps outside. Then getting to her feet she saw that an orange glow lit the room, and that outside everything was confusion. The townspeople were racing away from the square to help the military battle the fires, and the few soldiers left to guard the prisoners looked a little frightened. If ever she could escape, now was the time.

First she had to extinguish the lamp. On her way to the desk to do this, Damaris caught up the dagger on the chair and muffled the military cloak about her. Then, dousing the flame she went swiftly to the window and looked about. It wasn't very high off the ground, and no one stood guard below. Carefully, willing herself to make no sound, she sat up on the sill and swung her feet over into space. For a moment she sat there listening and then let herself drop.

The fall was jarring, but she was unhurt. For awhile she stayed crouched silently, but there was no sound except for the panicked shouts that came from the firefighters. Now, she told herself, but before she could get up to run she heard a shout. "The prisoners! The condemned prisoners have all escaped—they've gone!"

For a moment there was a stunned silence, and then a muffled shouting came from the still guarded royalists in the square. Cheers, shouts of joy and triumph shattered the night. Several soldiers left the burning buildings and hurried to reinforce their fellow guards. They passed very close to her, and she held her breath, praying they would not see her.

For a moment she thought her prayers had been answered, and then the last soldier to pass her stopped. Panicked, she saw him turn and come back to where she was. She clutched the dagger tightly, until a soft curse in the darkness brought recognition: the man standing not two yards away from her was Tam Linker.

For a second, he simply stared at her, and then it seemed to her that he grinned before he wordlessly turned and hurried after his companions.

He was going to let her get away! Staggering a little, she got to her feet and drawing her cloak tightly over her hair and clothes began to slip away through the darkness. Doing her best to avoid the bright orange glare of the fires, she edged out of the square and then sped silently through the deserted streets toward the outskirts of Long Marston. The town was deserted; everyone seemed to be firefighting. Breathing a prayer of thanksgiving, Damaris left the town.

She didn't stay on the road long. Sense told her that the soldiery would be after the escapees as soon as they got the fire under control and that the safest course would be to strike out over the downs and try and find a place to hide. The going was much harder here. Briars tangled in her skirts, tall grass rustled about her as she hurried, and the night wind pushed back the folds of her cloak and wrapped its long cold fingers in her hair. Above, a half moon rode tattered clouds and shadowed the beginning of woodlands a half mile or so away.

There'd be shelter among the trees, she thought. Her legs ached with weariness but she pushed herself to more effort. Once she reached those trees she could rest. She repeated this litany over and over in her mind as she came to the ends of the downs and felt the cool shadow of the welcoming trees.

It was cool here—and so quiet. Damaris sank down under a large tree. The air was scented with pine, with crushed leaves and grass, with the very distant tang of burning. It was still too close to Long Marston, Damaris thought. She'd have to go on. She was just getting to her knees when she heard the hoofbeats. She listened intently, hoping against hope that she was in error, but there was no mistaking that sound. A horseman was coming toward her through the woods and coming fast.

"No," she whispered out loud, and the spoken word fuelled her rising panic. She couldn't be taken again, must not be returned to Clandennon. She must hide, and quickly. Clutching her dagger, she got to her feet and hid behind a screen of trees. As she did so she saw the horse and rider burst into view through the branches and tangled vines of the woods before her. Go on, she urged them in her mind, but when they were directly in front of her, the horseman called softly to his mount and pulled in the reins.

She wasn't conscious of moving, but she must have, for a stick broke under her heel. The rider lifted his head and swept the woods about him and spoke in a quiet, deadly voice. "Who's there? I have my pistol trained on you. Move and you're a dead man."

Faint moonlight glinted on the barrel of the pistol, but it was not this that made her gasp. She felt as if she had gone suddenly boneless, bloodless, and put her hand against a nearby tree to steady herself. "Jonathan," she breathed.

She heard the swift answering intake of his breath. "Sweet Christ," he swore, and he dismounted and came toward her. He still held his pistol, and the ragged moonlight that streamed through the trees caught his hard-planed face but left his eyes in shadow. "Damaris!"

She simply looked up at him. He had been in her mind and heart, and now he was here. How and why didn't seem to matter. She started toward him and then he said, "What are you doing here? Were you released?"

Reality came crashing back and she felt dizzy and sick. How could she have forgotten their last meeting? He was not her savior, nothing but a roundhead and an enemy. She tried to frame a lie that might save her, but could not force her brain to think of one. "No," she tried to say bravely, but the word came out in a small whisper. "Clandennon . . ."

She couldn't say more, but his eyes narrowed as if he read what she could not put into words. He stepped nearer to her and she could see the killing rage in his eyes. "Did he harm you?" he demanded.

She shook her head, but he looked into her face and saw the horror there. The thought of Clandennon putting his hands on her filled him with such a wave of fury that for a moment his mind went black with it. In that second he could have strangled the man, or any man who hurt this woman.

"I got away," she was saying, still in that small, frightened voice. "There were so many prisoners, and they were going to hang twenty-five of them while we watched. And then—and then there were fires, and in the confusion the condemned prisoners escaped. And so did I."

He seemed to force himself to remain calm as he listened to her. "Then you're a fugitive and Clandennon will be after you."

"Will you let me pass?" she asked very low. "Please, will you let me go on?" He shook his head. Well, what else could she have expected? She wanted to beg him not to give her back to Clandennon, but she knew it would be useless. She knew what he thought of her. "I see. You have—your duty."

Unwillingly, he felt admiration for her courage, and something else—the familiar twist of the heart that he could not overcome. He said, "I can't let you go on, not alone. This wood becomes a forest and you'd lose your way. It's no pleasant place to be lost. There are brigands hiding here, and highwaymen—brutes who'd make Clandennon look like a saint by comparison." He looked down into the pale, upraised face, the deep, beautiful eyes, the tender mouth. "I'll go with you and see you safe."

"But . . . !" She pressed her hands to her shaking mouth, disbelieving, hoping.

"Yes, I know. That makes me a traitor to Cromwell." She heard the bitterness in his voice as he turned away from her. "Still, I can't leave you here in danger. I did promise your father that I would try and see you safe."

It was the oath that bound him, nothing more. She realized that she felt no more joy but a sudden and terrible despair. She saw the glitter of his eyes on her and lifted her chin bravely. He must not know how she felt—must never know.

"You said yourself that your promise was given to Master Langley and not to Colonel St. Cyr," she reminded him. "You don't have to take me anywhere, Captain Hartwell. I can go on on my own."

She tried to turn away, but her shaking legs wouldn't support her, and she staggered a little. Blindly reaching out for support, she felt his arms go about her.

She was shivering so hard that her trembling seemed to impart itself to him. Jonathan felt his own arms tense as he registered the warmth of her slight body. The night suddenly seemed to be scented with the fragrance of flowers and sunlight that emanated from her. "How can you go on alone?" he demanded, roughly. "You're ready to drop."

"I'm not!" With an effort she pulled herself erect and apart from him. She wrapped her own arms about her body, desperately trying to deny the effect that his strong arms had on her. "Your oath wasn't binding, and both of us know it. Please go away and leave me be . . ."

He ignored the desperation that had crept into her voice. "Don't talk like a fool," he snapped. "You're worried that my pledge to your father isn't binding, is that it?" His voice rose in wry self-mockery as he said, "I, known as Jonathan Hartwell pledge you, Damaris St. Cyr, to take you to a place of safety and to do all in my power to get you safely away to France." He then broke off to add, "Now will you come with me?"

His face was like stone, and she knew why: he had given her his pledge, and with it he was forsworn. A part of her ached for him even as she rejoiced for herself, and as he began to walk toward his horse she whispered, "But your duty, Jonathan . . ."

"Don't you trust me?" His voice had a mocking note. "I'm pledged to help you, remember? Even the word of a forsworn roundhead is binding, Damaris."

Without further question, she followed him to the horse and was lifted up behind him. "We must ride hard and fast," he then said. "Do you feel strong enough for that?" She murmured assent. "Then hold on."

She felt the curve of his powerful back against

her breast, as they began to move forward, and she clung to the sinewy strength of his lean waist and drew in a deep breath of his never forgotten scent. The horse began to go faster and she leaned against him so that the movements of the horse and the feel of his body against her became the only part of the world that mattered. And now that he could not see her face, she pressed her cheek against his back and at last admitted to the sweet wild joy of knowing that she was with him again.

They rode for several miles in silence, most of the time bending low over the saddle to avoid the low-growing branches of the woods. After an hour or so, they broke into a narrow clearing. Jonathan pointed silently to a long, slender ribbon of road that led through the tall trees.

"How well you know the way," she murmured. "But is it safe?"

His voice was firm. "Yes, it is."

"How can you be so sure?" she asked, and he turned to look at her over his shoulder.

"You forget who I am. I have access to a great deal of information, Damaris, including little known forest roads." Forest roads where royalists hide—the words weren't said aloud, but she knew they hung between them. "I know for instance that your Stuart king is in France. He sailed about a week ago from a little known harbor called Shoreham, and from there reached Fécamp in France."

"Thank God," she cried. "And the other

hunted royalists—Reisling and the Duke of
Buckingham and the Earl of Larraby?"

"Reisling escaped us," he replied grimly. "He
is probably with his so-called royal master if he
didn't drown on the way. No doubt the others
have also gone that route by now."

She wanted to cry thanksgiving again but held
back in some confusion, knowing that what
made her rejoice hurt him. Instead she began to
think of Charles safe in France, of the coming
restoration. She did not realize that her eyes
were closing and that she was slumping forward
against him until he halted the horse and dismounted to take her up in front of him.

"Now you can sleep," he told her.

There was no feeling in his voice; he might as
well have been talking to a comrade-in-arms or
to any chance-met stranger. But his warmth was
comforting and the way he gathered her against
him brought her a sense of safety she had never
thought to have again. And yet, though she
knew herself safe, she could not sleep. All her
senses had come wide awake so that she had
never been more aware of his nearness. Realizing this, she broke the silence. "Where are we
going?"

"I had hoped to cross these woods and make
for a place of safety that I know, but the ride is
too long and the horse will be tired carrying both
of us," he replied. "We'll make camp in a clearing about a mile from here," he said.

Turning the horse from the path, he urged it
back into woods so dense that no moonlight

filtered through. Jonathan dismounted and led the horse forward until the ground began to incline downward. After some time the undergrowth thinned out until they came suddenly into a ring-shaped clearing. It was bordered with white birch and tall oaks and carpeted by sweet grass that had turned silver in the moonlight, while in the distance there was the murmur of flowing water.

Damaris was astonished at the unexpected beauty of the place. "It's an enchanted spot," she exclaimed.

Moonlight dazzled silver into his eyes when he looked up at her. "You could be right. It's said that the queen of the little people and her attendants come here to dance on Midsummer's eve. Local people fear this place and give it a wide berth, which is all to our good."

He held up his arms to help her dismount and for a moment held her as she slipped to the ground still in the circle of his arms. She felt the hard beat of his heart against her breasts, and she held herself stiff and rigid in his hold. Then he moved away, and she felt unaccountably bereft.

Angry with herself, she walked away from him on the pretext of examining their campsite. It was even more beautiful than she had first thought. Autumn flowers seemed to lift their faces to drink in the silver moonlight, and as she walked and crushed the grass underfoot, a clean herbal fragrance arose. At the edge of the circular clearing she could see Jonathan leading his horse to the stream among the trees, hear him talking to the animal as he fed and tethered it and draped it with a blanket. When he returned to her, he carried yet another blanket over his arm.

"We can only rest a few hours since we must ride before dawn." He held the blanket out to her, adding, "Put this on the grass and it will make a soft bed. The cloak you wear will keep you warm."

Their hands met as she took the blanket from him. Her whole being registered the heat of that touch. Her eyes flew to his face and what she saw there made her draw in her breath sharply before he turned away and walked to the edge of the clearing. "Where—where are you going?" she faltered.

"I'll keep watch while you sleep," he replied. "Rest, Damaris. You're safe here with me."

The words came without her conscious will. "I've always been safe with you, Jonathan."

She'd spoken so softly that she did not know he heard until he repeated the word. "Safe," he said, and then he gave a bitter, mirthless bark of laughter. "Well, you're right at that. I always seem to be a fool where you are concerned."

She couldn't stand the bitterness in his eyes. She took a step toward him pleading, "No, not a fool, never that. I know I lied to you but I never—Jonathan, surely you know I trust you with my life, that I always have."

For a moment she saw his eyes change. Yearning, tenderness, passion all were ignited there.

Then he looked away from her, and when he spoke his voice was harsh. "You want me to say it? I will, then. You trusted me to come back to try and help you—and I did. Knowing you were in Clandennon's hands galled me like a wound. I could not think of duty, of honor—of anything but you. And so I came to Long Marston to try and free you in spite of all I'd sworn to do."

There was a heartbeat's silence and in it she could hear the sigh of the wind and the drowsy chirp of autumn insects. All about her the silver world throbbed with moonlight and the pain that was in his voice. She could not bear that pain. She forgot everything, pride, the differences between them, even the promise she had made to the dying colonel, and all her heart was in her voice as she said, "Jonathan, hold me." And as he made no movement toward her she ran to him, and hugged her arms about him, holding tight. "Please," she whispered, "take me into your arms."

Chapter Eleven

FOR A MOMENT HE DID NOT MOVE, AND THEN HIS arms circled her, drawing her to him hungrily. Home—the word formed in her mind as she rested her cheek against his shoulder. I'm home.

"You must have known I would come for you," he was saying against her hair.

She stroked the muscled arms that held her, moved her hands over his shoulders, touched his lean, hard jawline with remembering fingers. "I thought of you. When Clandennon called me and when—back in the woods there when I heard you coming. I thought you despised me, but it didn't matter. I wanted to be with you anyway."

His mouth touched hers, a swift, remembered kiss and then claimed her lips. Sweet and firm and sure, his tongue curved the perimeter of her lips, touched and caressed the satin of her inner mouth. She breathed from his lungs and clung to him while he felt the tremors of her body ripple through himself. She was like life, he thought dazedly, like water, like air, like fire. She was everything that he wanted or could ever want. "God pity me," he muttered, "it's as if you've bewitched me."

"Then I too am bewitched. You said that this place was enchanted." Her voice shook and her breasts were heaving against him, their very softness an invitation. He kissed her again, drinking the sweetness of her lips. As though reclaiming her, his hands roved over her back and down her hips, and then up again over her ribs and her breasts.

"My heart," he named her. "My love."

His love . . . all that had happened, all the grief and the fear seemed seared away in the fierce spurt of her joy. She felt weak and dazed with want of him. She had never felt like this, never, and her mouth clung to his and her hands stroked his broad back and his narrow, tense hips and strong thighs. She was impatient with the clothing that they wore, impatient at the distance that still separated them, and she tugged wordlessly at his doublet.

He shrugged it off. While covering each other with mute, passionate kisses they tugged at clothes, at buttons and hooks. The discarded clothing fell to the silvered grass. As his flesh came bare to her eager lips, she kissed his flat male nipples, bent to rub her lips against his lean-muscled belly, ran her delicate fingers across the hard tension of his thighs. And as her riding habit and shift slid away from her and to the ground he lifted her into his arms, his mouth curving around the roundness of her breasts and closing about the eager nipple.

Now they were consumed with a desperate sense of urgency, a need to be still closer. But when the last of their clothing fell from them she was surprised that he did not at once lower her to the ground. Instead, he held her nestled against him, loving her mouth and shoulders and breasts, clothing her with his kisses. "You are so beautiful," he murmured, and his deep voice shook with yet controlled desire. "A man could lose his soul for such beauty."

"Strange talk for a Puritan," she teased breathlessly, and he kissed her again.

"No, not strange. We are taught that Solomon felt awe when he saw the lovely queen of Sheba." And he quoted, "'Behold, thou art fair, my love—thy lips are like a thread of scarlet . . .'"

He lowered himself to his knees, taking her with him. She circled his strong neck with her arms and buried her face against his shoulder. He moved to spread the blanket on the grass beneath them and she heard his deep voice say, "'Thy lips are like the honeycomb—honey and milk are under thy tongue—'"

She leaned back onto the blanket. For a moment she registered its roughness under her naked back and felt the underlay of cool, fragrant grass beneath. Then all feeling was lost except for his weight as he leaned over her, his mouth on hers, his kiss on her breasts, moving lower to adore the concavity of her navel. He lingered there, taking his pleasure and then rubbed his mouth against her thighs. She moaned and moved against him, whispering his name in the rich silvered darkness.

"Jonathan, come to me. Love me," she begged him, but yet he held back, worshipping her with his mouth and his hands until she caught her fingers in his crisp dark curls and tugged to draw him toward her.

"My dear one." He spoke the words softly, wonderingly, almost like a prayer. "I've wanted you and loved you so long."

"And I love you . . ." Once spoken, she repeated the sweet words again against his lips. "I love you, Jonathan. But I thought you hated me."

"I was angry because I thought you had used me, that it had all been a game for you and that you had kissed me and laughed behind my back."

"It was never a game." She began to touch and kiss him in her turn. Everything about him was sweetly familiar, the slightly salt taste of his skin, the smooth silk of his muscles, the hard demand of his passion.

Lightly, she curved her fingers about this

power and gloried in the urgency of his desire, the way he came swiftly to kneel between her parted thighs. "I've wanted you so long," she heard him whisper. "Dreamed of this—" and as he spoke he raised her hips and she drew him to her. Into her.

She tensed at the first shock wave of his body's invasion and at the shadow of pain. He grew still within her and waited. She could sense the tension in his back, rigid with the effort of control and with concern for her, and suddenly nothing was as great as the fierce want that racked her. She moved against him and heard his deep male growl of pleasure as their bodies merged into one, and she called him her lover and her heart, her man and her soul, until she was conscious only of him and of the strong, heavy stroking of his love. Of the wild beating of her blood that merged with his, faster and still faster until all that they had been burst into a flame. Into conflagration. Into one.

She came to awareness of herself again only gradually, and her first waking sensation was that of a warmth and a well-being that she had never known before, a happiness that seemed to bubble up from some untouched and hidden source deep within her. From that wellspring ripples of pleasure still eddied through her, and she felt refreshed, rested. And loved. Drowsily she snuggled closer to the strong male body beside her.

"Jonathan," she murmured.

"I thought you slept." Had she been asleep? She opened her eyes and saw his profile against skies that were fading from cobalt blue to gray. How could she have slept after that explosion of joy? She rested her head against his chest while his arms took her to him possessively. When she moved, her foot touched his. She sighed. It seemed at that moment that nothing in life could ever hurt or grieve her again.

"Jonathan," she repeated, saying the name with love, as she had always longed to say it. When he smiled his face looked younger, happier.

"You're a woman of few words, but I'm content, dear one." She pressed closer to his big body and he held her so tightly that she could feel against her the urgency of his want of her. But when he spoke his words were regretful. "We must go."

"I know." But he didn't move and neither did she and instead turned her cheek to kiss his chest. The crisp chest fur made her sneeze, and she laughed and kissed again. "I wish we could stay here," she sighed.

He tucked the cloak more securely about her. "You'd soon tire of sleeping on the grass on a rough blanket, and the nights will soon turn cold. Though I vow that all I need of warmth could be found in your arms."

Unthinking she said, "I vow that you cannot be a roundhead to speak like this."

"But I am." She felt the tension in his arms at once, a tension that warned her of something she had managed to forget for a moment. No matter what they felt for each other, the differences between their worlds yawned wide. Unhappily, she watched as he sat up, his naked back and shoulders dark against the gray dawn.

Then he bent to kiss her, and the mood snapped. His mouth on hers was eager, passionate, and she curved her arms about him and clung to him as he drew her up with him and wrapped the cloak about her shoulders against the morning chill. "Dress, dear one, and quickly —we've a long ride ahead of us." He rolled away from the blanket and cloak and pulled on his garments with swift, economic movements. "I'll see to the horse while you make ready."

She hurried to clothe herself and to help him, but he had the horse saddled and some bread and cheese and apples for their breakfast by the time she joined him. As they ate and drank cool sweet water from the spring, he told her the way that they would travel.

"Several miles to the southwest is a small village that I know of and a house that once belonged to my parents. Because they used it as a place to be alone and be together, nobody besides the family and a few trusted servants know of it." He smiled as he spoke, and she saw the warm affection in his eyes.

"Your parents must love each other very much."

The light in his eyes grew somber. "They died some years ago, about the time that Charles I lost his crown. In a way, it was a blessing. My father was a man of peace, and this prolonged violence in England would have distressed him. As for my mother, she was a gentle lady, and she could not long live without my father." His eyes came up to her and he smiled again. "You would have liked her, Damaris."

She was touched and yet made thoughtful. Were these parents the reason why Jonathan was like no Puritan she had met? "Once in Arbor Cottage, no one will harm you," he was saying, "but to get there we must ride several hours through this wood and then across some flat-lands. We had better make a start." She followed him to the horse but as he helped her mount she turned and looked at him.

"Will you stay at Arbor Cottage also?" He nodded. "Will we stay there long, Jonathan?"

He seemed to hesitate. "It's unwise to predict the future, Damaris. Let's just see what happens," he said.

They fell silent again and she sensed that he listened and watched with great concentration as they left their enchanted valley and rode back into the woodlands. The air seemed different here in the gray dawn, and mist hung damply across the trees. She clung closer to Jonathan as they rode along and drew some comfort from his unyielding back against her breasts, but the silence remained unbroken until they had left the woods and were riding across meadows kissed by the first sunlight of the day. Then she said, "The countryside is so different here. It's hard to believe that that valley ever existed."

He seemed to intuit the meaning behind her words. "We will find it again someday, dear one."

"Someday," she repeated. "Someday when the civil war is over." She paused and then said slowly, "I know that you are Cromwell's man, Jonathan, but can you condone his cruelty to those who believe in the king?"

He was silent a moment and then said, "The Lord Protector feels that we, like ancient Israel, must smite our enemies." She sensed a disquiet beyond the words as he added, "He believes that the Lord is our sword arm and our shield."

"But what do you believe?" she challenged. He was silent. "Is it justice that Cromwell's officers patrol the streets to make sure English people keep his smallest laws and that he levies fines on those who so much as leave their houses on Sunday? Is it freedom when he hunts poor men and women down and hangs them without a trial simply because there is suspicion that they have helped the king?"

He gave a low laugh and turned to kiss her. "I never argue politics with a lovely woman." She began to protest, but then he said in a changed voice, "Hush—we are not alone."

Several men in roundhead uniform were

crossing the meadow toward them. They had dogs with them, and they were beating about them with huge oaken staves. "What are they doing?" she exclaimed.

"They're hunting." The grim note in Jonathan's voice left no doubt as to what the men were hunting. He reined in his horse and sat watching the men as they approached while Damaris shifted uneasily behind him. "Say nothing to arouse their suspicions and show no emotion no matter what they say," he warned her. "Clandennon is the kind of man who has spies everywhere, and if they suspect you are a fugitive he'll learn of it before nightfall."

He raised his voice and hailed the men. "Ho, there. What do you seek in the grass? Snakes or quail?" he shouted.

The men stopped and stared and then one burly fellow replied. "Neither, sir. We hunt traitors."

"Have we seen any of them around, m'dear?" Jonathan turned to address Damaris with careless amusement. "What do these traitors look like, sirrah?"

The man jerked off his hat at Jonathan's lordly tone. "They're escaped royalists, sir." Encouraged by Jonathan's nod, he grew more talkative. "We've just had word from Long Marston that scores of royalist prisoners have escaped the hangman, and there's worse news. It's said that one of Charles Stuart's especial friends is in

England and that he's helping these traitors to get away from the authorities and take ship to France. Perhaps you've heard of him, sir? The earl of Larraby's his name."

Jonathan nodded gravely. "I see. Well, let us not keep you from these duties, sirrah. I would stop and help you but . . ." He shrugged and glanced back at Damaris and then winked. The man grinned broadly in understanding and saluted before moving on to join his companions. As he did so, Jonathan touched his spurs to his mount again.

"Poor men." She didn't know she had spoken aloud until he turned to look back at her. "I hope they don't catch them. I hope they escape to France. I hope that they do have help to get to France."

"Noble sentiments but hardly wise," was the dry reply. "They'll be caught, poor fools. They'll make for the woods and they won't know their way. They'll be captured before too long and probably executed before week's end."

"You were the one who told me not to predict the future. For all you know, the earl of Larraby may be waiting for them in some arranged place. I pray so."

"And do you think that one man can fight all of Cromwell's England?" he demanded. "I've heard of this Larraby. He may be a brave man, but he's also a fool. He should know there is very little he can do for his master's henchmen." He half turned to her to add, "But you admire him, don't you? You would. Women always want heroes even in a dirty civil war."

This cold cynicism was so unlike him that she spoke up heatedly, "Yes, I admire the earl of Larraby. I would do everything I could to help him—even to risking my life."

"Be careful what you say, Damaris. Remember who I am," he said and urged the horse faster. "Besides, there's little you could do for Larraby. If he's not careful the man might find his own neck on the headsman's block."

He sounded so callous that she could not keep back a cry of protest. "How can you speak like that? Royalists are men, too!"

"They're my enemies." The words caught her unawares like a slap across the face. "England is at war, Damaris."

His voice was suddenly cool on her name. Damaris, not 'my dear one' and not 'my love'—her breath pained her suddenly and as if he read her thought he spoke quietly. "Understand. I will see you safe, but beyond that there are no promises that either of us can keep."

She knew the truth of his words. Though she still felt the wonder of last night's loving, that enchantment was past. He had sworn to take her to safety, but that was all, and beyond that, there was no ground where they could meet. Beyond that their loyalties would always find ways to part them.

She heard him draw a deep breath that could have been a sigh as he spurred on the horse, and she sensed instinctively how dear his words had cost him. She was tempted to burrow her face against his back and tell him she cared nothing for king or Cromwell or country, that all she wanted was to be with him. Was greatly tempted —but remained still. She, too, had a duty she was in danger of forgetting.

Chapter Twelve

As Jonathan had predicted, they rode all morning and through most of the afternoon. Once as they traveled through meadowlands they saw a party of horsemen riding to hounds, and later they spotted a troop of roundhead soldiers marching along the downs. It was to avoid these troops that they turned away from the set route and detoured through wooded valleys and small hills. The hills led to a forest so thick with ancient trees that they could hardly see the sun, and Damaris broke the silence that had fallen between them to ask if they were lost.

He shook his head. "In a little while, we'll come to a path that will lead us to Arbor Cottage. As I've told you before, I doubt if even Clandennon will be able to follow you there."

She wished the journey were over. Her back and neck ached from the long hours of riding pillion, and even worse was the strain that had grown between them. The tension hadn't been eased by the silence they had maintained for most of the day, and now as the end of the journey approached, she could feel the unease growing stronger. If only she hadn't been so outspoken, she thought unhappily. She should not have brought their differences into the open when he was clearly flouting his duty to see her safe.

But before she could tell him how she felt, they emerged from the woods, and late afternoon sunlight fell against the curve of a little-traveled trail. It disappeared over a rise in the ground, and as they followed it Damaris could smell woodsmoke. So could Jonathan—he gave an appreciative sniff and grinned. "Old Larkin and his grandson must be working late today. Usually they finish their woodcutting long before sunset."

There was a gladness in his tone that she hadn't heard before, and he urged his tired horse up the hillock. On the summit he drew rein and simply announced, "There it is."

She looked with weary relief at the village that nestled in the hollow. It was a very small place but it also looked prosperous, surrounded by wide fields of wheat and pasturelands where cows and sheep cropped peacefully. These broad green acres were neatly bordered by orchards, and in the far distance beyond the trees she could make out the roof of a larger house. "That's Arbor Cottage," Jonathan said briefly.

He dismounted and began to lead his horse forward, and as he did so a young boy came out of some nearby trees. When he saw Jonathan, his eyes widened until they seemed to be in danger of popping out of his head. "Sir!" he exclaimed, "Yer've come back! We've worried . . ."

"No need to be. And no need to raise the dead, lad." But the boy was already running back among the trees screaming for his grandfather. Jonathan looked up at Damaris and smiled ruefully. "The people of the village have known me since I was a boy. They feel it's necessary to make a great fuss over me whenever I visit."

The boy, now followed by a white-haired gaffer, hurried back into sight. The old man bowed deeply and then scanned Jonathan's face anxiously. "Ye be all right, sir?" he demanded.

"Never better. Larkin, this lady will stay at Arbor Cottage for some time." There was a warning in those words, Damaris knew. The old man's eyes went wary, and he stopped talking and bowed again. "Will you run ahead and tell Mrs. Carme to put some supper on to cook, lad?"

The lad scampered off immediately. "How have things been here, Larkin?"

"Good enough, sir, though Will the farrier has some complaint about John the shepherd. It may be wise to speak with them. And the Widow

Smythe's youngest son has a great desire to go to sea. That matter requires yer attention, too."

Jonathan turned to Damaris. "The master of Arbor Cottage has always been considered a kind of local magistrate," he explained. "Larkin makes sure that I have plenty to do when I visit."

She didn't care for the way the old man eyed her with a speculative disapproval. No doubt he took her for some woman of easy virtue, for what lady would gad all over England alone with a man? She thought of last night, and her weariness increased. Perhaps Larkin was right after all.

Jonathan seemed unaware of her discomfort and continued to talk with the old man for some time about local matters. It seemed like forever before he finally seemed to remember she still sat on the horse.

"The rest can wait," he told Larkin. "Just now I must get this lady safely to Mrs. Carme. Later, we will talk again." He led the horse past the bowing gaffer and down into the village, but here again they were delayed. Men and women with children clustered about them had come out of their houses and had lined up in the street to greet Jonathan. The men bowed, the women curtseyed. Jonathan greeted each villager by name, and when he came to a woman at the far end of the respectful line he paused. "Larkin says that you have a boy that needs to go to sea, Mrs. Smythe," he said.

The woman was plump and had round red cheeks, but her eyes, Damaris noted, were wary as they turned from Jonathan to his companion on the horse. "He's been driving me loony, that he has, master."

"I'll see what can be done." Jonathan seemed deep in thought as they finished the walk through the village, and Damaris did not break the silence. Instead she looked about her as they followed the path into woods filled with the scent of goldenrod and of the apple orchards that surrounded the house. Only when she got a look at the house did she break the silence.

"You call this a cottage?" she exclaimed.

It was a two-story home built along spare and elegant lines very much out of keeping with the cluttered architecture of the day. From where she sat her horse she could see the western front of the house with its projecting bays which were filled with an array of plants and flowers. An arched loggia ran across the central block of the house, calling attention to the high sweep of roof. Everything that met the eye spoke of proportion and grace and of dignified wealth, and as they came closer she could see carved into the stone of the archway the design of a spreading tree over a sword which she had first seen on Jonathan's pistol.

"My mother was of a knightly house and that is her family crest," Jonathan explained. "Arbor Cottage was a gift to her from my father, and as I told you it was a peaceful retreat for them both."

"It's beautiful. It reminds me of the house we lived in long ago when Mother still lived. That place wasn't half as beautiful or as grand as this, but it had the same feeling of peace."

"Peace—a rare commodity these days." His voice was dry again.

Before she could respond to this, the front door flew open and a slender, gray-haired woman in dark clothes came hurrying and curtseying down the steps of the house. "Master Jonathan, my lady. 'Tis good to see you here at Arbor Cottage, sir. It's good to see you safe home."

Damaris watched Jonathan's face as the old lady spoke and saw the tightening of his mouth at the last words. Though he smiled and gave her fair greeting, his eyes remained somber, and as he helped her down from the horse, she felt a familiar tension in his arms. He was right, she thought unhappily. Peace was a rare commodity —and while England was at war there was no place that could be called safe, or even home.

Mrs. Carme urged Damaris to rest before the supper hour. "You're worn out, my lady," the old lady scolded in a half maternal, half respectful way. "I'll have Carme bring up the bath to your room, and you must soak in it and let the knots in your muscles ease away. Master Jonathan says as you have been in the saddle for most of the day and most of last night, too?"

The last sentence had been turned into a question, and Damaris murmured assent. It seemed incredible that she had ever been pursued through Long Marston, ever had needed to race for her life across the downs, or cowered in terror in the woods. Here in the guest chamber of Arbor Cottage, there was no inkling of war or violence or fear.

All about her here was luxury. As the smiling housekeeper left her, Damaris walked about the large chamber and admired its exquisite appointments. She had never before seen rugs on the floor, though she had often seen them pad chairs or chests in the homes of more wealthy friends. Neither had she seen such a profusion of silk and satin, for the drapes of the room were made of rose-colored satins that rustled when she touched them, and the bed hangings were of silk that reflected rosily from gilt mirrors that sparkled on the walls and against the window glass as well. From the window she could see both the gardens below and the sun that sank slowly into the dark apple trees that edged the grounds. She stopped to watch the sunset for a moment, and then was sorry that she did. The crimson ball of fire reminded her of a malevolent eye, slowly winking out into the dark.

The housekeeper's husband, a tall, well-muscled fellow for all his graying hair, now brought in a large bathtub which two young maids filled with warm water and rose petals. It was heaven, Damaris thought, to step out of her travel-stained clothes and sink into the comforting water. She was leaning back in the tub, inhaling the subtle scent of roses, when she heard a knock on the door.

"Come in, Mrs. Carme . . ." But it was not the housekeeper who stood on the threshold of the door. It was Jonathan.

He had already bathed and changed, she saw instantly. His dark hair curled more closely about his fine-shaped head, and the white cambric shirt he wore was open at the neck against the beginning shadow of chest fur. A hint of a smile curved his lips when he saw her eyes widen at sight of him. "I'm sorry," he said. "I did not mean to disturb you. I meant only to ask you how you fared so far."

"I fare very well," she said and eyed him with some apprehension. In spite of his words, he didn't seem about to go away. He looked so overwhelmingly large and male in this feminine setting, the rose silk and satin of the room a foil for his dark masculinity. She curled herself further under the lip of the big tub. Last night, she would have held out her arms to him eagerly, welcomed him. But last night was long past.

"I had hoped to dine with you. Unfortunately there's village business that can't wait." Jonathan tried to make his voice sound casual, but he found that was hard to do in this woman's presence. She had never looked so lovely, her eyelids all but translucent from the warm water, her mouth soft and full and ripe for kissing. Her glorious hair had been caught up on her head to avoid wetting, but one golden-red tendril fell against her creamy skin. There was an ache in him to touch that skin, to kiss the damp shoulders and to seek with his lips the rosy curve of the breasts that he glimpsed below the surface of the water. And—sweet Christ, he knew such thoughts led to disaster; their talk this morning had proven that. He must keep his distance for both their sakes.

She wished he wouldn't look at her so intently. The light in his gray eyes was as palpable as a caress, and that silvered gaze touched her face and then moved down. She felt her nipples tauten as if he had touched them. Her loins were heavy, honeyed, waiting. "'Behold, thou art fair, my love . . .'" The words he had used last night came back to her, and she shivered in spite of the warmth of the water.

Abruptly, he turned away. "I'll leave you now," he said, and she was conscious of a wrenching disappointment. Though part of her wanted him to leave and to remove this confused push-pull of her senses, she spoke to forestall his going.

"Does this village business you mention have to do with Mrs. Smythe's son?"

He looked swiftly and searchingly back at her and she noted the slight narrowing of his eyes. "How did you know?"

"She seemed very distressed. Is it such a terrible thing to go to sea?"

"These aren't normal times," he explained. "If the lad goes to sea, he may never return. But if he's set his heart on this, nothing I can say or do will stop him." He paused and pulled open the door. "Dine well. I'll see you later in the evening."

She thought of his words as she dried herself on the soft towels Mrs. Carme had brought and dressed in a borrowed gown of watered silk which the housekeeper said had once belonged to Jonathan's mother. He seemed, she thought, most concerned for the villagers. As he had once said, the civil war had cut through the differences of wealth and class, so that people from all walks of life served Cromwell. Jonathan, no doubt, had been a country squire before becoming Cromwell's captain and special emissary, a rich country squire loved by his people and conscientious in his duties. She told herself that this curiosity about Jonathan was useless and could lead to nothing, but over the rich and solitary dinner Mrs. Carme brought up to her in her elegant room, she found herself asking anyway.

The housekeeper looked surprised. "Master Jonathan a squire? I doubt that would be the word. His father was master of the village in his time, and when he died Master Jonathan took over his duties."

That was all she would say, and Damaris noted the same questioning, appraising look in her eyes that old Larkin had given her. Still, the old lady fussed around the stout oak table, placing yet more delicacies before her guest and she beamed when Damaris praised the roasted capon and the fricassee of eggs, and finally the excellent quince pie that had been made, Mrs. Carme said, from fruit picked near the cottage itself.

"Master Jonathan's favorite pie. I thought he'd be here to eat it, but he's always been one to set duty above pleasure," she sighed.

When Mrs. Carme had gone, Damaris walked to her window and pulled back the curtains to look outside. Under the moon the expanse of orchards and woods seemed different somehow, shadowed and dangerous. "Danger . . ." She said the word out loud and frowned because till now the word had had no meaning here in this elegant house. Now, it echoed warningly in her mind. Danger to whom? she wondered and shivered, wishing that Jonathan were back from his talk with Mrs. Smythe's errant son.

He had said that he would return after the meal, but the hours passed and he did not come. She told herself that she was foolish to suppose anything could have happened to him here among his own people, that he was probably being forced to listen to some long-winded complaint by one or another of the villagers. Mrs. Carme said the same thing when she came to clear the supper things away.

"Go to bed, my lady, and sleep well," she urged. "The master sometimes stays up half the night listening to yon villagers jaw about their problems. None of them think that he might be tired and might like a rest, too."

Damaris smiled at the old lady's tone and was grateful to seek her bed. It was soft and comfortable, and she was half asleep even before her head touched the down-filled pillows. She slept without dream, deeply, an untroubled sleep from which she woke with a start. For a moment she was disoriented, and then she remembered where she was. She also realized that hoofbeats under her window had wakened her.

Jonathan had returned—she almost closed her eyes to sleep again when she heard him calling for Carme. There was something in his voice that kept sleep away, and she heard him say, "Well, it's done."

Carme said something she couldn't make out, and then Jonathan spoke again. "It wasn't easy this time, as you know." A pause and then she heard him laugh. "The Lord Protector should reward me for this night's work."

The Lord Protector—Damaris's heart gave a tremendous hammerblow that threatened to tear through her ribs. She jumped out of bed and ran to the window, and looking out saw Jonathan dismount from his great dark horse. As she watched, he handed his cloak and his sword to Carme. "It needs cleaning," he told the man grimly.

"Oh, sweet Jesus." She didn't realize that she had whispered the words aloud and her own voice frightened her. Even here in the peace of Arbor Cottage, Jonathan's mission for Cromwell threatened her. If there had ever been doubt, she was now sure that he was a tracker, a hunter, especially dangerous because he was a special emissary from the Lord Protector. He'd been out looking for escaped royalists tonight, and he'd found them.

She continued to watch him as he spoke in

lower tones to Carme and then came into the house. She could hear his footsteps downstairs, then more low conversation, and then the stairs creaking under his weight. She listened to his steps coming nearer and wondered what she would do if he sought her tonight.

For a moment he seemed to pause before her door and she held her breath. She had not thought to lock her door, and anyway, what lock could stop him if he wanted her? And worse than that was her own reaction: even knowing where he had been and what he had done, she could feel her treacherous body respond to his nearness.

"Sweet Lord," she breathed again. "Please." She didn't know whether it was a prayer to keep him away or to bring him to her, but after a moment he walked past her room, and she heard another door open and shut. Then there was silence. She stood where she was, listening intently for new movement from him, but there was no sound. And then she thought, I can't stay here. I must go away.

Madness to stay here with him knowing what he did, what he had to continue doing to serve his Puritan master; madness to stay feeling the way she did whenever he came near. Tomorrow, she swore, she would ask him to fulfill his pledge and get her to safety. Perhaps away from him there would be balance in her world again.

She went back to bed but during the remainder of the night she started awake at each real or imagined sound. When she slept it was only fitfully, and her dreams were confused. In one of these nightmares she found herself back in the woods near Long Marston with Clandennon on her trail. He had a pack of hounds with him, and as they gained on her she cried out to Jonathan for help. But he did not come, and when she turned about to see whether her enemy gained on her, she saw that the hounds were almost upon her and that one of them wore Jonathan's face. . . .

In terror she awoke to early morning and the liquid trilling of birds. A scent of late-blooming flowers and cool country air drifted through her half-opened window, and a bar of palest sunshine lay across her bed. She closed her eyes and tried to rid herself of the dream, but its horror did not fade. Instead, it mingled with the real horror of what she had discovered last night, of what she knew about Jonathan.

Resolutely, she rose and washed at the basin in her room, then hesitated before dressing in a sprigged muslin gown that Mrs. Carme had laid out for her. It was a lovely thing, pale green embroidered with white flowers, and as she brushed back her hair before one of the gilt mirrors she wondered what Jonathan's mother would have thought to know what her son did for the Lord Protector. And what would her own father have thought? The widening of her own black eyes reflected in the glass gave her the answer.

She would waste no time but talk to Jonathan

now, this minute. She went downstairs and found Mrs. Carme, who indicated that the master was walking in the apple orchard. "He likes to see the fruit ripen on the trees," she continued fondly. "He was up early, though he got in late, Carme says."

"The villagers must have kept him late," Damaris said. The housekeeper nodded, unaware of the edge in Damaris's voice.

"Aye, so they did. A great one for doing his duty, Master Jonathan," she said.

In silence Damaris left the house and stood for a moment in the bright sunshine, looking out into the garden and the orchard below. It was hard to think that evil existed on this cooly glorious autumn day. Then she sighted Jonathan and last night's scene played over in her mind. Not that there was anything sinister about him now; he was walking toward the house munching on an apple, his dark hair blazing like black gold in the morning sun. But when she looked again, there were subtle signs that he had hunted well last night. There was a spring to his lithe stride, an arrogant cock to his powerful wedge of shoulder. All that for running some wretched royalist to earth—Damaris clenched her hands at her sides as she went to meet him.

Halfway down the garden path he saw her. "Good morning," he called, and she heard a new cheerfulness in his voice. "Did you sleep well?"

"I did indeed. And you?"

"Never better." He was telling the truth, and it sickened her. "I thought you would be asleep still, or I'd have asked you to walk with me. The orchards are truly lovely in early morning, and the apples are sweet." He pulled a rosy fruit from his pocket and offered it to her. "I picked it myself."

She ignored the gesture. "You swore to take me to safety, Captain." She spoke so abruptly that he stared at her in astonishment and she added, "You swore to see me to safety."

"And so I will, but arrangements must be made. It's not so easy to find a ship that will take you to France these days. Ports are being watched for escaping royalists." He shrugged and added, "Besides, you're safe here."

Memory of what he'd done last night made her shake her head. "No, I'm not. How can I be when my host hunts down royalists and brings his bloodied sword home for his servant to clean?"

For a moment astonishment, incredulity and something else, something shadowed and elusive, flared in his eyes. Then he took another careless bite of his apple. "Indeed? And what brings you to this interesting conclusion?"

The crunch of those strong white teeth into the fruit and the cynicism of his tone infuriated her. "I heard you return last night. You boasted to Carme that Cromwell would reward you for your 'difficult' night's work." Her voice shook in spite of herself. "I had thought you were different, a decent man caught up in this bloody civil war. Not like the others, not like Clandennon. But now . . ."

The gray eyes held hers so that she could not look away. "And what do you think now?"

"I think you're worse than he is. He's a brute, a beast, a sadist—but he isn't a hypocrite."

Half turning from her, he sent his half-eaten apple spinning away among the trees. "Well spoken, my fiery royalist." He didn't even make an attempt to deny anything she had said, and she felt a terrible dull ache begin inside her. She realized now she had hoped against hope that she had been mistaken, that there was some other explanation for what she had seen and heard.

"I must get away." She hadn't meant to speak her thought aloud but she must have, for he turned to face her again.

"I can understand that my company would rankle you—and so we will end this little interlude." He spoke calmly and without emotion, and she understood that he did not care whether she stayed or went. Those moments in the enchanted glade had been mere amusement for him, and she had been a fool to ever believe otherwise. He was saying, "I will do my best to make arrangements to get you away as soon as possible. Unfortunately, that might not be possible for some time. Will that content you?"

Nothing will content me as long as I am near a man like you. He saw her thought in her dark eyes and felt bitter anger stir in him. Christ, what did the woman want from him? She knew what he did and knew, too, what he risked for her and continued to put at risk. To the devil with her, he wanted to cry, yet when she squared her slim shoulders so bravely and walked away from him, he knew those weren't the words he wanted to say.

"Make sure you are ready to leave when I give the word," he snapped, and Damaris, registering the coldness of his words, did not see the way his eyes followed her until she was out of his sight.

Chapter Thirteen

DAMARIS SAT BY HER WINDOW AND STARED INTO
the darkness. She didn't like to admit to herself
that she was waiting for Jonathan, but there was
no other explanation for this vigil. He had ridden away after supper, a silent meal which they
had shared in the large airy room downstairs.
The silence between them had been awkward
and hard to bear, and she had been glad when
immediately after supper he had risen to an-
nounce that he was going riding, though, knowing his errand, "glad" was not an appropriate
word.

It was very late and Mrs. Carme and the
servants had long since gone to bed. Outside her
half-open window, nothing stirred except for
cool autumn breezes that carried on them a hint
of wood smoke and the scents of pine and earth.

They reminded her of the forest, and she caught her lip in her teeth. That night in the forest was madness that she didn't want to remember, would not remember ever again as soon as she got away from this place and the proximity of Jonathan Hartwell. . . .

Her thoughts went to powder as she caught the faint sounds of hoofbeats drumming against the hard road. He was returning. She didn't want to think of what he had been doing, but her mind conjured images nonetheless. They grew even more vivid as horse and rider trotted out of the concealment of the orchard and approached the house.

Carme came quickly out of the stables, and not wishing to be seen at the window, Damaris drew back as Jonathan passed almost directly beneath her. From where she stood she could not see him, but she could hear him. "Don't bother about that," the deep voice snapped. Apparently things hadn't gone so well for him tonight; he certainly wasn't laughing or talking about a possible promotion from his chief. There was a murmur of voices and then loud protest from Carme.

"But, master!" The horse whickered then, covering the man's next words so that Damaris could only hear the end of the sentence. " . . . not tonight," he was finishing.

"You've got your orders. Remember that I'm to be obeyed in everything I say." The brusque words were hurled out in a tone she had never heard Jonathan use before. She leaned forward against the windowsill, but he was no longer outside—instead, she heard his footstep on the stairs. His unsteady footstep. Did Puritans drink, and was that perhaps the reason for his ill nature, Damaris wondered. *In vino veritas,* her father had always said. You always found out the truth about a man when he was drunk.

Heavy footsteps punished the landing, then came across the hall and stopped. She stood very still and didn't realize she'd been holding her breath until the hard knock came on her door. What to do, she wondered. She had no desire to talk to a drunken Jonathan. As she hesitated, he knocked again even more sharply.

"I know you're awake," he told her. "I saw you by the window. Open the door, Damaris." There was a little pause and then he added, "Unless, of course, you don't want to discuss your leaving Arbor Cottage."

She hurried to open the door and then was sorry. He looked different covered from neck to boot-top in the dark riding cloak. Though she wasn't sure if he were drunk or sober, his eyes were hard gray stones, and he was very pale, as if something about this night's business had upset him terribly.

"I'm glad to see you're dressed." His eyes ran over her without a shred of desire. "You can leave." She echoed the word blankly. "Yes, leave. You made it plain enough this afternoon that you were in a hurry to be gone."

"You said that it would be difficult to arrange . . ." Her words broke off as he leaned heavily against the wall by her door. She couldn't smell liquor, but his next words were a little slurred as if he had trouble forming them.

"Difficult, yes, but it's done. You'll be taken through the woodlands toward Exeter and from there southeast to a small fishing village called Silverneck Wells. A ship will be waiting for you there. It'll be a long ride, but you will be able to reach the sea in thirty-six hours' time. Can you do it?"

"I can ride as hard as you can," she retorted.

"I won't be going with you. There are certain other matters I have to attend to here."

The way he said it made her positive that some royalist had escaped him and that he was anxious to get back into the chase. "Very well," she said, despising herself because even now she couldn't remain indifferent to him. "I can travel myself as long as I know the way . . ."

"Carme will go with you. He has his orders." He spoke abruptly. "Now get your cloak and anything else you value."

He stood half wedged against the doorjamb and the wall and watched as she gathered up her few belongings—her small supply of money, the cloak she had brought out of Long Marston and the small dagger. She tried to act casual under his watchful eyes, but it wasn't easy. She had the feeling that the silver-gray gaze was boring into her. Nor did he make things less difficult when she was ready. He simply said, "Hurry. Carme is waiting with the horses."

Approaching the door, she hesitated. He obviously wasn't about to move aside to let her pass, and she had the sudden fear that he would reach out to her. She trembled as she stepped past him, breathed the familiar scent and felt his nearness keenly. But she sensed that something was terribly different about him. It was almost as if the vitality of the man, as much a part of him as breath itself, was dimmed tonight. Then he said, "Godspeed, Damaris," and she turned involuntarily to look back at him.

She caught her breath, her eyes widening at the weakness in his voice. And the man wasn't white, he was gray. As gray as Father was, she thought, and then understanding burst into her mind. "You're wounded," she heard herself gasp.

"Nonsense." It was an attempt at a sneer, but she saw him stagger as he spoke. She moved quickly, but not swiftly enough to forestall his slumping to the floor. Pulling open the cloak that covered him, she cried out when she saw the huge crimson stain over his heart.

She didn't realize she'd been shouting for Mrs. Carme until the housekeeper appeared at her side. "My sweet Lord," Mrs. Carme exclaimed in horror. "I knew this day would happen—I knew!" Almost in tears, she leaned forward as Damaris tore open the blood-soaked doublet and shirt, exposed the jagged, blood-pumping wound high over the left ribs. Then she keened out loud. "He's dying. Oh, Lord, he's dying."

"He needs a physician. Your husband or one of the servants must ride for one immediately." Damaris cut through the woman's loud wails.

Her own heart was pounding violently, but if she gave way to hysterics, this man would die. She picked up her own discarded cloak, balled up a section of it and pressed it down hard on the pumping wound.

"What are you doing?" Mrs. Carme cried, but her husband shouted from below the stairs to leave my lady alone.

"She's trying to stop the bleeding, I know that much," Carme said. His face was haggard, his graying hair rumpled, but at least he wasn't going to pieces like his wife. Damaris again called for a doctor, but Carme shook his head. "The Master gave orders—no doctor," he said. "The Master has to be obeyed in everything."

Were they all mad? "He'll die unless he has someone to take care of this wound," Damaris cried. Under the hard pressure of her fingers, the wound still bled.

Neither the man nor his weeping wife moved, and she realized that they weren't going for help. Jonathan would die anyway unless she managed to stop this bleeding, and he looked so white that perhaps he was already dead. She felt for his pulse. For a moment she could not find it, and panic assailed her, but then, she felt it—the beat was weak and thready beneath her fingers, but he still lived.

"Get clean linen, hot water, get something for him to drink. And bring me the strongest spirits you have in the house," she ordered.

By the time the housekeeper had returned with supplies, the flow of blood had almost stopped. Damaris was encouraged enough to remove her now blood-soaked cloak and swiftly substitute clean linen. Then, remembering what her father had taught her about battlefield first aid and blood poisoning, she poured almost half of the strong-smelling liquor over the linen and the wound. She also sent her first wordless message to Jonathan: I'm not going to let you die.

Satisfied that she had done as much to cleanse the wound as possible without touching it, Damaris instructed Carme to carry Jonathan to his bed. It was the first time she had been in his room, and even at such a time she found herself thinking that it fitted Jonathan well—an elegant but thoroughly masculine domain enriched by fine portraits and comfortable chairs that all bore the crest of the tree above the sword.

Mrs. Carme hovered tearfully near as her husband gently deposited the wounded man on the canopied bed. "My lady, will he live?" she questioned.

Carme answered his wife's question. "The wound is high, and so it missed the heart. It seems clean and he's a strong man. But he has lost so much blood . . ." He broke off to look at Damaris.

She knew that the wound had been made by a royalist blade, but she couldn't find any satisfaction in that thought. Suddenly, she realized that if Jonathan died, something unnamed within her deepest self would also ceased to live. Why this was so she had no idea, but she recognized the truth of it, and she answered Mrs. Carme's question with quiet force. "He's going to live," she said.

Jonathan's life hung in the balance through the next three days. Fever swiftly followed the shock of losing so much blood, and it went so alarmingly high that for all her brave words, Damaris was frantic. She told the Carmes that she would go seeking for a doctor herself, but both the housekeeper and her husband were adamant. Even now, the master's commands had to be obeyed.

"Besides, you cannot leave him, my lady, dear," Mrs. Carme remonstrated. "He's so much easier when you are with him."

That was false. Jonathan didn't know who sat beside him, for he raved with fever. He didn't know, either, who prevented Mrs. Carme from using prevalent remedies, like applying splurge and Burgundy pitch to his feet.

Instead, she horrified the staff by stripping Jonathan and sponging him with cool water. It was a trick she had learned from an old soldier who had been under her father's command and who had lived near them in York, and she prayed that it would work against the raging fever as she bathed the great body over and over again. She also tried to force all the cool liquids that he could gulp down into him. With this Mrs. Carme concurred, lending any assistance that she could give, though she protested that the master would die from repeated bathings.

Sometimes, as she sponged him, weary but unwilling to allow less skilled hands to assume the task, she heard him mutter broken stuff about Cromwell and the war and Charles II. She paid no attention. Sometimes, he called her name, and the way her name broke on his feeble lips tore at her heart. He was so weak, so very pale. Yet, she insisted that he was going to get well.

She clung to this belief all through the fourth day of his sickness, but by evening of that day her faith weakened. Part of this weakening came from her own exhaustion. Though she had caught short naps by his bed, she had not left his side, always afraid that if she were out of the way Mrs. Carme would start using her ghastly remedies. Tonight she was so tired that she did everything by rote—forced liquids down his throat, soothed his hot body with cool compresses and spoke to him in the weary litany she had perfected through the long hours of caring for him. "Jonathan, you can't die. I won't let you."

She wondered why had she been so angry with him and then recalled that it had something to do with royalists and roundheads. How unimportant that was now. Politics and wars and even duty were nothing compared with Jonathan's life. And more than that—she loved him. "I can't let you go not knowing," she told him wearily. "I've always loved you, yes, from the first time I saw you at the Silver Dragon Inn."

And then, again, the litany that was almost a prayer—"You can't die. I won't let you."

After she had done sponging him, she slumped wearily into the chair by his bed and fought sleep as she watched the rise and fall of his chest. As long as he breathed, as long as he was alive, she would battle off despair and fight for him. But not even the power of her will and her love could keep her eyelids open, and slowly, irresistibly, she dozed.

"Damaris . . ."

She came awake suddenly, heart pounding. She sat up in her chair. Surely she had heard him call for her? Now it came again, the painfully weak whisper that had no delirium in it. She got up quickly from the chair and bent over him, and he said, "You are here. I thought—I dreamed. Thought—you'd gone."

She felt his forehead and then, mistrusting the evidence of her hands, touched it with her lips. The skin was still warm, but the terrible fever had abated. As she leaned back to look at him, the faintest color stirred under the stubble of days-old beard on his cheeks.

One weak hand raised and touched her cheek. He looked at the moisture on his fingers and then at her. "Why?" he murmured, and she knew he asked why she wept. Unable to speak, she shook her head. "Why?" he persisted.

"I was afraid for you. Afraid that you might die." Suddenly, the fears she had battled all this long time overcame her, and she hid her face against his sheets. As she struggled with her emotions, she felt his hand touching her hair.

"Behold . . ." She looked up quickly and saw his lips forming words. "Behold, thou art fair, my love . . ."

His whisper stilled, and she knew he'd fallen asleep. She knew she should call the Carmes and share her good news, but she couldn't. Not yet. She leaned over him, exulting in his improved color, the stronger beat of his pulse, his cooling skin. She watched him as he slept and knew that while he needed her, nothing else mattered—not the king, not her promise to her father, not even England itself.

She bent and kissed his now quiet lips. "God pity me," she whispered aloud. "I love you more than anything on earth."

Chapter Fourteen

AT FIRST, JONATHAN WAS TOO WEAK TO DO MORE than drift from sleep to wakefulness while Damaris watched, grateful beyond words for the gift of his life. Then, once having begun to mend, his superb constitution began to heal rapidly.

They spent those days of convalescence in quiet happiness. She would read to him while he watched her face and listened to the low music of her voice fill the long, golden afternoons. When he was stronger, he told her about his childhood and the humorous events that marked his growing years. She in turn related stories she had half forgotten of the days when her mother was still alive or made him laugh by imitating her father's more comical comrades-at-arms. By tacit consent, they did not speak of the war or of the events that led to Jonathan's wounding. And though love for each other showed in every action, every touch and word, they neither discussed the future nor their feelings for each other.

She managed to keep him bedfast for three days, but on the fourth morning after his awakening, she came into his room to see how he did and found him dressed in shirt and breeches and standing by the window. "Are you trying to kill yourself?" she cried.

He turned to her and spoke quietly. "It's time I was up. It will soon be time for me to get back to my duties again, Damaris."

The words thrust through the fragile happiness of the past few days, and she knew that by breaking their unspoken agreement of silence, he was telling her that nothing had changed or could change between them. "You mustn't fear," he was going on, "I won't come to harm again."

"Why must you to talk about this now?" she protested.

He came to her and took her hands in his, kissing the knuckles and then turning them to kiss the palms. She registered the remembered warmth of his mouth as he added, "I have my work to do for the Lord Protector, Damaris. I've never pretended to you or lied to you, and I won't start now."

"But you aren't strong enough, and the wound has not yet healed. You lay near death so short a time ago."

He stepped away to stare through the windows again. There was something intense and almost fierce in his expression, though his voice was calm. "I will go softly, don't fear. I will not soon forget that you gave up hope of safety to nurse my wounds. I know you have promises to keep in France, Damaris."

"Promises?" she echoed.

He smiled a little. "To your father. Aren't you entrusted with information from him to take to your so-called king?"

"But how do you know?" she cried.

An eyebrow went up, the corner of his mouth tugged down in wry amusement. "Why else would Clandennon be so eager to get you back into his clutches? Besides, from the little time I spent with your father, I'd guess him to be the kind of man who'd risk his life for his chief." He paused. "It's true, isn't it?"

She didn't bother with denials. "And even so you would have helped me get to France?"

"I gave you my word, remember? I seem to have little willpower when it concerns you, Damaris." He smiled, easing the strain. "Enough of this now. It's a beautiful day, and I want to be outdoors. Have I been a good enough patient to deserve a short walk outside?"

She protested this foolhardiness vigorously and, when he would not listen to her, summoned reinforcements from Mrs. Carme. The housekeeper raised such a hue and cry that Jonathan was forced to give up the idea of setting foot outside Arbor Cottage that day. Next morning at dawn, however, Damaris heard footsteps pass her door and go down the stairs. Knowing that it would be impossible to try to stop him, she hurried to dress and followed him out of the house and into the apple orchard where the cool early light was just beginning to pick out the shape and color of the fruit.

He stood with his back to her, and she realized how strong he had grown, saw with both joy and sorrow that he held the great wedge of his shoulders at the old imperious angle and that his stance was one of command. When he turned to her, his customary agile grace was back in his step.

"Awake already?" He held out his hands to her as she went toward him. "I had meant to be quiet on the stairs. Was I so noisy?"

She shook her head. "I felt you would be up and out of doors today."

"Then you know me well enough to know what I have hungered for." With one hand he cupped her chin and tilted it up to him, while with the other he drew her closer.

With delicious boldness, his mouth found hers. His tongue tip circled the perimeter of her mouth, teased her tongue, drew honey from her eager inner mouth. He stroked back her hair, moved to caress her back, sweep down over her hips. But when he sought the swell of her breasts, she pulled back murmuring protest.

"No, Jonathan. Your wound—we must be careful."

For a moment he held her, and then he reluctantly loosened his clasp about her. "I think you are too careful, beloved physician," he murmured. "Still, I won't argue with you now." Swiftly he kissed her again, touching her temples, the deep dimple at her chin. "Very well, since I'm to do your bidding, will you at least walk with me to the village?"

"The village! Jonathan, that's a mile away!"

He was laughing at her, but there was something his eyes that told her his mind was made up. "What's a mile? Will you come with me, or has lolling about in Arbor Cottage made you soft?"

"I'll come." He would go anyway, and if she went with him she could at least see that he did not overtax his strength. He offered her his arm and as she took it she added, "But we must walk slowly—for my sake. I cannot match your long legs."

They started decorously enough, but soon she was hard pressed to keep up with his long stride. He seemed to grow stronger as he walked, and she saw the driving determination in his face harden. "I am well," he told her when she tried to caution him.

It was still early when they reached the village, but farmers were already tilling their fields, and their wives and children were busy with household chores. The villagers greeted Jonathan with enthusiasm, and Damaris found herself surrounded by a respectful circle of the women. Mrs. Smythe came forward to drop a deep curtsey and ask if my lady would not accept a cup of herbal tea in her home. "The Master will be talking with the men, my lady," she explained. "It will be some time before they are finished with their business."

Damaris saw that Jonathan was surrounded by a small group of men. Thinking that from Mrs. Smythe's home she could keep watch on him and not be observed, she accepted the older woman's offer and was led toward a straw-thatched stone house.

The house consisted of one room only, but everything within was clean and orderly. The air was scented with herbs and spice, and a plump cat yawned on the well-swept hearth. Damaris took a chair near the door and looked about her with pleasure.

"What a pleasant place this is," she exclaimed, and Mrs. Smythe beamed agreement.

"Indeed it is, my lady. Peaceful like. The master has made it so, of course. Else we'd have been beggared or heaved upside down by the war—like some of the other villages and towns."

From where she sat, she could see not only Jonathan and the men about him but the rest of the village, fair and rich in the early sunshine. She wondered again how he had managed to keep the civil war away, and as she did so realized that several newcomers had joined the men. For a moment she thought that these were villagers also, but a second look gave her the lie. Though dressed in simple homespun, these newcomers were of no peasant stock. They carried themselves too proudly and with a military air.

Soldiers, she thought, roundhead soldiers . . . and then she suddenly knew how the master of Arbor Cottage had kept war and violence away from his people. By cooperating with the round-head army, he had probably been able to negotiate concessions for the village. Because they worked together, the village might not need to pay high taxes or send any of their sons to war. Well, why not? Jonathan was Cromwell's man; he had never lied to her about that.

And now what, she asked herself. She knew that if she spoke her suspicions aloud, the bond forged between herself and Jonathan would twist and snap. For a moment she thought of leaving and of going away to France, but all her heart cried out against this move. His near-death had proved that she could not lose him, not yet, and if the price had to be her silent compliance to what he believed in and what he did, so be it.

As if he had read her thoughts, he broke away from the men around him and came toward Mrs. Smythe's cottage. He leaned against the lintel of the small place and for a moment they looked at each other. She saw a brief, shadowed look fill his eyes while he in his turn read knowledge and decision in her face.

Then Jonathan smiled. "Are you enjoying the hospitality of the village?" he asked her. "We will soon go back. Mrs. Carme will have my head stuffed for her dinner if I am not about when she calls for breakfast."

She paced him on the way back to Arbor Cottage and for the rest of that long day she watched him. Outwardly she talked and laughed, too, because he was in good spirits, teasing the flustered Mrs. Carme at breakfast and then insisting on escorting Damaris around Arbor Cottage. He showed her the herb garden where his mother had loved to spend her summer mornings, green lawns in back where his father had played tennis. He even discovered a lute that his mother had played in her youth and attempted a romantic song that made Damaris laugh.

"Fie on you for your laughter," Jonathan told her severely, though his eyes danced. "That was a song with which my father wooed my mother."

"And did the lady need so much wooing?"

His expression softened, as it always did when he spoke of his parents. "Aye, she did. Her father was a knight, purse-poor but rich in an ancient name, while he . . ."

"Was not a nobleman?" she supplied as he hesitated. He shrugged, and she said, "I think I understand. I was too young to go to the first King Charles's court, but my father told me that the lords and ladies of England are very careful who they marry. Marriages are made for dower or for land—or for an ancient name, or so my father said. Noblemen and women don't marry except for such."

They had strolled out to the apple orchard and

now he sank down on the fragrant grass and drew her down to sit beside him. "My mother did marry my father, nonetheless," he said reflectively, and she felt the silver warmth of his eyes on her.

She didn't wish to pursue the subject. Marriage, love, permanence—all these were not a part of her and Jonathan's world. He seemed to share her mood and lay silently with his head in her lap as she sat with her back to an apple tree. She smoothed his dark forehead and wound the crisp curls about her fingers until Mrs. Carme called them in to supper shortly after twilight.

Tonight's meal was a merry one, partaken in the large and pleasant room that took the place of the central hall where the housekeeper served up delicacies like venison and a rack of lamb smothered in herbs and sauce, but though Jonathan praised her cooking, Damaris saw that he ate sparingly. She did not guess the cause until the meal was over and they were alone. Then he rose and came to stand behind her chair and put both hands on her shoulders.

"I must ride tonight," he told her.

She felt as if her heart had tumbled from its place in her chest and was falling into black void, and she realized that she had known that this moment would come ever since she had seen the soldiers masquerading as villagers that morning. Her lips felt numb as she whispered. "Tonight? but you cannot. Your wound . . ."

"Tonight." His voice was very firm, and his hands, too, holding her where she sat. "Perhaps

I should not have told you, but I did not wish to lie to you."

He gently withdrew his hands and walked away from her toward the door. Only then could she manage a whisper. "Jonathan, be careful."

He did not answer her, and she didn't know whether he had heard. She sat where she was as she heard his footsteps dying away outside and the sound of hoofbeats. She listened to him riding through the orchard and drew a deep painful breath and thought—only let him be safe. And by that pitiful prayer she knew that she cared for nothing but for his safe return.

She got dazedly, stiffly to her feet and went to her chamber. There, sitting by the window, she watched the long silver road grow gray, then dark, then black. A crescent moon was late in rising, and its poor light showed little, but she sat with the lamps unlit, straining her eyes into the dark. No one disturbed her, and the house was still. She was sure that somewhere in the house the Carmes kept vigil, too, but this knowledge did not make her feel any less alone. An hour passed, two—and she grew tired of sitting and began to pace her room.

Please, let him be safe . . . as her mind formed the litany over and over again, she could envision him lying somewhere, bleeding from his reopened wound, could see him . . .

Hoofbeats! Her head flew up, listening, and then she ran to the window and opened it. A long, low cool wind sighed through the room and brought with it the far away clip-clop of hooves.

A horse was coming, but she had no way of telling whether its rider was hurt or whole.

With a muffled cry she ran to the door, pulling it open, and with her skirts bunched in her hands, she flew down the stairs to the outer door, and, tugging it open, raced down the pathway through the apple orchard. Her breath burned in her throat, came in shallow gasps as she ran. Please let him be safe . . .

The hoofbeats sounded louder now, and as she reached the end of the orchards and the beginning of the woods she saw horse and its rider turn a corner in the road ahead of her. Jonathan sat his horse erect, his cloak swirling about him, his head bare to the cool autumn wind. He was unhurt. Unhurt. She gave a low moan of relief.

Soft though it was, he heard it and drew rein at once. "Damaris?" he questioned, "Why are you here? Is something amiss?"

"I was worried . . ." She had started to shake and could not control the trembling, and when he trotted his horse toward her and leaned down to give her his hand, hers was like ice. He frowned as she set her foot on his and was lifted into the saddle before him, and he wrapped the cloak about them both. "Christ, sweetheart, you're frozen," he exclaimed.

"Are you hurt?" She could not rid herself of the picture of his red blood pouring from his side. It remained with her until they had reached the stables where he tossed the reins of his horse into Carme's waiting hands and had gone into the house. "Are you hurt?" she asked again.

He drew her up the stairs and into his room. There he lit the lamp and then as it flared, dropped the cloak and held wide his arms. "See if I bleed," he said.

He was half laughing, but she was wholly in earnest as she pulled up the shirt from his breeches, fumbled the buttons open and pushed the cloth aside to reveal his chest. There were no telltale signs of blood on the bandage, but she was not content until she had worked the bandage loose and the jagged, healing scar came to view. She felt such relief that her legs threatened to buckle under her. "Thank God," she whispered. "I was so afraid."

"Why? There was nothing to fear." He was laughing again, and there was a trace of male smugness in his tone. He compounded it by adding, "There was no fighting tonight, and even if there had been, I would have been a match for any."

"I must have been insane to worry!" Anger flared through her as she remembered tonight's terrible waiting. And for what, when he in his male bravado and pride did not even worry about himself? "I can see that you are perfectly able to care for yourself, sir, and I will leave you."

She turned on her heel to leave the room, took one step toward the door and was held back by his arms. "Damaris, don't go," Jonathan said.

At his words the tears filled her eyes. A reaction to her fear and worry, they streamed down her cheeks. She tried to hold them back but that only made it worse, and she bent her head and sobbed aloud.

"My brave darling." His arms went around her waist, tight under her breasts, and he drew her to him. For a moment she stiffened, still angry, and then she leaned against him. He kissed her hair, the nape of her neck, her shoulder, and drew in the lavender fragrance of her. He knew with a humility strange to him that these tears forced from her could not have been called forth except by love. "I love you," he told her.

He turned her gently and drew her against him, and she registered the hard muscle of his chest and shoulder against her cheek. She turned that cheek and ran her lips across his bare flesh, mutely assuring herself with her lips and hands that he was well, whole, alive. And here. Her mouth touched his nipples, the fur of his chest, lifted first to his strong throat, and then higher for his kiss.

The force of that kiss was almost bruising in its intensity. He may have made light of it, but from the way his mouth claimed hers, she knew he had played with death tonight. His tongue pillaged and adored the recesses of her mouth. His teeth nibbled delicately, insistently, on her lower lip. She breathed from his lungs and felt lightheaded with the warmth that was sweeping her veins, turning to heat, to flame.

Still kissing her, he began to work loose the buttons of her bodice. This time she did not protest but helped him as her shoulders, then her breasts came bare. He bent his dark head, then, rubbing his lips and tongue against the sweet eager roses of her breasts before drawing each into his mouth. She murmured her pleasure at his suckling, and her dark lashes swooped down to hide her eyes as she drew his head closer against the sweetness of her waiting breasts. But when he claimed her mouth again, her hands were free to run the length of his broad shoulders, the musculature of his back, the perfect, sinewy line of his lean waist, the tension of his still clothed hips. She tugged at the buckle of his breeches, and he helped her loosen them. Then she in turn shrugged away her dress.

It sighed to the floor and was followed by her shift. But as he moved again, drawing her to the great bed, she awoke to reason. "Jonathan, your wound . . ."

He hushed her. "My wound will take no hurt. I have wanted you so long, my dear one. Needed you here like this."

Making no further protest, she let him pull her down onto the bed and sank against the pillows to look up into his lean, tense face. As she did so a fragment of something she had read a long time ago filled her mind. "'My beloved is chiefest among ten thousands. His hands are as gold rings.'" She kissed his hands as she murmured the rest. "'His belly is like bright ivory, and his legs as pillars of marble . . .'"

She drew away from him a little, leaned above him as she kissed the flat male nipples, moved down to touch her lips to his flat belly. He reached for her to draw her to him again, but she shook her head. "Please, let me. Tonight you must care for your wound. Let me."

She knelt above him, loving his body, the dark perfection of it, the curve of silken muscle, the length of limb, even the healed scar. Lightly, she rubbed her lips about the scar, kissed the concavity of his navel, and then followed the dark line of hair to the hardness of his manhood. She touched this power lightly with her lips and felt his instant reaction. Delighted, she teased with her tongue.

"Is this the way you care for me and my wound?" His voice was tense with control and yet there was laughter in it, too. "Are you trying to kill me by sweet degrees?"

"What good would you be to me dead?" How good to laugh in the midst of passion, better still to see the tenderness in his eyes as well as desire. She tasted him again, loving the hard power of him. Then he drew her up against him so that she straddled him. For a long moment they looked deep into each other's eyes, and then she lowered herself upon him, drawing him deep within her.

She murmured her pleasure at the sure, deep fullness of his love, and he drew her closer and began to kiss her breasts. My love, my dear one . . . their words were no longer understandable, except to them. The words were new, used only by them. Shuddering with the sweet wild fire that was sweeping them both, they moved slowly at first, seeking to draw out the ecstasy that was like pain, wishing the moment never to end. But the fire within them changed from flame to conflagration, and he held her closer as they were whirled faster, higher, higher and faster still, until their world and their universe churned into maelstrom.

And as they shattered together at the height of the storm and fell into stillness, they were still together.

Ripples of pleasure still flowed through her as she awoke to brightest sunshine. It dazzled her eyes and she closed them, turning on her pillow to seek Jonathan. He wasn't there. She sat up, and the sheet that covered her fell to her waist so that a cool breeze from the half-open window teased her kissed-tender nipples.

He was standing by the window, looking out. Sunshine dazzled over his broad wedge of shoulders and strong back, over the narrow hips and long, powerful legs. Something in the tension of that familiar stance woke memory in her, and she did not want to remember. Throwing back the sheet she got out of bed and went to him, wrapping her arms about his waist and pressing herself close against him. "Good morrow, love," she murmured. "How do you feel?"

"I'm in need of you." Swift to react, he moved a strong arm to anchor her against his back so that her softness was pressed against him. Her questing hand found proof of his needing, and she laughed softly, contentedly. "It seems to be a condition that persists," he told her.

"The condition must be catching. I, too, feel this need." He turned to her then, wrapping his arms about her properly, bringing her into even closer proximity with his want. "Jonathan, be careful. Your wound mustn't reopen."

There was laughter in his voice. "My wound does very well. It's the rest of me that needs a lot of help."

She snuggled closer, wondering at the force of her answering desire. They had dozed and loved and dozed again last night, and each time together had been somehow different, even sweeter than before. "I want you too. But that's not all, Jonathan." In his arms it was easier to find the words. "Last night when I feared you were hurt or even killed, it mattered nothing to me whom you followed or to whom I owed allegiance. My promise to my father meant nothing. The king meant nothing." He began to speak, but she went on heedlessly. "I want nothing but to be with you."

She thought he would kiss her then, or at least draw her closer. Instead, his arms loosened about her. "That can't be," he said.

"Jonathan . . ." But he let her go and walked to a chair by the bed. He dropped heavily into it, and after a moment he began to collect his scattered clothes.

"It's not possible." His voice had a quiet finality to it. "We have our loyalties. No matter what we feel for each other, they exist. They will always exist."

"But I love you . . ." she began, and he shook his head.

"If you gave up your king for me, or I played my master false for you, we would grow to hate each other in time. Respect would go and then love would follow." She started to protest, but his somber gray gaze checked her. "I know you, dear one. I know the courage in you, and the heart. And you know me."

Dully, she realized the truth of his words. Even with her heart full for him, she knew that if she turned traitor to all she had believed in, to all her father had died for, some part of her would die. And it would be the same for him.

"I love you, Damaris, and before God, you are my heart and my soul. I would lay down my life for you gladly, but that is all that is mine to give."

She went to him and knelt beside him, looking up into his eyes. She chose the words carefully as if she were making a vow in church. "And I will love you as long as I live and wherever I live. Even if you are here in England and I—and I have to go to France, I'll love you and be true to you."

He bent to lift her onto his lap. Cradling her against him, he stroked her hair and kissed her. "Someday," he said, "there may come a day when there will be no need of barriers between us, no divided loyalties, nothing but Damaris and Jonathan." The emotion in his deep voice reached deep into her, and she ached with love for him as he spoke against her ear. "Enough, now. Let the future care for itself. You're here with me and in my arms, and by God, that's all I care about."

His mouth took hers. His tongue sought hers. Her arms went about his neck as he pulled her to sit astride him.

She formed words against his lips. "Truly, you did well to warn me, sir. Your wants are endless —seemingly!"

His deep laughter was joyously male. "Tell me, dear one," he asked as his body claimed hers, "would you have it otherwise?"

Chapter Fifteen

DAMARIS STEPPED BACK AND GAVE THE LONG table an anxious look. She had spent the better half of the past hour decorating it with wheat and flowers tied up in bright ribbons, and now it looked as cheerful as the other tables spread across the village green. "Well, Sir Table, are you fine enough?" she murmured aloud.

"Finer than any I have seen, but not as fine as my lady." She had not heard him come up behind her, but he had been so much in her thoughts that it seemed natural that he should be there, that his arms should go about her waist, drawing her to lean against him. She raised a hand to touch the strong lean line of his jaw, and he kissed the palm of that hand. "You smell of flowers and sunshine, dear one."

"I should indeed. I have been so much in the sun gathering flowers for tonight that I must be growing freckled like a bird's egg."

He turned her around and pretended to examine her face carefully. "You're right," he told her. "I see three freckles here. And here on your cheek." He followed the words with kisses. She laughed in mingled pleasure and protest, and he wished they were alone so that he could kiss her properly. He had never seen her look so lovely, her dark eyes shining with happiness and anticipation of the simple village festival to come, her mouth smiling soft for him.

"What are you thinking?" she was asking, a loving music in her soft, low voice. "You look very serious all of a sudden. Has Larkin burned up the ox that is roasting in the village? Or do you perhaps disapprove of my freckles?"

"I'm thinking that you've never looked so lovely." Nor had he ever seen her so carefree, so full of youth and laughter and simple joy. This time they had had together at Arbor Cottage had transformed them both, and he knew that he himself had never felt as happy as now or as fortunate. The Carmes and the villagers had taken Damaris to their hearts, acting as if she were truly the mistress of Arbor Cottage. She was never idle, and she sang softly to herself as she went about learning the mysteries of cooking quince pies from Mrs. Carme or discussing the properties of herbs with the old gardener who brightened up whenever she was near.

Even old Larkin had been won over by her and spoke of "my lady" with a kind of gruff adoration.

When she asked diffidently if she might help in preparations for the October festival, the last bright event before preparations for winter began, the village women had been delighted and so had he. Jonathan knew that she had made this simple annual event special, as she decorated the tables with flowers and wheat, twining flower wreaths for the women's hair as well. She had made one for herself also, and it perched at a jaunty angle amidst her red-gold curls as she smiled up at him.

He smiled back. "Does it seem strange that I love you more each day we spend together?"

"No, for I feel the same." She caught her breath at the expression in his eyes and wondered if it were possible to be any happier than she was. Her heart was full of him, and of this perfect blue and gold day, the second to last day of October; full of the scent of goldenrod and of woodsmoke and the warm, comfortable laughter of the village women as they prepared for the feast. She drew a deep breath and started to think back on the weeks they had shared together at Arbor Cottage, then put the thought away. It wouldn't do to reckon such golden happiness by mortal time.

Careless of the watching and obviously approving villagers, he drew her closer and kissed her smiling mouth. "It should be against the law to look as delicious as you do," he groaned. "I'm tempted to scoop you up and carry you back to Arbor Cottage where I can show you how much I love you."

Laughing, she drew away from him and went back to her work. "Now you certainly sound like some great lord of his land," she teased him gently.

"And you would prefer that to my being Cromwell's officer."

His voice changed, and when she turned to him she saw a shadow in his gray eyes that had been absent through all these enchanted days and nights. It made her remember what she did not want to remember, and she took quick refuge in a jest. "No, I would not, Captain, sir. If you were some great lord, you wouldn't even look at me."

"Why do you think that? You're a colonel's daughter."

"True, but as I said to you before, great lords look for titles or dowry. I have neither, I'm afraid." She straightened a sheaf of wheat on the table. "We have no centuries-old name, and the little money we had was given to Charles II to help in his restoration." She looked back over her shoulder at him and smiled. "You see? I'd be no match for any lord."

She was glad to see that he was smiling again. "Then I'm glad I'm no aristocrat. Think of what I'd be missing. The taste of your mouth, your warm, seductive body and the way you move when I please you." He did not touch her, but his voice caressed, adored. "Not to be with you in that way would be worse than being cut off from paradise."

She did not hush him but stood there drinking in his words. Her eyes were wide with love for him and suddenly so full of shared desire that he felt his senses swim for want of her. He yearned to hold her to him without the barrier of clothes. He wanted to kiss the heavy silk of her hair and her soft mouth to willing surrender and seek the eager roses of her breasts. He wanted to lose himself and find himself in her, and the desire was so strong that for a moment it seemed as if the village and all in it disappeared, that only they were alone in the universe.

Then he heard some of the men calling to him, asking his advice about the roasting ox, and reality flooded back. He sighed and smiled ruefully down into the lovely, upturned face. "It seems that I must now play the role of cook," he said. "There'll be time later, dear one."

But not time enough. The words came from nowhere, cast a shadow against the perfect day. She struggled against it, seeking out Mrs. Carme among the other women to offer help to carry in the mountains of good, simple food, the collops of beef and the pickles, the mounds of golden custards and the fruit stewed with honey and smothered in cream; but though she talked and discussed and even laughed with the women, her eyes kept returning to Jonathan. Some strange emotion that was not quite fear and deeper even than desire, made her want to run to him and put her arms around him and hold him close.

She was glad to put such thoughts away as the festival began. The villagers had dressed in their best because it was a day to show off. Farmers had contributed their finest vegetables to the feast; the sweetest butter and finest milk had come from the villagers who tended the cows. As they all waited shyly for Jonathan to take his seat at the central table, they compared notes: old Larkin had cut the wood to roast the ox; Mrs. Smythe had woven the linen for the head table. And, they all pointed out with affectionate approval, "my lady" had decorated all with her own hands. There were many nods and smiles and small curtseys when Jonathan seated Damaris next to him.

"The people love you," he told her as the feasting started, and several tankards of ale were raised to the master's and my lady's health. "Larkin has become your champion. He scolded me severely for letting you work so hard with the other women for this festival. Ladies, according to Larkin, should sit still in fine chairs and be waited on hand and foot."

She chuckled and looked about her at the contented faces, the happy, scrub-faced children. The sun was not far from setting, and there was a thick golden glow over everything turning all that she saw to such incredible beauty that she felt tears fill her eyes. She was flooded with such love for everyone and everything, that she could not explain her emotion, but when she turned wordless to him he understood. "I know, dear one," he said, and the clasp of his big hand was as tender as a kiss.

The feasting now got underway with both good food and laughter. Larkin, bolstered with several mugs of ale, got up and sang a comic and rather risqué song about a pair of reluctant young lovers that caused the villagers to howl delightedly while maidens blushed and glanced at the young men out of the corners of their eyes. The song also seemed to be some kind of signal for some rustic musicians to bring out their wooden instruments and to begin to twang out some boisterous tunes. Soon, many of the younger people left their places at the table to begin an energetic country dance.

Damaris and Jonathan watched for a while, clapping in time and laughing as youths swung their partners about and used any excuse to steal a kiss or a hug, but when old Larkin hopped spryly up to Mrs. Smythe and offered her his arm in partnership, Jonathan leaned over to whisper, "Well, my love? shall we chance it and join this madness?"

His eyes were merry, and hers mirrored both his amusement and tenderness. "Why not? Perhaps it is time that Larkin realized that ladies do other things beside sit on fine chairs." There was loud applause and clapping as they joined the dancers. Hopping, retreating, prancing with the rest, Damaris felt as if she were suddenly ten years old again and as carefree as a child. And when the dance was over, she half collapsed against Jonathan and noted that he too looked young and refreshed.

"You did that very well, my lady," he told her. "Your bright eyes and pink cheeks make you very lovely. I'm emboldened to ask you for yet another dance."

The music was starting again, but this time the tempo was different. Instead of the spirited jigging of the last dance, this music was sweet, even dreamy. As Jonathan took her hand Damaris could almost hear words in the slow, tender strains, words of love written especially for her. As they began to move together through the measured steps, she felt tears touch her eyes for the sheer beauty of those unspoken words.

"What is it, dear one?" he asked her.

"I don't know, I can't explain," she murmured. "It's the music, Jonathan. It fills my heart with both joy and sadness." She tried to laugh. "Perhaps I've drunk too much ale."

Drawing her away from the dancers he put his arms about her. "No, I feel it too. It seems to know how deeply I love you and how barren my life was before you came to me. How great is the gift of this time we have had together."

She looked up at him uncertainly. All the laughter had fled from his face leaving it stern and even remote, the eyes shadowed with more than the twilight that had slowly begun to creep across the merrymakers. "You almost sound . . ." She checked herself, but the thought continued in her mind. He almost sounded as if he were saying good-bye.

He drew her even closer, and she registered the odd tremor in the arms that held her, sensed his thought matched her own as he whispered, "My love, I would be with you. I want to love you."

Before she could respond, Larkin's apologetic voice cut in. "Master, your pardon. Saving your presence, sir, a word with you . . ."

For a moment he continued to hold her, and she could feel the steady beat of his heart against her breast. Something in his embrace, something in Larkin's voice brought a sense of foreboding, and she wanted to hold Jonathan back even as he drew away. "Don't go," she nearly cried, but he had already released her and was turning to Larkin.

"A moment only," she heard him say. "My lady is tired and wants to return home."

She watched him walk away through the uncertain twilight and tried to read the expression on his face. She could not hear the words the men said to each other, but when he came back to her, she knew that the news was bad. "Damaris, Larkin will see you home safe to Arbor Cottage tonight," he explained. Her eyes asked an unspoken question and he said, "I must ride."

Her head began to swim. "Tonight?" she heard herself ask dully.

"At once. My horse has been brought here. I don't want to spoil the festival, so I'll slip quietly away. If they notice, tell them that I was weary from my wound and had to return home."

Before she could answer, he had gone. Without kiss or touch, she thought dully. "Be careful," she whispered into the suddenly empty dark and felt fear flood through her, cancelling all the happiness and the security she had felt this day. Behind her, the musicians swung into another song, and one youth began to sing. "'So come and kiss me, sweet and twenty—love's a stuff will not endure.'"

The remembered words brought a loneliness which was physically painful. She started to turn away and then saw that Larkin was standing at her elbow, watching her. "Couldn't his precious duty have left him alone for tonight at least?" she cried.

The old man hesitated. "There was no choice, my lady," he then said. "There's someone nearby who commands his presence."

She forgot to be wise. "Some wretched royalist prey, no doubt," she snapped.

But he was shaking his head. "No," he said in a low, unhappy tone, "'tis not. 'Tis Captain Clandennon."

"Clandennon."

It was hours since she had returned to Arbor Cottage, and yet the sick horror Damaris had felt then had not eased. After Jonathan's depar-

ture she had returned to the head table and
pretended to enjoy the songs and the dances that
went on endlessly. But while she clapped her
hands and nodded her head, something in her
brain kept screaming. Clandennon was nearby—
and Jonathan had gone to work with him.

When evening fell and the villagers lit bonfires so as to continue dancing, she pleaded
weariness and asked Larkin to escort her back
to the cottage. The sight of the flames and the
prancing dancers reminded her vividly of that
day when she had watched Charles II's effigy
burn to cinders under Clandennon's cat-eyes,
and even when she had reached Arbor Cottage
and her own room where she could be alone,
that terrible picture remained. Jonathan had
been disgusted with Clandennon's cruelty that
day, and she knew that he loathed the thin
officer as a man. But they served the same
master. The thought that Jonathan might have
to help carry out Clandennon's wishes made her
want to retch.

She tried to knit her thoughts together, but
nothing fit. She knew that she must make plans
to leave Arbor Cottage. If Clandennon were
near, it must be because he'd picked up her trail
somehow. She had lived in a make-believe world
for the past happy weeks, she thought miserably. Because she could not bear it, she had made
herself forget that they would always be on
opposing sides of battle lines. And yet, how could
she think of Jonathan with anything but love?
My beloved, my enemy—she paced back and

forth in her room, the thoughts echoing in her mind till she was exhausted with the strain.

Physically drained and emotionally spent, she sank into a chair by the window and waited for Jonathan's return. Sleep was the farthest thing from her mind, and yet she must have slept, for when she opened her eyes again, she awakened in his arms. No lamps were lit and she could not see his face, but she could feel his tension when she murmured his name. His reply came swiftly. "I did not mean to waken you, dear one, only to see you comfortable. You need your rest."

He was placing her on her bed, lowering her head onto the pillows. He would have retreated then, except that she caught at his withdrawing hands. "Were you with Clandennon tonight?"

She prayed that he would deny this, but he didn't. "Who told you about Clandennon?" he asked sharply. Then, when she didn't answer, he said, "So you know. I wanted to spare you as long as I could. I wanted you to sleep sound for a little while longer."

"When?" she asked him. It was the only word she could manage, and he understood.

"At dawn. I've made arrangements for you to meet a ship at Silverneck Wells." She listened to his deep voice say the words and wondered why she felt so calm. Or perhaps she was simply numb. "I will ride with you this time," he was continuing. "I'll see you safe, don't fear."

Still, the numbness persisted. She had known this moment must come, and yet she could not take it in. In spite of his words, fear such as she had never experienced before was filling her, and through the panic she could hear Jonathan's quiet voice.

"It won't be as dangerous as you think, dear one. Clandennon is sly and shrewd, but I still know of ports which are clear of his men and of a ship's captain who will take you to France." She did not answer, and he frowned into the darkness. He could not see her face, but he read panic in every line and curve of the body he knew as well as his own.

"It isn't danger that I fear." Her voice was almost inaudible.

"Then what?" But he could read the words in her mind before she spoke them.

"I can't bear the thought of leaving you." She clasped her arms about his neck and clung to him, and he lifted her from the pillow and held her cradled in his arms. "God help me, I love you more than anything," she wept, "and now I must leave you."

And he must let her go. God above, he cried silently in his heart, it is almost more than I can bear. The warm, slender body in his arms became a source of almost unendurable pain, and he lifted his hands to unclasp her arms around his neck. "Damaris, you must rest. We will have far to ride in the dawn. Your life may depend on it."

But more than her life depended on holding and being held close, and she would not let him go. When he kissed her cheeks he tasted not tears but sunlight and the scent of flowers and the joy that had been theirs to share during these too brief weeks. "I want to remember," she whispered, "I want to remember how much I love you."

She heard the sound he made deep in his throat as they kissed again and again, their lips passionate and tender, gentle and tempestuous. Their bodies seemed to obey one mind as they helped each other with their clothes, and as these barriers were removed, their blood sang with warmth and need for more kisses, more touch, more of the vital essence and spirit of each other.

"Behold thou art fair, my love," he whispered to her, kissing her mouth and then bending to kiss her breasts and take the taut, waiting nipples into his mouth. Greedy for her honey, he nuzzled and kissed and adored while her hands moved up to stroke the lean line of his jaw, run delicately over his lips and then slip down over his chest and lean belly to touch and cradle him.

She would have drawn him to her and into her, but though her touch was like flame, he would not give in to her desire at once. He kissed her breasts again, suckling her and teasing until she moaned with a want that was almost pain. Then he roved his mouth lower, teasing the hollow of her navel, the joining of her thighs, adoring the secret shadow of her womanhood. He could hear her throbbing whisper, "I want to remember how much I love you," and he knew that they would both remember this. He would carry to the grave the feel of her silken body, the honey of her, the way she whispered his name. And this, and this—his mouth continued its exploration of her until she moved against him, and her slender fingers tugged at his hair.

"Jonathan, my love, my heart, please. Come to me," she begged him.

Want for her was like an aching flame in his loins, but he was careful when he began to love her. Almost as if this were the first time, he held himself steady within her. This too, he would remember—the warm satin that sheathed him with such love and such trust. The tumbled silk of her glorious hair that kissed his face and shoulders, the urgency of her hands on his back, the sounds she made, the rise and fall of her smooth, firm breasts against his chest—and above all he would remember the love he felt for her beyond all sense and thought of self.

He could not tell her all that he felt. He couldn't find the words, even though he struggled to form them. He could only show her with his body, and she understood. She exulted in his weight, the slow, strong strokes of his loving. She wanted him to come deeper, nearer, make her a part of himself so that this too brief love of the flesh could express all the wanting and the loving of their hearts. Wherever I am you will also be, she wanted to cry out to him as they moved together. I will remember you always, no matter where I am because I am you and you are me. Jonathan, my love, my dearest love, I must leave you but I can never leave you. . . .

Knowing that this was the last time for them,

they tried to spin it out forever. With kisses and broken lovewords they strove to delay the moments of fire and gold, tried to hold onto one more minute and then one more second. But they could not. Their kisses intensified, their bodies caught flame, seared and blazed into one. And when the fires slowly burned out leaving them spent and yet still together, he finally found the words.

"I've never felt less like a Puritan," he murmured against her ear, "yet now I remember a psalm that fits the way I feel. Dear one, even if you were to take the wings of the morning and dwell in the uttermost parts of the sea, even there shall my right hand hold you. I will be with you and you with me forever. For always, Damaris."

"Forever," she echoed, and kissed his strong shoulder beneath her cheek and struggled with the tears that were tearing at her heart.

Chapter Sixteen

It was remarkable, Damaris thought, how everything came back so quickly. The feeling of nameless apprehension, the chill and then the sweat of riding hard against the wind, and the way her body became accustomed to the saddle so that hour after hour she kept pace with Jonathan over the wilderness of downs and hills and through the winding back roads that led to Silverneck Wells. Even the cold hardness of the pistol he had again handed her now felt familiar against her waist. She'd thought that she had forgotten about these things at Arbor Cottage, but now it was the peaceful life there that was fading so quickly away. She looked at Jonathan as if for reassurance.

He was riding a little ahead of her, his big body tuned to every sound and movement about them and for the slightest sign of pursuit or ambush. They had not spoken very much since they'd begun their ride half an eternity ago, and since then dawn had paled to day, given way to twilight and to night again. They had rested a few hours in a small inn whose proprietor Jonathan obviously knew, and she had fallen asleep for a few fatigue-sodden hours while Jonathan dragged a pallet to the door, stretched himself across the doorway, and slept also. But hardly had sleep come when he was shaking her awake again. "Time to ride again, dear one," he had said, and she had clung to him for one long moment before they mounted up again.

Now the second day had ripened to late afternoon, and they still rode. It was a gloomy, overcast day, and it was already turning dark although it was hours to sunset. She could still see no sign of the sea, but she imagined that the air had changed somewhat, and that the rain-heavy wind that was blowing from the east also had salt on it. As she drew in a deep breath, testing it, Jonathan slowed and half-turned his mount so as to draw abreast of her.

"We'll soon be there," he told her. "We've made good time."

She knew he was being purposely matter-of-fact and forced a smile as she nodded. They would soon be there. It would soon be over. He seemed so calm and remote on his dark horse that she felt him slipping away from her already. She spurred her horse forward and closed the gap between them, but he didn't reach out to touch her. "The wind seems fair for France," he muttered.

"France." It was echoed with such despair that he jerked up his head to look at her closely. The strong wind had torn aside the hood that covered her head, and her magnificent red-gold hair was blowing like a flaming flag in the wind. Under it, her face was pale, grieving. He forced himself still. This was no time to take her into his arms.

"France and safety," he told her with some force. When she still didn't respond he went on, "You never told me. Is there someone there whom you know, someone who will take care of you?"

Nodding, she tried to gather her scattered courage. "Lady Blount," she told him. "Her husband was a brother officer of my father, though the Blounts were well connected and we were not." She even managed a smile. "I remember that my father talked wistfully of marrying me to the Blounts' son Philip for awhile, though nothing came of that. He was, of course, of the nobility, and anyway I had no desire to marry Philip, though I always thought him a good friend. He married a Frenchwoman, a countess, and he is lucky in his choice. Ysoud is as kind as she is beautiful."

He saw the way her shoulders straightened and loved her all the more for her bravery. "So you will go to Lady Blount?"

Again she nodded. "She has lived with Ysoud and Philip since her husband's death, but she has always been a champion of the king. She told my father that if we went to France, our home was with her."

"Then you'll be all right," he said, relieved. "You'll be in good hands."

Not wanting him to see her struggle with her tears, she spurred her horse forward away from him. She could hear him calling to his horse in his deep voice as he followed, and she knew he was deliberately giving her some time to compose herself. "Stay close to me now," he then said. "We'll be coming to the dunes very soon."

They were cresting a hillock as he spoke, and as they reached the top she saw a mile or so away, the sullen, gray line of ocean that seemed to vanish into the equally gray and sullen sky. A stronger wind had begun to blow, and she could smell the brine. As she started her mount down the slope toward the sea, Jonathan caught her reins.

"Slowly," he told her, and she saw him sweep the near distance with his eyes. "Stay behind me, and keep alert. There are too many places hereabouts for an ambush, and we must be watchful."

He trotted his horse forward and she followed silently. She saw that his free hand rested on his pistol butt, and she felt the despair of parting give way to wariness and caution as she looked about their bleak surroundings. Jonathan was right. This mile ride to the sea was seemingly open and safe, but there were many places where waiting men could hide. There were small clumps of wind-stunted trees and bushes, rocks from which nervous seagulls flew shrieking, and then just before the sea there were rolling dunes crested with sparse tufts of marsh grass. As they approached one of these large dunes, she heard a noise. She whispered a warning, but Jonathan, too, had heard the sound, and he drew his pistol, pointing it full at the shadow of the dunes.

"Who's there? Stand where I can see you."

"God's teeth, Captain Hartwell. If you shoot me, there'll be no more deliveries to France," a new voice exclaimed.

Damaris watched Jonathan's set face relax slightly. "Come around the dune so that I can see you," he ordered, and when a short, bandy-legged little man had swaggered into view he added, "Unwise to skulk behind sand dunes in these times, Master Rogers."

"I was waiting for you—and keeping watch. I'd heard rumors that there are a few unfriendly souls who mightn't take kindly to your lady's leaving these shores." He touched his cap to Damaris, and she revised her initial opinion of him. Small he might be, but the small gesture had set up a ripple of muscle in the man's shoulders. He looked to be as strong as an ox.

Jonathan dismounted, took Damaris's reins and led her horse forward. "You've heard right. That's why my lady must be aboard your sloop and away from here as quickly as can be managed."

"Aye." The little man jerked a thumb backward. "My men are making ready *The Discovery* now. The wind is fair, and we'll be underway within the half hour. With your leave, I'll go on board now. Do you follow."

He swaggered away, and Jonathan silently led Damaris's horse around the dune. From here she could see the sea much more closely, and now she could hear the dull roaring sound it made. She could also see the fishing sloop bobbing close to the shoreline. She had expected to see it there, of course, and yet the reality of it struck her almost as painfully as a physical blow. Jonathan misunderstood her involuntary intake of breath.

"It's safer than it looks, dear one. I would not hazard your life if I were not sure of *The Discovery*'s seaworthiness."

"It's not that. Jonathan, you know it's not that . . ." He held out his arms, and she dismounted, tumbled, fell into them. He held her desperately close for a moment and then let her slide down to the ground still within the circle of his arms. "You know," she murmured against his shoulder.

"Yes." The bleak word conveyed everything he felt—fear for her, sorrow, resolution.

She looked up at him intently as if seeking to imprint his features in her mind and her heart. She would remember forever, she knew, the way his dark hair blew against the wind, the way his hard-planed face, harsh now with anxiety for her, could turn soft and young and loving when he smiled. She reached up and touched his mouth, traced the lean, strong line of his jaw. He caught her hand in his, imprisoning it against his cheek.

"Damaris," he began.

And stopped. He turned away from her, his chin lifting, his eyes narrowing. "What . . ." she began, but the tightening arm about her shoulders hushed her. And then she heard it, too.

"Men on horses," she whispered.

Swiftly he caught her by the hand and began to hustle her toward the sea. "It doesn't matter. You'll be long gone, and I, too, God willing."

"Ah, but God is not willing, Captain Hartwell."

The new voice came from behind them, and Damaris stifled a cry as she wheeled about and saw him. He was standing on top of one of the nearby dunes, and he held a large pistol leveled at Damaris's heart. He laughed to see their faces.

Silhouetted against the sullen sky in his swirling military cloak, he looked like a large, bony crow, and the effect was heightened by his rasping voice. "God is also not mocked, Captain," he said, sardonically. And then he ordered, "Drop your pistol, sir. On the ground where I can see it. So. And now, your sword. Remember, there's a bullet in my weapon for this pretty redhead for whom you seem to have sold your soul. Ah, good. Now kick the weapons out of your reach."

"How came you here?" To Damaris's surprise, Jonathan's voice was almost conversational. Only the white line of his mouth belied the easy tone he employed. "Did the master of *The Discovery* play me false?"

Clandennon shook his head. He was laughing soundlessly, and even at this distance Damaris could see his cold-burning green eyes on her. "None played you false—Captain." The title was purest mockery. "You have been clever, I grant you that, but not clever enough to fool me. When there was a rumor of a roundhead officer and a red-haired woman riding together, I had it followed by my spies. It wasn't so difficult to find your approximate whereabouts—a few more days, and I'd have discovered exactly where you had gone to earth. You saved me the trouble by breaking and running, you and your redhead vixen."

Damaris had one moment of pure thankfulness that Clandennon didn't know about Arbor Cottage or the village before her mind came back to the terrible danger in which she and Jonathan now stood. Two other Commonwealth soldiers had now come up on the dune to stand behind Clandennon, and at his command, they began to climb down the dune toward their prisoners. Without turning, she could hear redoubled activity on the fishing sloop. No doubt its master was in a hurry to set out to sea and avoid involvement in what was happening here.

Jonathan was saying, "You'd have been better off hunting down enemies of the Commonwealth."

Clandennon's eyes blazed. "Men like you are the greatest enemies to the Commonwealth. I and these two here have ridden hard to intercept you before you set sail. When the rest of my troops arrive, it will be my pleasure to take you and Mistress St. Cyr to London. There, she'll be forced to tell her secrets in the tower and your head will grace a traitor's pike."

The sound of hoofbeats was closer now, and as she glanced at Jonathan she could read his thought. He wanted a weapon with which to face Clandennon. Her hand moved under her cloak and clasped the cold handle of the pistol he had given her.

"Stand away from Hartwell, Mistress Vixen!" The sharp, rasping voice came simultaneous with her thought. "Get away from him or I shoot you now."

There wasn't time to think of some plan, only time to act. As the two guardsmen closed on them, she gave a low moan and pitched forward as if in a faint, tumbling to the sand directly in front of them. At a loss, they looked back at Clandennon, and in that split second, Jonathan lunged forward, pushing one of his adversaries into the line of Clandennon's fire. There was the report of a pistol and then a howl of accusation. "Jesus, Captain, you hit Melchior!"

"Get his weapons, you damned fool!" Clandennon raced down from the dune, his now useless pistol smoking in his hand. The second guardsman lunged forward, but Jonathan was quicker and the man went sprawling, a knee in his gut.

Jonathan snatched up his sword from the

sand. "And now, you filthy bastard," he told Clandennon softly, "there are old scores to pay between us."

Damaris, on her knees in the sand, hefted Jonathan's pistol. It was getting even darker, and a fine, misty rain had begun to fall, making it hard to see. And in that premature dusk she could hear the thunder of hoofbeats—very near now. "Jonathan—I have Clandennon covered. He won't dare move while we go on board the sloop."

He did not take his attention from Clandennon. "It's too late for that."

As he spoke, the first of the riders cantered onto the sand toward them. "Jonathan, hurry!" she cried, and at that moment she felt arms clamp about her. An iron grip seized the hand with which she held the weapon. She kicked backward, but the voice in her ear was familiar. "Lady, you'll only lame me if you do that again. It's Captain Hartwell's orders," the master of the sloop was saying.

"Let me go. Let me—" but the arms that held her were inexorable. "Jonathan, why?" she cried as she felt herself being dragged away. "You can still get away . . ."

The answer she got was the ring of steel on steel. She could see him in that fading light, a shadowy and yet powerful figure with sword upraised to parry Clandennon's vicious thrust. "We must wait for him," she begged Skipper Rogers.

"Them's not his orders, lady. If we stay, those

bastards as are coming now will stop us from
sailing. He knowed that something like this
might happen, that's why he ordered me to grab
you and set sail at once if there was any hint of
trouble." She fought as she was carried backward until she felt wet splash her ankles and
knees, and then she was being bundled up a
ladder and onto the deck of the sloop where the
pistol was taken away from her. She managed to
break away and tried to get back on shore, but
the master of *The Discovery* caught her again.
"He's paid well to take you to France, and I'm a
man who keeps his bargains," he said.

From where she stood on the deck she could
hear the savage grunts of the combatants as all
their force and muscle and will went into this
fight. It would be to the death, she knew, knew
too that the conflict was unequal because
Clandennon's men were even now pouring out
onto the open beach, and surrounding him. "Oh,
Jonathan," she whispered.

As if he had heard her, she heard his answering shout. "Godspeed, Damaris."

She fought like a madwoman, clawing at the
hands that held her, ready to throw herself into
the sea to go to him, stand with him, if needs be
die with him. Fought to no avail as she heard
orders being given, felt the sloop gliding out to
sea, heard Clandennon's shout to his men.

"Stop the sloop. St. Cyr's daughter is on
board . . ."

St. Cyr's daughter—that was who she was,
and why she was going to France while her lover

fought for her life and her freedom. It made no sense. Jonathan had turned traitor to his own kind so that she could keep her life and her loyalty to Charles II. Ironical that all she wanted to do now was to stay here with him. . . .

She could no longer see him, and the sound of his bitter conflict was hidden by the sounds of the sails flapping in the wind that carried the sloop to France. But when she closed her eyes, she could still visualize him to the last detail. And she knew that for as long as she lived she would always remember how she had sailed away and left Jonathan to die for her.

Chapter Seventeen

"Eh bien," Ysoud Blount was saying in French, "There is the chevalier Chassin and Sir Brian Rourke with my husband. I fear you must tell your story again, *cherie.*"

Damaris gave an inward sigh. She had told her story many times in the last few days, and yet each time she framed the words, they brought fresh pain. She had had to recount the details of the battle of Worcester and her escape across England to old Lady Blount's son Philip when he journeyed to meet her at the port of Lacroix. And since then, since being brought here to the Blount's home in the luxurious Marais district of Paris, she had had an insatiable audience in the jewelled members of the French aristocracy who frequented the salon of the "Maison de Blount" and who seemed to be fascinated by her adventures.

Ysoud's blue eyes were sympathetic. "It is hard to recount again and again this story of your suffering. This I know. I also know you would gladly tell all your adventures to the king."

Frail Lady Blount, ensconced in a comfortable seat by the satin-draped windows of the elegantly appointed room in which they sat, nodded agreement. "It is a shame that His Majesty is so ill. But do not fear, dear child. He will soon give you the audience you desire so much. His cold should be better in a few days."

But a few days might be too late, Damaris thought bleakly. Since arriving in France her first and dearest wish had been to be given audience with Charles II. Philip had tried to arrange such a meeting, but the dispossessed English king was not well. He had a bad cold, she was told, and could not possibly grant an audience for several days.

She shifted unhappily on the comfortable gilt and satin chair in which she sat and tried to smile at the chevalier Chassin who was bowing over her hand. She looked, she knew, nothing like the salt-bedraggled waif that had stumbled into Philip Blount's brotherly embrace a scant handful of days ago. Ysoud and her gentle mother-in-law had done their best to welcome her and to see to her every possible need. This included the gown she wore of emerald-green

Lyons velvet which highlighted the creamy pallor of her skin and served as a foil for her glorious hair. It was cut scandalously low by English standards, and at any other time she would have been embarrassed by the look of admiration the chevalier accorded her white shoulders and the silken swell of her breast.

Now, all her concentration and her energy was on one thing. She must see the king. Not only to tell him the secrets she carried, but to plead Jonathan's case and to beg him to let her return to England. Surely, the king would understand? He had been a fugitive himself, it was said, and his story of escape was as romantic as a ballad out of ancient chivalry. Surely . . .

She realized that everyone was looking at her. Obviously, the chevalier had said something she hadn't heard. "My mind was elsewhere. Please forgive me," she stammered.

The chevalier bowed. He was a courtly man nearing middle age, and he was also, according to Philip, one of the most influential peers at the French court and a confidante of the powerful prime minister, Cardinal Mazarin. Behind him, the elderly British knight cleared his throat.

"It is understandable," he said gruffly. "You've been through a great deal in the last two months."

Sir Brian Rourke was as rumpled and as rough-hewn as the chevalier was smooth and polished, but he looked at Damaris in a kindly way. Philip Blount said, "We all know that. Damaris, I hope you don't mind that I've asked the chevalier and Sir Brian here to hear your story. Chevalier Chassin expressed a great interest in hearing of your adventures, and Sir Brian has a vested interest in all news that comes out of England these days. His family is distantly related to the earl of Larraby. You've heard of him, of course."

"Perhaps then you could help me to get an audience with the king," she exclaimed, and the old knight looked somewhat uncomfortable.

"A lot of people want to see the king," he muttered.

The chevalier now spoke in slightly accented English. "His Brittanic Mahesty is really not feeling well, mademoiselle. He has but recently escaped from England himself, and has only been here in France for some weeks, and the hardships he has endured has weakened his superb strength." He paused. "Perhaps if you recounted your story, Sir Brian could carry it to him."

Ysoud ordered refreshment and while they were brought and offered, Damaris steeled herself to tell her story once more. She had thought to tell it with cool dispassion, giving only the important highlights of her escape from Worcester and her flight across England to Silverneck Wells, but the chevalier wouldn't let her get away with this. The Frenchman asked questions when Jonathan entered the story and made Damaris describe him in detail. Later he stopped her again to demand a blow-by-blow account of the adventure by the river.

Damaris soon found herself being carried away by her own words. As she told them about Long Marston, she felt again the terror of that night. She told them of Arbor Cottage and the peaceful English village where she had been so happy, and though she did not speak of her relationship with Jonathan, none could mistake the love or the agony that trembled in her voice when she described that last scene of parting on the beach. "I had to sail away and leave him there. I wanted to jump into the sea, but the sloop's master held me back. I had to go and not know whether he was killed or imprisoned . . ."

Her voice trailed away into total silence. She realized that she had kept her audience spellbound, and that tears were streaming down Ysoud's cheeks. Lady Blount's eyes, too, were wet. But it was Sir Brian who seemed to have been most greatly affected.

"You say this Captain Hartwell was a roundhead?" he demanded. "I cannot believe that a Puritan officer would so forget his duty to Cromwell. To help you, perhaps, but to pledge himself to see you safely to France and to even give you one of his own weapons—"

"But he did all these things—I will show the pistol if you like." Knowing that Sir Brian could influence the king in his judgement of Jonathan, she hastened it from her chamber, and the old knight stared at it for some time, frowning. He then traced the crest of the tree and the sword with his thumb.

"And what is this?" he demanded.

Damaris explained and was cut short by the chevalier Chassin. "The fellow was of good blood," he exclaimed. *"Bien entendu,* I am not surprised. He seems to have played the part of a gallant gentleman of noble birth."

Damaris saw her opportunity and spoke with urgency. "It is because of this gallant gentleman that I must see the king. As I told you, I left him fighting for his life on the beach. Clandennon's men were upon him even as we sailed. If he were taken prisoner . . ."

Sir Brian said, gently, "He could be dead, ma'am. No man wants to be taken alive by such a beast as this Clandennon. I've heard of his reputation for taking royalist prisoners and treating them with utmost cruelty, and before he took me, I would fight till I was cut to bloody shreds."

Within her heart she spoke a litany that she remembered from another time. No. He isn't dead. If he were dead, I would know it, somehow.

"I can't believe that he is dead," she said with a firmness she didn't feel, "and something must be done to save him. Please, Sir Brian. Beyond my small service to the king, my father has been his loyal supporter all his life. We have never asked for anything. And—and it is possible that Jonathan, brought here to France, could aid His Majesty."

Sir Brian conceded, "It bears thinking of. I

will do my best to persuade His Majesty to see you."

Before she could express her thanks, the chevalier rose to his feet and, taking Damaris's hand, bent to kiss it. "I think that you are a brave lady and a gallant one," he declaimed. "*Eh bien*, I have envy for this Jonathan Hartwell. A man could do much worse than die for such a woman."

Next morning she received word that Charles II would grant her the audience she had so long desired. It was set for three o'clock in the afternoon, and she waited feverishly for the hours to pass. "You will make yourself ill," Lady Blount scolded, but Ysoud understood.

"Dear mother, think of how I would feel if Philip was shut away in some terrible roundhead prison," she said as she embraced Damaris and kissed her pale cheek. "I, too, would be frantic with worry. But you must not fear, Damaris. It will be well for you and your handsome and brave captain. I know it will."

Ysoud's certainty helped, made her bear the slow passage of time, and she also helped Damaris choose suitable clothes for the occasion. They settled on a decorous dress of wine-dark satin ornamented with lace at the wrists and a felt hat with a sweep of wine-colored feathers. "*Alors*, it is said that Milord the British king has an eye for lovely ladies," Ysoud said when Damaris was ready. "If this is true, *ché-*

rie, you had better take off this dress and wrap yourself in rags. He will want you for himself and not lift a finger to help your captain if you look like this, for you are very fair."

"Behold, thou art fair, my love . . ." She could almost hear the deep voice speaking somewhere close to her as she left the luxurious house to climb into a carriage where Sir Brian awaited her to escort her to the Louvre where Charles II and his mother, Queen Henrietta Maria, had taken residence. It was not too long a journey, and before long their carriage was traversing the Rue de Rivoli.

Damaris watched the imposing, grayish building come into sight against the deeper gray of the Seine. A bank of fog had rolled in from the river, and perhaps it was this backdrop that gave the Louvre its impression of cold and haughty royalty, but as they crossed Pont Neuf, she found herself glancing toward the more magnificent and much more pleasant-looking edifice of the Palais Royale to the north.

"You won't care for His Majesty's surroundings either," Sir Brian said rather grimly. "Though he has many friends in France and his followers would willingly die for him, he has little money of his own. All that he has and will have has been channeled into regaining the crown. He makes light of personal discomforts and says that he won't rest easy until he steps on English soil again." The English knight paused and then said with fierce pride, "That is why he refuses all offers from supporters like the Blounts who would gladly see him quartered in more comfortable quarters."

She was silent as they were met by an official escort which had obviously been waiting for them and which guided them down the long and winding passageways of the Louvre until they approached a suite of rooms. The entrance to this suite was attended by French guardsmen who sprang to attention as the small party approached, but when Sir Brian stepped forward to explain his errand, the guards stepped away from the doorway.

Damaris's pulse beat painfully as she preceded the old knight into what looked to be an anteroom. There were several Englishmen present, and Damaris recognized a few: there was General Danby, one of Charles's most able commanders; the dashing Major Carlos who had escaped from Worcester with him; and several peers of the realm that she knew by sight. She realized that these constituted Charles's guard of honor, and she curtseyed deeply as Sir Brian explained her errand.

General Danby would have gladly detained her with talk of the battle of Worcester and of her father, but now the inner door of the suite opened, and the king's personal servant ushered Damaris and Sir Brian into the royal presence. She sank to the floor in a deep curtsey before the tall, dark man who sat near the fire and the frail dark woman beside him.

"Your Majesties," she murmured.

There was an instant's silence, and then Charles Stuart sneezed. It was, Damaris realized, cold in the room in spite of the blazing fire on the hearth. It was also very dark. Though the forbidding grandeur of the Louvre and Sir Brian's words had warned her, she had not expected the royal quarters to be so bleak. Everything was dark, from the heavy cloth that draped the windows, to the cumbersome furniture of the room itself. And yet the man by the fire was royalty—it was in his carriage and his every movement. When he held out a large, aristocratic hand to her, she bent to kiss it reverently. Here was the only man in the world who could help her.

"Mistress St. Cyr, I must apologize," the king was saying. He had a pleasant voice, deep and unpretentious, and though he was not handsome in any sense of the word there was great charm in his heavy-lidded black eyes and his wide smiling mouth. "I greet you with a vile cold in the head, exacerbated no doubt by my wild crossing on the channel. I have heard of your adventures from Sir Brian here, and I heard of your gallant father's death. We both share the loss."

"Colonel St. Cyr was a gallant gentleman." Henrietta Maria, too, could not be called beautiful, but her eyes were as lustrous as her son's. "I understand his daughter is as valiant." She, too, held out her hand to kiss.

The formalities over, Charles II insisted that Damaris sit down. "We aren't at court, and even if we were, I would never insist on strict protocol as my French cousin Louis does," he told her. "Oddsfish, the youth is fanatical. He will not even bow unless it is prescribed according to etiquette." When Damaris had reluctantly seated herself in a straight-backed chair, he continued, "Sir Brian told me that your father sent me word through you."

Though her own personal mission was hammering at her brain and heart, Damaris began to give the message entrusted to her. It seemed so long ago, a lifetime almost, since she had knelt beside her father and heard his dying voice damn the duke of Deerforth. Now as she repeated those words, she saw the young king blanch.

"The hearing is not pretty, sire," she apologized.

He shook his head as if at a loss. "It is hard to believe that a man I trusted as a brother played me false. And yet, Naseby did the same and so many others. And I can see now why we failed so miserably at Worcester." A deep frown furrowed his brow and he murmured, "Even in death, St. Cyr served me well. He was always a gallant gentleman, your father." She heard the warmth and sincerity in his voice and saw that his color was coming back and that his large, intelligent eyes were resolute as he added, "I promise you that the information you risked so much for will be treasured—and used. By God, it will be used!"

"What will you do, sire?" Sir Brian asked.

"The duke of Deerforth is still in England. We thought him a fugitive from Cromwell, but now we see why he chose to remain." His voice tightened angrily. "There are still ways of reaching across the channel and making the traitor pay."

Charles II seemed to consider, and then he shook his head. There was a wry pull to his mouth as he said, "Too many have lost their lives in this business, Brian. Derby has died for me, and poor Francis Yates, and God alone knows how many others—and I will not sit on a blood-soaked throne. When I return to power, it may well be that these sometime traitors will be my most avid supporters."

"Sire!" Even the hairs on the elderly knight's head seemed to bristle with indignation. "You would forgive Deerforth!"

"He has betrayed you, my son," the queen put in. "It was most fortunate that this brave girl escaped from your enemies with her information, for otherwise it could have fallen into their hands and been used against you. Deerforth might have been moved to strike openly against you while you are in exile."

The king smiled outright, and Damaris felt the compelling charm of him, the effortless charisma with which Charles II would always command loyalty and love. "No, Deerforth I will not forgive. He has sold himself for gold to Cromwell, and he will suffer—but not at the headsman's block." He paused and added, "I'll borrow a line from old Cromwell himself and say that to err is to be very human while to forgive divine. And kings have divine right, don't they?" He became serious. "If I'm to heal the wounds of England, I must bring friend and enemy together somehow, under one rule. That will cost money—and Deerforth has wealth. As I said before, he will pay a great deal."

Before she could lose her courage, Damaris said, "Your Majesty is very wise. You may have more friends among your enemies than you think." She hesitated, but the king encouraged her with a nod. "It was because of such a man that I managed to escape from Puritan England."

She told her story again, careful this time to point out all of Jonathan's efforts in her behalf. As she spoke, the king leaned forward in his chair nodding sympathetically. Once he interrupted. "A tall dark-haired man with broad shoulders and gray eyes—oddsfish, a figure out of a romantic tale, is he not?"

"An unlikely Puritan, indeed," Henrietta Maria agreed. "I had thought all of them close-cropped and severe, hating beauty and without a drop of chivalry in their bodies."

Charles nodded at Damaris to continue and sat listening as she ended her tale. When she had finished, he drew an appreciative breath. "A gallant gentleman," he said.

"I thought this, too." At her side, Sir Brian spoke gravely. "I knew that this story might entertain Your Majesty."

Damaris clasped her hands in her lap and met

his dark eyes beseechingly. It was all or nothing, and she prayed for his understanding as she said, "Sire, I love this man. We love each other. I left him fighting Clandennon so that I could get away. He's a traitor to his own kind now, and—and I fear for him. I ask your permission to return to England to see if I can help him."

"It's out of the question." He spoke regretfully but firmly nonetheless. Damaris hadn't expected that swift reaction, and she blinked at him. "What could you hope to do—alone?"

She had thought of this and had her answer ready. "Sire, he has friends. The villagers near Arbor Cottage would risk their lives to free him. Something can be done. Something must be done." He was shaking his head and she said desperately, "Are there not brave royalists who help their fellows escape? When we were going toward Arbor Cottage, we met some soldiers who told us that the earl of Larraby was nearby, that he had helped many royalists get away. Perhaps he could help . . ."

The king now rose and went to the windows from which he stared out into the foggy November day. "Even if he could do anything, Larraby is too valuable to me to risk in such a mad adventure. And besides, it is getting harder and harder to leave England. Cromwell has all ports watched."

A deep silence settled in the room. She could hear the snapping of fire, and the smoke that wafted back into the cold, drab room made her eyes ache.

"You won't help," she whispered.

"I am sorry," Charles II said. He seemed to mean it. "I can understand your feelings, but reflect—I myself am an exile, living on what amounts to the charity of my friends. I must conserve all that I do have to help my known *friends*—not roundhead officers. Besides, I am in a strange position here in France. Politically, I am very vulnerable."

Sir Brian explained. "His Majesty means that there is civil unrest in France also. King Louis and the Cardinal Mazarin are pitted against the Frondeurs, led by the powerful Prince Condé. He has Spain on his side, and this Spanish influence is much feared."

The king did not turn from the window but said, "My brother, the duke of York, is considering fighting under Marshal Turene to defeat the Frondeurs. And since King Louis pledges me his help if the Fronde are defeated, I am naturally on the royalist side. I've been asked to mediate between the king and the Fronde, and that makes me unpopular with the Parisians. My movements are now carefully watched by both sides."

Henrietta Maria now interposed. "Both sides in this civil unrest woo my son, and both suspect him of actions that might be construed as harmful to their cause."

Charles turned from the window. "I'm in no position to aid you. I can't give you money, and I will not risk my brave friend Larraby. Nor can I, with these damnable political factions watching me, give you permission to sail back to England lest such permission be thought by either the royalists or the Frondeurs to be a hostile act."

She had meant to go down on her knees before him and beg him, but his calm reasonableness took away that last option. It was hopeless. A sob rose into her throat and she struggled with it. She would not cry before her king and his mother.

Unexpectedly, she heard Henrietta Maria sigh. "It is hard to be a woman and torn away from the man you love with all your heart," she said, and her voice was sad. "It was so for me once, and I still remember the pain. Yet this Puritan captain gave his life for you, so that you could be safe. Think of this and be comforted. If he is the gallant gentleman you describe, he, too, will be content."

"There's little with which to reward you for your bravery and loyalty now, Damaris." The young king was smiling at her again, dark eyes showing his approval. "But be aware of my abiding gratitude."

He gave her his hand to kiss again. It was a gesture of dismissal. She curtseyed over it and felt his fingers squeeze hers sympathetically.

"You're not the only one to leave a heart in England," he told her quietly. "The only advice I can give you is to go on, somehow. Look forward, not back—" His voice lowered even more, and then she heard him add, "unless you wish your heart to break."

Chapter Eighteen

DAMARIS SAT IN THE BLOUNTS' FORMAL FRENCH garden and looked with unseeing eyes at the activity about her. Even in this pale November sunshine, gardeners were busy trimming the trees in the orangerie beyond the marble fountains and readying the beds for spring flowers. She could hear them talking and laughing, and once in awhile the youngest of them would whistle a cheerful tune.

It almost broke her heart because she had no cheer left. She had clung to hope at first, but it had been dashed to pieces so many times since her audience with the king yesterday that she felt almost physically bruised. She had first begged the Blounts for help in getting to England, but Philip had demurred, pointing out the danger in such a step. "Cromwell's men would only catch you and imprison you, force you to confess such things that would be damaging to His Majesty," he had said, and though Ysoud had been sympathetic, the Frenchwoman had explained that she could not go against her husband.

"You have only to lend me a horse and let me ride to Lacroix," Damaris begged, but Ysoud had cried out against such folly. The streets of Paris, she had told Damaris, were dangerous. No one ventured out in them alone after dark. And Frondeur checkpoints were everywhere these days, to detain and search and sometimes even arrest suspected royalists. What else could be expected of Frondeurs who had become so bold that they had demanded the resignation of the powerful royalist Minister, Cardinal Mazarin? If some Fronde officer got it into his head that Damaris was an English spy hired by Mazarin, she would be in terrible trouble.

Undaunted, she had then asked Sir Brian to come and see her and she'd put the matter before him—and he, too, had refused, saying that the king's commands had to be obeyed. She couldn't blame the old knight for his way of thinking. That was how her father would have reacted, how she herself might have felt if Jonathan Hartwell hadn't ridden into her life. Now, she couldn't focus on anything besides him and her need to get back to England and try to save him.

If he still lived. The thought was so terrible that in desperation she closed her eyes and let his image fill her mind. After all that happened, it was wondrous comfort to pretend that he was with her, that he stood in this garden, and the pretense was so real that she could almost see the way his dark brow quirked up in amusement, or how the silver light played in his eyes when he kissed her. And his mouth on hers—memory brought her the feel of his arms about her, the cool sure sweetness of his kiss.

"Are you dreaming here in the garden?"

The deep voice made her gasp and whirl about, and her hands flew to her trembling lips. He had been so vivid, so entirely real in her mind that for one wonderful second it seemed as if some miracle had brought him back to her. Then she realized that the cultured voice had a touch of an accent.

"Chevalier Chassin," she stammered.

"Alas, I am not he for whom you wait. I am desolate. I would give much to be in your thoughts like that, mademoiselle. As I said before, your Captain Hartwell is to be envied."

Thoughts of Jonathan were so much with her that she couldn't frame a courteous response. "Is a man who's been abandoned by everyone to be envied?" she cried.

"That is very sad." The chevalier offered her his arm, and when she had hesitantly taken it began to promenade up and down the garden with her. "Your audience with the king has made you lose hope."

She said tensely, "I must get back to England somehow. Chevalier, can you help me? There must be a ship. I'll pay the ship's master well . . ." She paused, mechanically tallying all her assets. She had only a little money, but there was her necklace of gold and pearls. Her mother's necklace, and it would hurt to part with it, but the situation was desperate. Mother would understand if she bartered memories for Jonathan's life.

"A ship," he was repeating. "*Dieu de Dieu*, mademoiselle, you would go back to that hell alone?"

"He is in that hell." She had clenched her hands tightly to stop herself from weeping. Tears wouldn't help now, she told herself fiercely. Strength was what counted. "Chevalier, I've asked Sir Brian and the Blounts for help, and they won't go against the king's command. But you're a Frenchman, and not sworn to obey Charles Stuart's wishes."

Amusement filled his worldly eyes. "That is true. Also it is true that I would rather obey a pretty woman. But it is difficult these days to leave the country. I myself am watched because I am a royalist and much feared by these dogs of Frondeurs who suspect my every movement. There has also been a new ruling that makes it impossible to leave France without written permission from the cardinal. This permission I can obtain from His Eminence, but still one must move carefully. A moment, mademoiselle, and let me reflect."

She watched him fearfully, holding back hope in case it should be dashed again but hoping anyway. Her heart was beating so wildly that she was sure he could hear it in the silence of the garden, and dark specks danced and floated before her eyes. Finally he said, "Perhaps something can be managed."

"You will help me!" she cried, joyously.

He smiled. "Don't look so happy, or your kind friends will suspect what is happening. They, along with the Frondeurs, will put a stop to what we plan." His expression grew grave as he continued, "This evening, the Blounts have been invited to a masque and ball at the Hôtel de Revie as have I. Do you know of this invitation?" She nodded and he added, "The duc du Revie is a most influential man in Paris, a royalist of great note, and there will be many guests at his home. The eyes of most of Paris will be on this affair. You will tell your hosts that you are going to the Hôtel de Revie—with me."

"But . . ."

"*Mais alors*, mademoiselle, you will not arrive at the Hôtel de Revie. Once we are in my carriage, we will leave Paris at once by the gate of St. Denis and make our way to the port of Lacroix." He patted her hand with an almost regretful sigh. "Come now and tell the Blounts what you have decided."

She could hardly contain her joy and relief, but she forced herself to cast down her eyes and appear sorrowful when she returned to the house with the chevalier. It was hard not to smile at Ysoud's surprise when Chassin explained that he had prevailed upon Mademoiselle Damaris to accompany him to the Hôtel Revie that evening, hard not to react to the relief that was very apparent in old Lady Blount's swift assent to the plan.

"But of course," she agreed, and Philip Blount was quick to add that he was glad Damaris had decided to abandon her hopeless cause.

"And you'll enjoy the entertainment tonight. The duc's masques are excellent and there'll be dancing—especially the gavotte."

"It will be my pleasure to teach Mademoiselle the steps of the gavotte," the chevalier said, and Ysoud gave Damaris an odd look as Philip explained that the gavotte was considered scandalous since the dancers exchanged kisses during the lively dance. She said nothing, however, and later came to Damaris's room to offer her several lovely dresses to choose from.

"I have heard that King Charles himself will be at the Hôtel de Revie," Ysoud said. "Ah, you are wise and practical, *chérie*. It is sad, but life goes on in spite of heartbreak."

Damaris longed to tell Ysoud the truth, but she didn't dare. The fewer people who knew about her plan the better. She was silent as, with characteristic generosity, Ysoud offered her considerable wardrobe to her guest. Damaris chose a simply cut dress of dark brown velvet that looked as if it could withstand travel and hard treatment.

It was hard to wait, and as the time passed, the waiting became even harder to bear. Damaris's sense of urgency mounted as sunset followed the age-long afternoon and the Blounts readied themselves for the evening's festivities, grew even more acute when Chassin's carriage failed to come for her at the appointed hour.

Philip and his wife would have waited with her or taken them with her, but she begged them to go on without her, and when they had reluctantly gone ahead, she paced the floor of the rich salon imagining all sorts of calamities until finally she heard a carriage arriving at the front door. But the chevalier was not in the carriage. Instead, a liveried servant presented a note. He was, Chassin said, desolated that he could not carry out his plan to escort mademoiselle to the picnic. He had been summoned into unexpected conference with Cardinal Mazarin about important state business, and there was no way he could extricate himself from this meeting. If mademoiselle wished, however, the carriage was at her disposal, and here with the note was a pass signed by Mazarin, authorizing her to leave France by way of Lacroix.

She read the note with outward calm. Inwardly, she was revising her plans. If the coachman knew the way, there'd be no difficulty reaching Lacroix harbor. She briefly remembered Ysoud's warnings about traveling alone in the streets of Paris and rejected them. She had faced too many dangers before this to be afraid, and besides she had Jonathan's pistol.

She gripped it under cover of her cloak as they started out, but she had underestimated the palpable menace that seemed to hover about the narrow, dark Paris streets. Groups of men lurked in doorways or watched sullenly from street corners, and when they saw the chevalier's coat of arms they seemed to grow even more menacing. Then, as they drove through an ink-black street, she heard the rush of feet and several men raced out toward the carriage.

One of them attempted to seize the horse's reins while the other clawed at the door of the carriage, actually pulling it open. She heard the driver swearing loudly and slashing about with his whip, and with all the force of desperation she seized the door handle and pulled it toward her. The intruder hadn't had a very firm grip on the door and he released it and fell backward, but not before she had seen his hating, lustful eyes and heard his cry—"Filthy *aristos!* One day, we'll knock you into the gutter!"

"*Canaille*—dogs," she heard the coachman snarl as they broke free and plunged through the dark streets again. That danger was over, she told herself, and soon they'd be outside the city, but the dark Paris streets and the violence they spawned weren't the only difficulty. As they were about to leave Paris, they came up to what looked to be an official checkpoint where the carriage was stopped.

"Chassin's carriage," she heard one of the checkpoint guards say, surprised as he held up a lamp to see the crest on the side of the carriage. "What's the chevalier doing on the road tonight? Nothing good, I'll warrant."

These must be the Frondeurs, of course, but

what did she care for France's civil unrest or its political parties? Damaris managed her prettiest smile as one of the guards opened the carriage door. "Good evening, monsieur," she said in honeyed French.

Holding his lamp up high, the guard stared at her. He then looked back over his shoulder at his mates. "Chassin's not here. It's a woman."

She saw curious, surprised faces fill the aperture of the doorway. They were country faces and somehow reassuring because they reminded her of the common folk of England who had been kind to her. Then these faces were displaced by a stern, pale aristocratic one and a cold, cultured voice demanded, "Where are you going, madame, in the Chevalier Chassin's coach?"

This one was no peasant. She detected a hardness behind his cultured voice, and she knew that he wouldn't be easily fooled. "I'm going to meet my lover," she murmured.

Unconsciously she had lifted her chin and lamplight caught the gleam of her hair, brought dark sparkle to her eyes. The men stared at her with admiration and one of them sighed. "Lucky fellow," he muttered.

"But why in Chassin's coach?" their leader persisted. "Is he your lover, *hein*?" Before she could frame an answer he turned to his men. "It is possible that that pernicious royalist is trying to smuggle information out of Paris in this coach or on this woman's person. She must be searched."

"That would be a pleasure," she heard a laughing voice say, but that was not what frightened her. If she left the coach, it might be seized by these Frondeurs. She might be detained. And even if they let her go, their search might take precious time. Clutching her pistol firmly Damaris raised her head haughtily. "Then step back from the carriage," she commanded in an imperious tone.

As the men involuntarily obeyed her, she shoved the pistol forward, pushing it almost into the face of the Frondeur officer. "Get out of my way or you will die," she snapped.

"*Sacre diable . . .*" But she didn't wait for the rest of his reaction. She caught hold of the carriage door and slammed it shut, screaming commands to the coachman as she did so. He whipped up the horses and they bolted madly forward. There was the crack of a pistol shot, and she heard the whizzing sound of the passing ball. Someone was shouting, bellowing for them to stop in the name of the Frondeurs. "Hurry, drive more quickly," she implored the driver.

"This is as fast as these horses go, mademoiselle." But he cracked the whip again and the coach maintained its headlong pace. It had started to drizzle a little, and as they left the city by the gate of St. Denis, it began to rain in earnest. To Damaris's nervous ear, the rain impacted on the coach roof like pursuing hoofbeats, and it was hard to sit still. Yet everything hinged on her remaining calm. They were still miles away from Lacroix, and there might be further Frondeur checkpoints for which she must make ready. And after that, there would have to be negotiations with sea captains at the port. She must moreover reload her pistol so that . . .

"Mademoiselle—mademoiselle, listen!"

There was fear in the coachman's voice and almost simultaneously she heard hoofbeats clear in the wind. "The Frondeurs are after us," the man was crying. "They ride like the devil."

"Can we outrun them? We have a head start." The coachman applied the whip, but the horses were tired and could not go faster. "They're gaining on us," Damaris moaned.

As she spoke, she heard one of her pursuers gallop past the carriage and order the driver to stop. They were caught, but there was still a chance. Damaris held back despair as she felt the carriage grind to a standstill. Perhaps the men could be bribed . . .

As the door to the carriage opened, she spoke in rapid French. "You will be well rewarded if you let us pass. I will give you gold and jewels . . ."

"Save your breath to cool your porridge, mistress." She started at the familiar English voice. "So. You flout the king's wishes and disobey his commands."

"Sir Brian," Damaris gasped.

"Didn't he expressly forbid you to try and take ship to England?" the old knight demanded angrily. "Fortunately, I had an inkling that you might try something foolish like this and when I saw Blount at the Hôtel de Revie and he told me that you were with Chassin, I put two and two together. You see, I knew Chassin was in conference with the cardinal." He shook his head in disgust. "That Chassin is a Frenchman and a romantic. It's just like him to help you in some hairbrained scheme to return to your roundhead captain."

There was a silence. In it she could hear the desolate sigh of the rain, the nervous whinny of horses. She felt spent, sucked dry of any last shred of hope.

He seemed to understand, for he gave her a look that was almost sympathetic. "Come," he said. "We must return to Paris immediately. His Majesty is waiting at the Hôtel de Revie to see you and learn why you dared to disobey him."

Chapter Nineteen

"ODDSFISH, MISTRESS, DON'T YOU KNOW THE meaning of the word 'no'?"

There was nothing approving about the king tonight, and the chill anger in his eyes was at variance with the merrimaking that was going on around them. He continued, "Did I not ask you not to try and return to England? Didn't I explain the reasons why I wished you to remain in France?"

She'd seldom been so miserable. She wished that a hole would spring up at her feet and swallow her whole. "Your Majesty did."

"And did I make things clear?" the king sneered.

"Quite clear, sire, but if you remember, I begged you to allow me to return. I still ask it."

She sank forward until she was kneeling before him at his feet. "On my knees, sire . . ."

There was a burst of music nearby and much applause to signify that a gavotte had come to an end in the great, glittering ballroom of the Hôtel de Revie. She had had a glimpse of that ballroom, gleaming with the resplendant luxury of three hundred white wax tapers and crowded with most of the nobility in France, before Sir Brian had conducted her here to this anteroom. She had seen that a stage had been set up at one end of the ballroom for the promised masque, and that musicians played while servants circulated with food and wine of every possible description. It had seemed incongruous that there could be a world where laughter and light-hearted song and dance could coexist with her heartbreak.

"Damaris, you try my patience sorely." Charles II had begun to pace up and down the small room. "Oddsfish, you do. If your father were alive, what would he say?"

"My father was a loyal man, sire, and I am loyal, too. I'd gladly give you my life. But I love this man beyond everything." He snorted impatiently, and she said, "If you loved someone with all your heart, Your Majesty, would you not try to be with her no matter what the cost?"

"God protect me from such love," he snapped. Then he said more gravely, "England is my love, Damaris, and will always be first with me."

"That's because you're a king, sire." She

couldn't believe that she was being so bold, but in the depths of his dark eyes she read something that encouraged her. "I'm not."

A little distance away, Sir Brian gave a scandalized snort. "Is that a way to speak to your king?"

"Nay, Brian, let the girl talk." Charles Stuart stepped closer to the kneeling Damaris and bent down. One long finger tucked itself under her chin, raised it. "So you love this Puritan more than life even though he's an enemy and an avowed traitor to his own cause. A man without honor." The words were harsh, but the king's voice had softened a little, and Damaris felt a rush of hope when he added, "What would you have done if you'd gone to England and found him ready to meet the headsman's ax?"

"I'd have been with him, sire."

He turned, shaking his head, to Sir Brian. "Women are infallibly romantic. It has never occured to this girl that there might be reasons why her captain might not want to see her again."

Was he jeering at her? She couldn't tell. "Sire, we love each other," she murmured.

The young king's wide mouth twisted in wry cynicism. "And do you say that that love is worth your life?"

She closed her eyes and remembered a deep voice speaking to her across distance and time. "Worth my life and my honor too," she managed to say. "Sire, please have pity and let me go."

She could hear Sir Brian clearing his throat

hard by, and then the king spoke again. "I cannot help you, Damaris, but there may be one gentleman who can. You yourself mentioned hearing of the earl of Larraby? He reached France today after many adventures and difficulties." Charles II shook his head as if in wonderment as he added, "Oddsfish, I'll swear that the roundheads wanted my good friend even more than they wanted me! And with good reason, since he's the one who played merry hell with Cromwell's security and smuggled so many royalists out of the country. He's the one man who can help you reach your Puritan lover."

Without thinking, she clasped the king's hands in both of hers. "Where is he? Sire, please, where can I find him?"

"He is here at the Hôtel de Revie. But," Charles II went on severely, "you must promise me one thing. You must abide by his word. If my friend Larraby says that it is hopeless, you must agree to forget your mad scheme."

Before she could answer, the door opened and a man entered the room. For a moment he stood by the door, his face in shadow, but even though much of him was concealed in a fashionable cloak that had been flung over his broad shoulders, she could see that he was a tall man with the long legs of a horseman and the upright carriage of a warrior. Her heart beat fast. Somehow, she must persuade this man to help her return to England.

"Welcome, my friend." Still holding Damaris's hands in his, the king turned toward the newcomer. As the earl approached, he continued, "This is Damaris St. Cyr, a headstrong woman who is also a courageous lady."

Before he had finished, Damaris cried, "Sir, I have heard your name all over England. You are my last hope. Can you help me?" He was silent and she resumed desperately, "I realize you don't know me . . ."

"Are you sure of that?"

The deep voice cut through the shadows, and she cried out in shock. It wasn't possible! But then the man stepped forward and she saw him clearly.

The gray eyes that held hers were the same. He was thinner, the dark hair that curled about his face longer. And he was dressed not as a roundhead captain but in court finery: dark Lyons velvet breeches and a matching jewelled doublet over white linen that ruffled icy Buckinghamshire lace at his throat.

"Jonathan?"

Her lips mouthed the word, but no sound came. She felt that the room was whirling about her and she couldn't catch her breath. She reached out and steadied herself against the back of one of the nearby chairs and heard the king say, "Nay, you mistake. This is my dear friend John Harcourt who is the earl of Larraby."

The words echoed and bounced against her mind; the world began to spin. I must not faint, she told herself, and dug her nails into the palms of her hands. The pain steadied her, but even so she couldn't speak to him as he stood before her in a silence that seemed as stunned as her own.

"You're alive," she finally managed to say. Her voice came out so small and still that she didn't even recognize it.

He began to answer, but the king spoke first. "Aye, but he could have been killed a hundred times during his adventures which began even before Worcester. For Larraby was charged with an important embassy to Holland in my name, and he did not reach England until after our rout at the hands of Cromwell. He could have come unscathed to France, but instead he chose to set his sword and his wits against Cromwell's hounds and rescue those of his companions and my followers that he could."

"Sire . . ." Jonathan started, but Charles II held up a long-fingered, ringed hand. He was in high good humor, his dark eyes snapping with mirth, and Damaris was suddenly aware that the door to the anteroom had opened and that several people now stood in the doorway. She saw Ysoud Blount's amazed face and Philip's, and then all the faces seemed to blur into haze as Charles II spoke again.

"Oddsfish, is this meeting of lovers not better than a masque?" he demanded of all present. "I knew 'twas Larraby that this young woman spoke of when Brian here told me the tale of the roundhead pistol which bore a royalist crest."

"The crest . . ." Her lips mouthed the words without sound and Sir Brian turned somewhat apologetic eyes to her.

"I recognized the design of the tree and the dagger, as I am distantly related to the earl of Larraby on his mother's side. It is an honored crest and an old one, but one not easily recognized these days as the Lady Mary, the earl's mother, was the last of her name. I told the king, and he . . ."

"And he commanded silence," Charles II interrupted. "I had no doubt that John would find his way out of this Clandennon's clutches without our help, and that while he was still in enemy hands there were good reasons for keeping silence about his birth and true identity."

His mother's crest—he had not lied to her, but he had not told the truth either. Damaris felt the whir in her head worsen as Charles turned to his friend. "It was like you to carry that coat of arms into war. You were always bold, my friend, and for all you've done you have my thanks. But," nodding toward Damaris, "in this matter you have more than my thanks. Had you not managed to spirit this lady out of England, St. Cyr's precious information would certainly have found itself into the wrong hands."

"Sire." As Jonathan bowed, the last of Damaris's illusions vanished. She knew now that it had been the importance of the secrets she carried that had made her precious to the earl of Larraby, and not her own person. No wonder he had never told her who he truly was.

He'd known that there would be a time when the lines of class and wealth would be drawn shut between them, and he had as good as told her so. Had he not told her that beyond getting her to safety there were no promises he could keep?

As the thoughts raced through her mind, he moved closer to her. "Are you all right?" he was asking, and at the concern in his voice something weak and foolish in her began to weep.

"Very well—my lord." She spoke so low that he could hardly hear, and she made an odd, groping gesture against her cheek as if to brush away tears. But she was not crying. She looked oddly fragile, her face paper-pale against her blaze of hair, and he wanted nothing more than to take her in his arms, would have, except that a brittle dignity about her forbade this. "I'm glad that you're safe," she continued. "I feared for your life, leaving you on the beach with Clandennon."

"Clandennon is dead," he was saying. "I killed him in fair fight though the cur did not deserve so clean a death. I also kept his men at bay until your sloop had sailed, but they surrounded me and finally took me prisoner." There was a stir of excitement from the nobility gathered around the doorway and he added, "They debated hanging me on the spot, but someone had the good sense to suggest conveying me to London. They shut me up in prison, but I managed to bribe my jailer and escape."

Admiringly, Sir Brian put in, "You make it sound easy, but I know 'twas not. Those royal-

ists whose hides you saved speak of almost
miraculous feats, my lord. Of being rescued
from the gallows in the nick of time, of being
hidden for days in a backwoods village disguised
as peasants, of being escorted by night to the sea
and waiting ships. They tell of ambushes where
you battled off scores of roundhead swords." He
shook his rumpled head. "Extraordinary."

It all fit, she thought. The mysterious escape
of Colonel Reisling in the same storm that had
brought Jonathan to Kirke Hall, the strange fires
at Long Marston that saved the condemned
royalists from execution and Jonathan's—no,
John Harcourt's sudden appearance soon after
in the wood. What Sir Brian had said also explained the military men in the village and
those midnight rides. And she had never suspected. She had begged, here on her knees, that
Charles permit her to go looking for a poor
roundhead captain, and here he was safe, powerful, and as far above her as the sky.

Suddenly, it was too much. The nearby music,
the fascinated faces of the French and English
nobility, began to close around her like a fist and
left her no room to breathe. Only half aware of
what she did, she curtseyed to the king, begging
his permission to retire. And then, blindly she
turned and walked away from the music and the
light. Away from him.

As she went, she heard the king say, "Come,
John, tell the tale. Leave nothing out. I swear
that I have not heard the like before and it
makes a rattling good story, better than these

masques the French seem so fond of. Battle and cunning, war and love . . ."

And all was fair in love and war. The words haunted her as she walked, stiff-legged, past the brilliance of the ballroom. She didn't know where she was going nor did she much care, and she followed a corridor that eventually took her to a door. Her knees felt rubbery as she opened this door and finally gained open air.

It had stopped raining but the sky was still without moon or star, and she was glad of the concealing dark. She had never felt so alone before; not even when her father had died had she felt this bitter emptiness. Then she had felt numb, but now all her senses were alive and awake, and they hurt. It was as if she were caught in a riptide of pain and memory.

She resisted remembering. What had happened between her and Jonathan Hartwell had truly been, as the king said, a masque. And now it would become a tale of romance to amuse the French court. It would soon be all around Paris that a pretty but penniless colonel's daughter had fallen in love with the Earl of Larraby.

She told herself that she would survive this. She would hold up her head and laugh and pretend she did not care, and she might even pretend that she had seen through the game from the beginning and thought it amusing to take on an earl as a lover. She lifted her head proudly for one moment—and then she heard deep laughter from behind her that reminded her of him.

That sound shattered her fragile courage, and she knew that she lied to herself. Clandennon himself couldn't have devised a more painful torture. She would see him often and hear his voice and not be able to speak to him from her heart. She would be close enough to touch and would not be able to touch.

I must get away from Paris, she thought, but even that thought brought no comfort. Wherever she went, the thought and memory of him would follow. He had told her how it would be: even if she took the wings of the morning and dwelt in the uttermost parts of the sea, the thought of him and the want for him and the need she had for him would always be a part of her. It was foolish to think of trying to get away from her own self.

"Foolish," she whispered.

"I agree," the many-shaded voice said behind her. "It's the height of idiocy to stand out here in the cold without so much as a shawl." She felt his warm cloak settle about her shoulders and drew in the remembered scent of him as he spoke again. "Good Lord, you're shivering."

Turning to face him was a mistake. The silver gaze drew her eyes upward to his face and she felt the lurch of her pulse. "I didn't hear you come up, my lord of Larraby," she forced herself to say. "But then, you seem to make a habit of appearing where you are not expected."

"You mean that scene in the king's presence. I had no knowledge of it, didn't even know that you were in Paris. I reached Lacroix this eve-

ning and was taken straight to the king, who
assured me that you were well and safe but
staying outside the city with the Blounts. He
insisted that it was imperative that I attend this
gathering tonight since the Duc is a powerful
supporter of the English court in exile." He
smiled, and the remembered softening of his
fine mouth tore at her heart. "I have feared for
you, sweetheart."

His hands rested on her shoulders, and that
touch was sorcery. But as he drew her to him,
she pulled away. "Don't call me that—you have
changed—everything has changed for us." His
denial was on his lips but she cried, "Jonathan—
my lord—I don't even know what to call you
anymore. And you lied to me."

He frowned but kept his hands on her shoulders. "For the same reason you lied first to me.
Because it was necessary. For the sake of our
royal master." She tried to draw away from him
but then he swore deep in his throat, and his
arms went about her, pulling her against him.
Hard, possessive arms crushed her softness to
his hard chest, and without her volition her face
lifted, her head tilted back for his kiss. She
sobbed once for the desire that would not die,
could never die, and let him have his will.

Her mouth remembered his. Welcomed it. Her
lips parted beneath his insistent tongue which
teased and touched her inner mouth with fire.
His hands on her shoulders and back and over
her breasts under the cloak spun spiderwebs of
flame. "Dear one," he whispered.

She tore away from him crying, "Don't pretend—my lord! I'm not your dear one. Maybe I never was. I was in love with my enemy the roundhead soldier, not with you!"

This time he didn't try to pull her back against him but looked down at her with that shadowed, troubled look she had so often seen in his eyes. "I could not have told Damaris Langley who I was, and later I was angry. I'd come to the Kirkes after freeing Reisling and his men because they were known royalist sympathizers. I sought to enlist their aid, but when I found you there and your father so ill, I forgot my own mission and stayed on only to help you. And when Clandennon came and I learned you'd played me for a fool, I felt you had used me and my feelings for you to gain your own ends. Yet betrayed or not, used or not, angry or not, I loved you."

She would have put her hands over her ears to drown out that deep voice, but he held her hands. She glared at him instead. "At least be honest now and admit that our loving was a romance, an interlude. Nothing more."

"Damnation," he roared, "will you listen to me? After Long Marston, I knew I had to get you away safely, not just because I loved you but also because of the secrets you carried. But I was wounded trying to get some royalists safely away, and my first chance to see you safe was lost." His voice softened as he added, "Those days at Arbor Cottage were among the happiest in my life—and the most painful, too, for I knew that every day you stayed in England put you at risk, and even so I could not bear to let you go."

She whispered, "Why didn't you tell me all this when we were at Arbor Cottage? Surely you had proof of my love then."

"I knew your spirit, too. Did you not tell me yourself that you would risk your life to help men like Larraby? I was afraid that if you realized who I was and what I did in England, you would try and help me. For your peace of mind and your safety it was better to let you think me what I was."

She felt exhausted, unable to battle against him and against herself. With bittersweet resignation she admitted that she was still his and always would be as long as he wanted her. For now, for a little while, for always—time did not matter anymore. What mattered was that he was saying, "I want us to be together, Damaris," and again cupping her face between his cool, strong palms.

He saw the change in her face and relief coursed through him as he read her thoughts in her dark eyes. When he had seen her first he had feared that something, danger or distance or time, had altered everything between them. He bent to kiss her upturned face and then he frowned. She looked resigned and beaten, and that look from Damaris hurt him to the heart.

Her voice wasn't right either. "I can't live without you," she was saying, "so it will be as you say."

"What is it that troubles you?" he demanded.

She didn't meet his eyes. "It's not important."
Nor would it be, she told herself staunchly. She
had told Charles II that she loved this man more
than her own honor, and that had never
changed. "Nothing troubles me," she told him.

"Now it is you who lie to me." One dark brow
slanted up, his silver gaze was both quizzical
and worried. Letting go of her hands he took her
gently by the shoulders. "Tell me, Damaris. No
more secrets. Do you not remember that night
when we swore that there would come a day
when we could be ourselves without barriers
between us?"

She winced at the memory, and the ache in
her heart loosed itself in words. "But there are
barriers," she whispered. "There always will be.
You are an earl and I—you recall my saying that
I have no dowry or peerage behind me?"

"Ah, so that's it." He sounded enlightened.

Now that he'd admitted the problem, she
thought, they might as well have it in the open.
"I think that the king knew this and that he
chose to keep your true identity a secret from me
because he felt that you would not wish to marry
anyone like me. It doesn't matter, I—I know that
the earl of Larraby must choose his wife from
among the nobility and I am content to be yours
in any way you choose."

There was a small silence, and then he said,
"Do you mean that even without marriage you
would come to me?" She nodded. "As a mistress,
you mean?"

Again she repeated her small nod. Then she heard an odd sound, and she realized that the earl of Larraby was laughing.

"Don't laugh at me . . . !" Her spirit flamed back and she threw back her head to glare at him, and then her anger died in wonder. His eyes were as warm as a silver lake in spring, and his mouth was tender. He looked younger, more carefree than she had ever seen him since those idyllic days at Arbor Cottage.

"My foolish love," he told her, "do you think I bested half of Cromwell's bully boys and braved the channel to offer you a divided heart? Aye, you'll be my mistress, and my bride, and the mother of our brats someday, too, God willing. But above all, you will always be my love."

His words took her breath away and she could only look up into silver eyes which told her that he spoke the truth. "You have not yet said 'yes.' Sweetheart, there are ways to convince you."

This time the remembered warmth of his arms took away all pain and doubt. She had the confused feeling that they were standing in the garden at Arbor Cottage and that the moon was golden and the English October rich about them. She was home, she was safe. She felt dizzied with the happiness that was coursing through her.

He said, "We'll be married in the presence of the king—he insists upon this. He now repents of the royal whim of bringing us unexpectedly together, for he had no wish to hurt you even for a moment."

"It doesn't matter." Now that they were together, she couldn't be angry at Charles II or at anybody. "Nothing matters."

"There is something that might matter." His altered tone brought her eyes up to him in some alarm and he added soberly, "Damaris, the earl of Larraby by rights has fair estates in England, and yet just now I'm a relatively poor man. The roundheads have confiscated all my lands except Arbor Cottage and the surrounding area, and apart from some small property that I hold here in France, I have little to offer you. When the king regains his throne I will see you honored as my countess, but until then, I might as well be Jonathan Hartwell in truth for all that I can offer you."

As he spoke, her heart turned over with love for him. "I would not call it little to have given me safety at the risk of your life, and shelter and love." A sense of mischief suddenly brightened her eyes. "Speaking of which, my lord, would you like me to recount your assets as a lover?"

His gravity disappeared, and he kissed her hungrily. "I would rather we show each other. It has been a long time and I have wanted to love you so long."

"And I," she breathed against his lips.

"Then let us leave the French to enjoy themselves and their masque without us." He lifted her into his arms and began to walk with her away from the lights of the Hôtel de Revie. She wrapped her arms about his neck, drawing in the essence of him, remembering him as he had been when they first met, first loved. As he walked they kissed again, murmuring to each other of their longing and of their devotion until Jonathan spoke crisply into the dark and a groom led a horse forward.

"I have no carriage to offer you tonight," he told her, "but it is not a long distance to the house that is mine here in Paris. Will you ride with me?"

"Anywhere," she agreed, and he set her on the horse and then mounted behind her, wrapping his arms about her as she leaned back against his remembered hardness.

"Do you recall, my love?" she murmured then, "you made me many pledges as Jonathan Hartwell, and I promised much in return. Would we have time to repeat these promises to each other tonight?"

His laugh was deep and warm and loving as he hugged her close and urged the horse forward into the velvet darkness. "Tonight and any night you choose, my dear one," he promised her. "We have forever before us."

Tapestry

HISTORICAL ROMANCES

POCKET BOOKS

If you've enjoyed the love, passion and adventure of this Tapestry™ historical romance...be sure to enjoy them all, FREE for 15 days with convenient home delivery!

Now that you've read a Tapestry™ historical romance, we're sure you'll want to enjoy more of them. Because in each book you'll find love, intrigue and historical touches that really make the stories come alive!

You'll meet Aric of Holmsbu, a daring Viking nobleman...courageous Jeremiah Fox, an American undercover agent in Paris...Clint McCarren, an Australian adventurer of a century ago...and more. And on each journey back in time, you'll experience tender romance and searing passion...and learn about the way people lived and loved in earlier times.

Now that you're acquainted with Tapestry romances, you won't want to miss a single one! We'd like to send you 2 books each month as soon as they are published, through our Tapestry Home Subscription Service℠ Look them over for 15 days, free. If not delighted, simply return them and owe nothing. But if you enjoy them as much as we think you will, pay the invoice enclosed.

There's never any additional charge for this convenient service—we pay all postage and handling costs.

To begin your subscription to Tapestry historical romances, fill out the coupon below and mail it to us today. You're on your way to all the love, passion and adventure of times gone by!

HISTORICAL *Tapestry* ROMANCES

Tapestry™ is a trademark of Simon & Schuster.   T100P5